ℐNNOCENT PASSION

Tucker remained silent, comforting her with his touch, with his arms.

Now two sets of intruders were stalking them. And Raven would be the focus of their attention once they learned that she held the key to the discovery of the treasure.

"You're safe. For now, Swift Hand doesn't know where we are," Tucker finally said, trying to concentrate on her fear and not the ever-present simmering of his own body. He understood that she didn't know what she was doing when she rubbed her breasts against him, when she leaned her head back to look up at him.

Tucker groaned and tightened his grip on her arms. His lips moved against her hair, drifting lower until he found her lips. They parted beneath the pressure of his touch, allowing their mouths to merge, to join, to bond.

He could hear her breathing change, feel her heart fluttering even as he told himself to stop, to pull back.

But he couldn't stop. . . .

BANTAM BOOKS
BY SANDRA CHASTAIN

Rebel in Silk

Scandal in Silver

The Redhead and the Preacher

Raven and the Cowboy

Raven
and the
Cowboy

Sandra Chastain

BANTAM BOOKS
New York   Toronto   London   Sydney   Auckland

RAVEN AND THE COWBOY
A Bantam Book / July 1996

ISBN 0-553-56864-7

Published simultaneously in the United States and Canada

Bantam Books are published by Bantam Books, a division of Bantam
Doubleday Dell Publishing Group, Inc. Its trademark, consisting of the
words "Bantam Books" and the portrayal of a rooster, is Registered in
U.S. Patent and Trademark Office and in other countries. Marca
Registrada. Bantam Books, 1540 Broadway, New York, New York 10036.

PRINTED IN THE UNITED STATES OF AMERICA
OPM   0 9 8 7 6 5 4 3 2 1

RAVEN
and the
COWBOY

Prologue

The dream came again. At first there was the fluttering sound of wings. Then came the elusive shadows that fled before her as she walked. For weeks it had been the same, but now it was different. Now there was a curious fear mixed with the anticipation.

She stood at the edge of the precipice, her arms extended, the wind against her back urging her forward. The river below was a glittering reflection of blue sky, snaking its way along the boulders, through cliffs as slick and straight as ice.

Unafraid, she waited. Then the dream changed. This time she answered the urging of the wind and stepped out into the vast open space beyond. And suddenly she was falling. Yet she welcomed the sensation, the presence of unbound joy.

She could live or she could die. The choice was hers. Miraculously, she began to move her arms. The updraft caught her body and cushioned it, lifting her into the current where she soared like a bird. She glanced down at her body; it was covered with glossy black feathers. Her arms became wings. Her senses sharpened; she could feel the movement of tiny animals along the water's edge.

She was now the raven for which she was named.

But why? What did the dream signify?

Beyond the cliff and the river, the mountains loomed like guardians over her, not friendly, yet not angry at her presence. They drew her closer, hypnotically luring her toward their lofty peaks.

Then she saw him, a man, a tawny mountain lion of a man, a cougar lying on the ledge. Majestic in sleep . . . or death. She couldn't tell.

Drifting nearer, she felt drawn by the force of his inner power, a self he protected, hid from the world. A self he'd closed off for so long that only the spirits knew of its existence. He was alive.

She flew to the ledge and settled down beside him, knowing that this place, this man was her destiny.

1

Spring, 1877

Raven Alexander knelt by the dying man, her clasped hands resting against her knees, her head bowed. The coals of a mesquite fire burned down, breathing little warmth into the shadows. But she did not feel the cold.

From outside the tepee came the sound of low, muffled drumbeats, growing slower and slower, like the ebbing of the old man's heart. Then came the keening of voices, high, tight with grief, blown by the wind.

Death was no stranger to Raven. Her mother had lost her life bringing Raven into the world. Her boisterous Irish father had been killed in a mining accident. Now she was losing Flying Cloud, the man she'd always called Honorable Grandfather.

Suddenly the old man opened his eyes and reached out to clasp her by the arm. "Come close, my child," he said, gasping for breath. "I have little time."

"Be still, Grandfather, you must rest." She tried to ease him back to the rug on which he lay, but he continued to hold tight.

"No, you must listen. I have told you of the wealth

of our people hidden in the sacred mountains to the south. The time has come for you to go there, to claim the treasure."

"I don't understand."

"The spirits will protect you, Raven. You must go."

Flying Cloud let go of her arm and collapsed back to the ground.

"Grandfather? Please, I can't leave you."

"I have prepared you for this journey all your life, Raven. You will find two men. One comes to you," he rasped, "in the form of the cougar."

"Cougar?" Over and over in recent weeks, she'd dreamed of a sleek golden mountain lion.

"He'll take you to the other, the keeper of the sacred treasure who will guide you to the place where the light of the moon touches the light of the sun."

"But I don't want to leave you now."

"Go, my child. Promise me that you will do this thing."

She had no choice but to follow the wishes of this man who'd been her rock in a changing world. "I promise, Grandfather."

With a heavy heart, Raven stood and backed away from the man she'd loved all her life. His last words followed her from the dwelling.

"Beware the bronze dagger."

In a small cantina just south of the border, Tucker Farrell watched the slim Mexican across the table blatantly deal his Spanish friend a card from the bottom of the deck. The Spaniard wore an open jacket, displaying crossed silver-trimmed leather straps filled with cartridges for the pistol at his hip. Not only was he a crooked card player, he was a bandit as well.

The dealer gave a sharp laugh as he slapped a card on the table before Tucker and moved on to the grizzled old half-breed miner who'd turned up earlier, and who, in order to get into the game, had bragged about finding a lost treasure.

Nothing new about that along the Rio Grande. Tales of lost mines and treasure were routine. Tucker studied his cards. He was holding a pair of fours. Another time, he might have stayed in, but he weighed the possible loss of his drinking money against his chances and threw in his hand. He might have won, but a sure bottle was worth more than a few hundred maybes.

The miner studied his cards, took two. When the old man raised the bid, he shuffled his cards several times, then pulled a nugget of gold from his pocket and threw it into the pot.

The two remaining cardplayers looked at each other and nodded. The onlookers grew quiet. Tucker would have moved away had he not been caught up in the tension of the play. The hand progressed. Consternation was obvious on the old Indian's face. Now the pot held two nuggets and what looked like a heavy gold watch fob set with a ruby.

A sick feeling hit Tucker in the pit of his stomach. The prospector was heading straight for trouble, and he seemed oblivious to the danger.

"The bet, it is to you, old man," the dealer said in heavily accented English. "What do you say?"

Tucker wondered why the miner took such a chance. If he had actually found a treasure, it had to be worth a lot more than a meager pot in a poker game.

Must be pride, Tucker decided. Hell, he could understand that. He'd felt the same way, until he'd lost his own self-respect and given up on finding it again.

"I have a name," the old man said, a sudden burst of

excitement giving him courage. "I am called Luce, the keeper of the mountain."

Just as quickly the bravado turned to uncertainty as he wiped perspiration from his forehead with the worn sleeve of his shirt. "I—I cannot cover the bet, not with what I have. But I give you my marker. I will return with the money, I swear."

"We don't take no markers," the dealer's sidekick said. "You'd better have money or it's all mine."

Tucker groaned and laid his hand on the pistol strapped on his left hip, hoping he wouldn't have to use it. The old Indian had been showing off. No telling how he'd come by his precious loot, but he was in the stew now.

"But I have more," the old man insisted. "I do. I will make my mark." He reached inside his pocket.

Tucker heard the sound of a pistol being cocked. *Ah, hell.* The bastards weren't going to let him get away. If Tucker didn't act quickly, the bandits would have more than the old man's IOU. Without thinking, Tucker reached for the bottle in front of him, knocking it over on the cards. The dealer turned his eyes on Tucker in disbelief.

"What the—?" the bandit swore, scrambling backward.

"Sorry." Tucker took his bandanna from around his neck. "I'll just wipe it up." He lurched to his feet, slurring his words just enough to convince onlookers that he was drunk.

At the same time, he stumbled, swept the nuggets and the watch fob into his pocket, and collapsed across the table, determined that the bandits not profit from their cheating.

Then, as if he were trying to right himself, Tucker pulled the table toward himself and, shoving the miner out the door, sagged backward, blocking the exit as he fell. "I think I've had too much to drink," he said with an affected laugh.

"Get out of the way, you idiot!" The two men tried to get past him, one of them firing at the escaping prospector. But in his efforts to apologize and stand, Tucker managed to delay both men long enough for the old miner to get away.

The tirade that followed was in Spanish. Tucker didn't have to understand the exact words to know the men weren't going to let him leave the cantina peacefully. It looked as if the half-breed wouldn't get his treasure back after all. Still, it wasn't until until they forced Tucker out of the saloon and into the plaza beyond that he realized what they had in mind.

The saloon emptied as the customers followed, expecting to be entertained by what was obviously a common occurrence in the village.

"You know what we do in Mexico to people who get in our way?" the dealer asked, a cruel grin exposing the stark white of his teeth against his swarthy complexion.

"It was an accident. I wasn't even playing. I'd already folded."

"You and the old man were in cahoots. I saw you steal the ruby," the sidekick said. "Get a rope for the *americano* outlaw, *compadres*. Then we go treasure hunting. Si?"

Suddenly the situation wasn't so funny anymore. Tucker opened his eyes and took in the circle of men. He was a lot bigger and stronger than the Mexicans, but the guns pointed at his chest evened that difference.

"You can't hang me." Tucker drew himself to his full height and looked the cocky little bastard straight in the eye.

"Oh, but we can, señor," the man with the pistol boasted. "We surely can."

Tucker swallowed hard. He might as well give them the nuggets. Unless a miracle occurred, he didn't have a chance in hell of living to return the gold. After all the bad things he'd done as a soldier in the name of duty, he was going to die for helping a man he'd never seen before.

"What the hell," Tucker said. "This place has definitely lost what little charm it had. The whiskey's bad, the games are crooked, and as for women, haven't seen one I'd mess around with since I left Amarillo."

Tucker didn't know whether his stomach, his pride, or his manhood was suffering more. As his captors slipped a rope around his neck, he knew he'd never satisfy any physical need again. Returning the booty wouldn't change anything. The only way he'd get out of there was to sprout wings and fly.

Then suddenly he heard a low rumbling sound, like the ripple of sails in the wind, that grew louder and louder. The onlookers grew quiet as angry shrieks cut through the air. The sky filled with hundreds of large, yellow-eyed, black birds. They settled in the tops of the gnarled mesquite trees surrounding the plaza and on the roofs of the buildings. Soon the hard-packed ground was black with the querulous birds, while others hovered above the circle of men.

The Mexicans looked at each other in alarm. Two of them dropped to their knees, crossing their chests. The others followed.

The birds continued to appear as if they'd been summoned, closing out the sun and leaving the plaza dark and cold. For a moment Tucker was stunned. Then, seeing he'd been given a chance, he slipped the rope from his neck and ran to his horse.

"Get me out of here, Yank," he whispered, throwing himself into the saddle and leaning against the animal's neck. The birds scattered before them as, for once, the horse followed orders and together they raced away from the village toward the safety of the hills to the northwest.

Behind him the unnatural shrieks of the birds still filled the air. Then, as quickly as they'd come, the flock swept across the sky before him in a dark swirling mass, blotting out the setting sun like a black-gloved hand.

A ripple of unease ran up Tucker's spine. He didn't understand what had just happened, but he knew that it was unnatural as hell, and maybe as close as he'd ever want to be to the place. If he'd been a religious man, he might have been unnerved. Now he galloped along an unfamiliar trail in the burgeoning darkness, his freedom in peril should the Mexicans decide to come after him instead of the old prospector.

After several hours of hard riding along the rocky terrain and through shallow streams, Tucker reached a point where he could look back over the area he'd covered. He couldn't see any evidence that he'd been followed. And there was no sign of the half-breed Indian miner.

The horse Tucker had given, in a moment of irony, the name of Yank was breathing hard. Tucker was edgy, not only from almost losing his life, but from the way in which he'd been saved. He'd seen buzzards and he'd seen crows. The flock that had dropped like a cloud over the plaza was neither.

Shaking off the sense of unease that had traveled with him, Tucker was satisfied that he'd escaped. It was time to give both himself and Yank a rest.

Remembering his mad dash to safety, Tucker swore and reached back to examine his saddlebags. The pint of whiskey he normally carried was still there. He retrieved it and, with his teeth, pulled the cork from the bottom and spat it into his hand. He wasn't normally given to heavy drinking, but he was not normally rescued by demon birds either. Tonight he could use a little courage. He lifted the bottle.

When the bottle was half empty, Tucker Farrell recorked it and stuck it back into his pack. Not only was he wide awake, but all his senses seemed enhanced. Once, in the path of a tornado, he'd felt a sudden tingle in his skin that announced some startling event. Tonight he felt it again.

The moon had risen full and threatening, showering the trail with moonlight, making him an easy target to anyone watching.

Even Yank seemed unusually high-strung. He stumbled and came to a stop as he encountered a rock that had fallen from higher up. "Get on, you stubborn mule," Tucker cajoled.

Yank, true to his name, bullied his Rebel master by following orders only when they suited him. Tucker swore. Getting himself killed was one thing, but injuring his horse was something Tucker would never do. It was time to find a place to bed down before he fell off and rolled back down the mountain to that godforsaken place he'd escaped from.

Tucker disengaged one foot from the stirrups, swung it over the saddle, and, leaning his upper body in the other direction, slid to the ground. Too late he realized that he should have dismounted on the side toward the mountain instead of the side toward the ravine. As he tried to balance himself the earth beneath his feet gave way and he slid straight down, bouncing only once before he hit his head on a rock and knocked himself out cold.

For most of her twenty-six years, Raven Alexander had been torn between two worlds. Three days ago she'd left them both.

Perhaps her life would have been different if her father hadn't been Irish and her mother, Pale Raven, half Arapaho. But her kinship with her mother's people and the Grandfather, Flying Cloud, had pulled at her, forcing her to follow a separate path.

The leaving hadn't been easy. She'd had to fight her older half sister Sabrina's disapproval from the moment she'd announced her mission. Expecting Sabrina to understand the difference in their backgrounds had always been impossible. Sabrina's practical Irish mother had instilled such responsibility in her children that Sabrina would always consider herself head of the family.

Raven should have left in secret. That way, she'd have been saved having Sabrina accompany her to Denver, trying one last time to change her mind. "Raven, you are not going to New Mexico, alone, on some kind of crazy treasure hunt."

Raven let her go on. All the Alexander sisters had learned that when Sabrina set her mind to something, there was no stopping her. Raven could only be grateful that the other three sisters had married and moved away. Otherwise she'd have been besieged on all sides.

"The country is changing," Sabrina had argued. "The Comanche and the Apache are at war. The ranchers in the Southwest are bringing in gunfighters to stop the cattle rustling. And you don't even know that the treasure exists."

"It exists," Raven explained once more. "And I must find the keeper of the mountain. He will show me the way."

Raven didn't know why she mentioned only one of the men. Explaining that she expected to find a man who came as a cougar was more than even she wanted to try.

"You're just going to ride off into the sunset and wait

for some old man to step up and say, 'Look here, girl, I'm
to be your guide.' "

Raven ignored her sister's logic. She knew he would
come. "It's the Arapahos' last chance, Sabrina. With the
gold, we can buy land, good land, where all can live without being dependent on either crooked Indian agents or a
government that changes the rules before the ink on the
treaty is dry."

"But Papa's silver mine is producing now, Raven. And
a share of it is yours. If you want to buy land, you can
have the money. You may be part Arapaho, Raven, but
you're Cullen Alexander's daughter too."

"Yes, my father was an Alexander, Sabrina, but *my*
mother was an Indian. My hair is as black as the bird for
which I am named. My eyes are brown and my skin has
been touched by the sun. We are sisters of the heart, but
we are different. We each have our own purpose in life. I
must follow my destiny."

"Destiny, smestiny! You sound like some highbrow
English novel. The Arapaho will be fine on that reservation in Wyoming. What you need is to come back home
and forget about the Indians."

"You forget, Sabrina, *I* am part Indian, more Indian
now than white. But more than that, I made a promise.
It was Grandfather's dying wish that I journey to the
mountains in the south and find the guardian. I gave my
sacred word."

"What guardian?"

"When the Arapaho tribe left the southern mountains, part of their people stayed behind to guard the sacred mountain. The secret of its location was left to those
in the south, but one member of each succeeding generation in the north was given the means to find the treasure. Grandfather passed that secret to me. All I have to
do is find the guardian."

"And how do you plan to do that?" Sabrina asked in disbelief.

"I don't know," Raven admitted. "Grandfather said the spirits would guide me."

Sabrina wrung her hands. "But why you?"

Raven tried to find the right words to explain. "Because those who are left are divided. Swift Hand and his followers want to challenge the soldiers. The elders are weary of fighting. There are fewer than a thousand Arapaho left, and they go to the reservation because they have no choice. I am the only one who can change that."

In deference to her sister's concern, Raven had donned proper traveling clothes and taken the stagecoach from Denver to Santa Fe. But her horse, Onawa, carrying her Indian dress and bedroll, was tied to the back.

More than once in the last two days, she had regretted her decision. Sharing her stage with a frightened mail-order bride and her small daughter and a newspaperman heading for Albuquerque made the journey seem endless.

"I'm Lawrence Small, a reporter for the *New York Daily Journal*," the thin young man said eagerly. "Are you a native of the West?"

"I was born here, yes," Raven had answered reluctantly.

"And do you know any outlaws or cowboys?"

Once she answered, "I'm afraid not," he lost interest in Raven and began to interview the woman who'd answered an ad from a rancher who needed a wife.

Raven longed for her horse. Even her bones were sore from bouncing around the hard seat. She'd long ago given up on keeping the dust from her clothing, and the only way she could control her hair was by braiding and covering it with the absurdly small hat someone had devised as a way to torture its wearer.

Long before Santa Fe, she decided to leave the stage

at the next stop, remove the travel dress with its tiresome bustle, and don her buckskins.

Taking in a deep breath of the crisp, cool air, Raven cast her gaze outside the window and studied the mountains looming larger in the lengthening shadows of late afternoon. It was early spring and snow still capped the tops of the peaks, giving their stark variegated edges the look of jagged hard candy dipped in sugar frosting.

She longed to lie beneath the stars in peaceful solitude. The moon would be full, a bright silver disk etched with lacy shadows, resting against a dark tapestry embroidered with pinpoints of starlight. The wind would sing to her. From the looks of the clouds beyond the peaks, she might even feel the cleansing rain sweep over the earth.

At times like this, the spirits would come. A kind of silver mist would fall over her, and everything would grow quiet. Then, from somewhere beyond her mind, a chorus of muted voices would begin to chant and she would experience what she had come to call her waking dreams, dreams so real that she could experience pain and fear. But all the while, she'd be divorced from danger.

Longing for some kind of reassurance, at the next way station she decided to carry out her plan. While the food was being prepared, Raven found a private place to change her clothing within a stand of cottonwood trees. The travel dress with the bustle was stored in the bedroll along with her slippers and petticoat. Her tired body welcomed the soft buckskin dress and moccasins.

When she started back to the shack, the child met her, eyes wide. "You look like a princess in a fairy story. Do you have wings to fly?"

"No, I don't fly, little one. But I am going to leave you here and ride my horse across the pass into the mountains."

By the time the driver started to get worried about

her whereabouts, the exotic Miss Alexander had been replaced by an Arapaho woman in a buckskin dress.

The stationmaster reached for his rifle.

The newspaperman gave a disbelieving whistle.

The mail-order bride fainted dead away.

Raven left her case and most of her clothing for the bride, mounted Onawa, and rode west toward the mountains, feeling freedom settle over her like a peaceful mantle.

This was her quest, her mission, the unknown she'd waited for. Energy bubbled to life within her, and she let out a cry of joy as the horse beneath her leapt forward.

"Aieee!"

On the third night, the moon rode high as Raven crested the peak, casting a light as bright as day. She could hear the labored breathing of her horse and regretted not making camp earlier. Traveling unfamiliar territory was difficult enough in the daytime. At night it was foolhardy. But Onawa never faltered, and as Raven climbed higher she had felt herself drift into a spiritual meditation.

Now the horse slowed her steps, slinging her head as if she were listening to some unseen voice. Raven, too, sensed something she couldn't identify. They rounded a boulder, and the path she followed went dark as it intersected with another. Her horse stopped, waiting for direction. A shaft of moonlight suddenly found an opening in the overhanging ridge above her, casting a circle of pale silver around her that increased Raven's unease. "Which way, Grandfather?"

But there was no answer. Never had she been so tired. Her food supply had been exhausted since she'd left the main trail the day before, and other than a few berries, she'd had nothing to eat since then. She could have foraged the countryside as she'd been taught by her mother's family. But she felt driven and she hadn't taken the time. The area where she rode had become more and more rocky, almost as if a playful child had picked up a handful of assorted boulders and dropped them in a heap. The trail was steep and barren, with little foliage and no wildlife, except for the wave of black birds that appeared periodically overhead.

Birds. For the past two weeks, she'd had recurring dreams about large black birds and a rangy, untamed mountain lion of a man with hair the color of the sun. Then the man had gradually changed into a sleek, tawny cougar whose power was as great as the control with which he contained it.

Always before, Mother Earth had protected and provided for Raven when she was alone. This time she seemed strangely distant, almost as if she were punishing the child of her loins.

From the time she'd left the stagecoach, Raven had moved south as Flying Cloud had directed, following some inborn instinct. Now she was confused.

"Oh, Grandfather," she whispered, "show me the way to the guardian."

You will know the way, my child. The secret is hidden in your heart, the path in your mind. The guardian is one of us. Soon it will be clear.

"You choose, Onawa." Raven allowed the horse free rein. For a moment the small mare hesitated. Then, as if she'd been nudged, she turned to her left, taking the trail that continued upward.

Raven felt as if she were being watched over, but she was receiving conflicting images of her protectors. She had to be careful. She'd walk for a while, restraining the brave Onawa, who seemed suddenly eager to move ahead.

Searching inward, Raven reached out to the spirit

world. Of late she was becoming more proficient at closing out the real world and taking herself to a place of communion with the spirits. Her sisters wouldn't have understood how she could feel the presence of those who'd gone before, of the mountain, the moon, even the wind. But she was gaining the ability to make herself silent and listen.

There was a dangerous stillness in the night, a dark, powerful force that lingered in the wind. Above, the stars hung like teardrops in the black sky, so close that she could almost reach up and wipe them away. It was only then that she felt the dampness of her own tears on her cheeks. For a moment she wanted to turn back, call out to Sabrina, tell her that she needed to be the little sister again. But that life was over and gone. Every step took her farther away.

The savage call of a mountain lion echoed down the canyon, bouncing off the boulders and raking her nerve endings. Then came the answer, a response just as intense, but less aggressive. He was calling to his mate and she was answering in kind.

In the silence, she could hear the gentle slap of water against the rocks below. The fresh wind added its whisper to the scuff of the horse's hooves and the animals' cries, all merging in a rhapsody of lonely sound.

Then a sense of purpose stole over her, a sense of direction, an eagerness that quickened her pulse. She was being drawn by something in the rocks above her.

Something, or someone, waited.

2

Swift Hand stepped into the tepee, lowered the flap behind him, and took his place in the circle of men surrounding the fire. He accepted the pipe packed with tobacco, lit it, and took a deep, slow draw, releasing the smoke to waft upward across his scarred face.

"I have had a vision, a way to take back the land of our people—our trees, our streams, and the buffalo," he said and passed the pipe.

Each member of the circle smoked and nodded his agreement.

"The Great Mother Earth will share her riches with us. She has provided a guide to show us the way."

The pipe circled the fire once more, then a third time before Swift Hand tapped it against one of the rocks and spilled the tobacco onto the coals. The remaining shards turned into curls of fire and disappeared in smoke.

He looked at the man seated across from him. "We will follow the white medicine woman. She will lead us to great wealth. Are we agreed, Little Eagle?"

The young man with the eagle feather in his hair nodded. "We are agreed."

Swift Hand knew that some of his followers were still skeptical, but they were determined not to be relocated to the Wind River Reservation with the elders. That land belonged to the Shoshone. The Arapaho would have their own land or they would die. No matter that Raven had been chosen, he knew in his heart that he was to take the Grandfather's place.

Sounds Loud, one of the older warriors, voiced the question shared by them all. "But does she know the place?"

Swift Hand stood and stared into the coals. "Flying Cloud made the child of his blood a medicine woman. It is she who now speaks directly to the spirits, who shares their great wisdom. But Flying Cloud's vision was tainted. It is wrong that a white woman knows our secrets. We will let her find the guardian of the sacred mountain, then we will claim what rightfully belongs to our people. The spirits will protect us."

There was a long silence, then an uneasy chorus of assenting nods.

"So be it," Swift Hand said. "We leave at first light to follow the path of the medicine woman who holds the secret of the Arapaho treasure."

Raven walked through the darkness, her feet moving with certainty on the mountain trail. Onawa's hooves moved beside her in tandem, almost as if the two separate travelers were one.

The trail was sheer rock, the surface hard. Low-lying clouds drifted like fog across the moon, filtering out more and more of the light. Now the wind picked up, lifting sand and leaves and flinging them against Raven's bare arms and legs.

For the first time, she was afraid. How would she find

these men who would lead her? Flying Cloud had told her no name. He only knew that when his people had drifted to the north, the chosen ones had remained behind to be caretakers of the treasure.

"You will know him," Flying Cloud had said. "The cougar will show you the way."

Now a storm was coming. There would be rain soon. And the mountain where she walked would be an unforgiving place to find shelter. She quickened her step. Then, as if a warm, hard hand had been placed across the trail, Onawa stopped.

Raven felt the wind die. Nearby, the cry of a cougar echoed through the rocks. Not a cry of attack nor an announcement of his power, but a different song—enticing, alluring, melodious.

She again recalled her dream of such an animal and felt disoriented. The darkness around her seemed to swirl and change, circling her like a whirlwind of clouds. She heard the chanting begin. But there was a new sound, a gentle, rhythmic movement almost like the beat of drums, as if she were back in the dream that had haunted her for days. A raven and a cougar, lying together. The cougar was grumbling in a low voice as he watched the wary bird, yet he did not harm her.

But this time she was awake. This time she knew that she couldn't move her arms and fly. Still, there was no ignoring the urge she had to move to the edge of the path. Cautiously she stepped forward, searching the darkness for the sight of the river.

The earth started to rumble, and suddenly the ground on which she stood gave way. This time she didn't move her arms, and there were no feathers on her body. Instead she bounced off a rock and landed with a jolt on a ledge below the place where Onawa stamped her feet and neighed softly in alarm.

Raven lay where she'd landed, her head aching. The chanting grew louder and the swirl of fog returned to envelop her, closing around her in a fitful sleep that took away all thoughts and dreams.

Across the valley, masses of rain-filled clouds boiled over the mountains and descended to the ledge where she lay. In the stand of trees farther up the trail, Onawa sought refuge beside another horse, both animals nickering nervously as the clouds approached.

But the rain held off.

It was the sound of thunder that woke Tucker, followed by hard, pelting rain that stung his face. He sat up, disoriented for a moment as he tried to remember where he was.

Rain. He was outside. But where was Yank? A flash of lightning lit up the sky, revealing the side of the cliff and an opening in the rock before him. He pushed himself onto his elbows, his head vibrating as if he'd been hit by the lightning flashing in the distance.

Gingerly he began to feel his way toward the wall, his hand encountering something in the darkness—something that ought not to be there. An ankle. A slim ankle leading to a foot encased in a soft moccasin.

Tucker froze. He wasn't alone. Wherever on the west side of hell he was, he had a woman with him. But why wasn't she having a reaction to his touch? Another jagged streak of silver split the sky and illuminated her face—he could see that she was an Indian, wearing a buckskin dress.

He must have had more to drink than he'd thought. Maybe he was hallucinating. Or this was a dream. No, the leg he held was real. It was warm and soft and feminine. But something was wrong. No woman would sleep through a storm.

As the rain streamed down his face, Tucker turned to look behind him. All he could see was rain and—space.

Space? His stomach contorted and his knees quivered. He said a small prayer of thanks that it was dark. He didn't want to know how high they were. They were on some kind of damned ledge and she was hurt or unconscious.

He blinked, trying desperately to close out the ringing inside his skull. Once a horse he'd tried to break had kicked him and left him like this. A couple of times, he'd tied on a good one, but nothing like this had happened to him then. Too much whiskey made a man weak, and Tucker Farrell never lost control.

The rain came down harder. The woman. If he didn't get her out of this downpour, she could die. Taking her by the arm, he tugged her against him. With one hand behind him and the other arm around her waist, he inched away from the edge.

At last, with one final jerk, they were inside the cave, out of the elements. Tucker shivered from being wet. His bedroll was on Yank's back, wherever Yank was. Tucker didn't want to think that the horse had gone over the edge with him. Tucker always took care of his horse. Just like his namesakes, the big black was indestructible. They were a good match, a Southern Rebel and a horse named Yank. Both were survivors.

The cave was small and damp. The woman, still lying against his chest, was cold. He shook her gently, waiting for a reaction. But the only response he felt was his own as the top of his index finger found the space beneath her breast.

"Ma'am . . . Lady . . . I beg your pardon, but would you wake up."

She moaned and turned slightly so that her face was against his chest. His hand, below her breast only moments ago, was now holding it. Tucker froze, waiting for her to come to her senses and chastise him for his liberties.

But she didn't wake. He had the absurd feeling that he'd been cut into two people. His head ached fiercely while the lower half of his body, very much alert, announced a raging male hunger. Until he understood what was happening, he'd force his thoughts and touch away from that need as he cradled her head and laid her down.

That's when he found it, the wound, blood now dried across a deep cut in her scalp behind her ear. However she'd come to join him in this godforsaken place, she, too, had come accidentally. Nobody deliberately fell off a cliff. But what was he going to do? The rain hadn't let up. It was too dark to see how to get back to the trail, and he wasn't sure he was steady enough on his feet to get them there. His head ached like the devil.

If he could find some dry sticks or limbs, he could build a fire. Reluctantly he let go of her and waited for the next flash of lightning. Once he was reasonably certain that they weren't sharing the cave with any animals, he began to explore, encountering the remains of a pack rat's nest.

In the cantina he'd had tobacco and matches. He reached into his shirt pocket, hoping they were still there. They were, along with the half-breed's gold nuggets and the watch fob. Now the bandits had another excuse for chasing him—the loot.

Shielding his meager makings of a fire from the wind, Tucker cupped his hands and struck the first match against a stone. It flared briefly, then died. There were only a few matches left. He couldn't afford to waste another. By touch he found a tuft of dried moss and encircled it with his legs, planting his back to the cave opening.

Over the moss he crumbled tiny filings of dried leaves.

Closing his eyes, he prayed for a moment of calm as he lit another match. This time the moss blazed up, igniting the sticks. Within moments he had a tiny fire going. By its light he could see other animal nests and a stack of pine cones. Wild animals hadn't been the only ones to use this small cave. He hoped the Indians in the area wouldn't decide to collect rent because he was using their firestarters. He also hoped he wouldn't pass out.

With a fire going, he moved the woman farther into the cave. The heat brought out the smell of whiskey sopped up by his shirt when he'd knocked over the bottle at the card game. He wished he had it back. It would taste a hell of a lot better on the inside than out.

Though meager, the fire soon warmed the air inside the small cave. Tucker sluiced water through the woman's head wound and winced at the depth of it. He didn't know why she wasn't dead. She could die still if he didn't get her warm.

Removing his sheepskin jacket, he covered her, checking beneath her wet clothing for a sign that her body temperature was rising. It wasn't. Finally, because he knew nothing else to do, he lay down beside her and pulled her against him. He didn't intend to doze off, but the heat from the fire and the woman's body soon made him drowsy.

As the storm raged outside, Tucker Farrell covered himself and the woman with his jacket. Then he did something he had never done with a woman before. He slept.

Sluggishly, Raven felt life return to her body. Half awake and half asleep, she snuggled closer to the source of the heat. The fire dried her skin and her hair. The rain ceased and the wind died down.

She dreamed of an old man. He was telling her a story about a lion and a raven. Foolishly the raven had chased after a small animal and been caught between two rocks at the top of a cliff. The cougar was reluctant to climb the rocks, but he couldn't leave the silly bird trapped. Finally, seeing the raven near death, the cougar climbed up and freed the bird.

The raven flew away, squawking loudly, then turned back and landed on the cougar's back. For the rest of the journey, the two unlikely allies traveled together, each owing the other his life.

By the time the sun threw brassy light across the canyon, Raven knew, even in sleep, that she was the bird and the presence beside her was the cougar.

Three hundred feet below, at the foot of the cliff, near the river's edge, Luce Santiago lay, his blood staining the cream-colored sand. He would die here. His father had warned him. Now he'd brought about his own downfall by bragging about his treasure. It had been the cheap whiskey and the looks on the faces of the men who'd wanted no part of the old man.

For too many years, he'd felt their disdain, been laughed at, forced to barter for food. For once in his life, he'd been as good as they, better even, for he was the guardian of the mountain of treasure that his father's father, the man who'd been part Indian, part Spaniard, had helped hide.

The words echoed in his mind from some long-past time. As a boy he'd been taken into the mountains, where he'd gone without food and drink to purify himself for what was to come. Naked and with his head shorn, the tattoos of his father's people had been etched over his body. Afterward his father explained that from this day forward, he, too, would become the keeper of the trust.

"When the time comes for you to die, you may reveal the secret, just as I have done for you."

"How?" he'd asked. But his father had only replied that when the spirits called to him, he should once again give up all earthly things. He should bathe himself, fast, shave the hair from his head. One would come to see that his body was buried at the base of the barren side of the mountain in respect to the spirits who'd trusted him with the secret. And he'd cautioned the boy that any man who touched the treasure would surely die.

The boy had believed his father and waited. Finally he'd lost his wife, his children, and he had grown tired and old. Soon it would be time for his spirit to leave. Just once before he left this hard life, he'd wanted to be a man respected.

Through the years, he'd crossed the mountain to the other side. Once, when the earth trembled, he'd found a way inside. Only one time had he allowed himself to remove a bag of nuggets and a piece of jewelry, just enough to buy food and supplies. He'd considered the gold small payment for his vigilant care of the mountain. But in the end, he couldn't resist taking the jewel. He'd thought he'd be safe. He would have been, had he not been foolish.

Now with a mountain of gold his for the taking, he would die here as poor as the day he was born. But not yet. The one who would bury him according to the ritual had not come—the next guardian of the sacred mountain.

When Tucker Farrell opened his eyes, it was morning. A woman wearing a butter-colored buckskin dress was watching him. She didn't look real, but he couldn't be sure. He closed his eyes again.

"Who are you?" he asked and waited.

No answer. Carefully he cocked one eyelid, allowing bleary light to seep through the narrow opening. So far so good. He tried the other eye. The woman was still there, serene and ethereal in the shadows, with sunlight glaring against the ledge behind her.

"Are you hurt?" she finally asked.

Tucker drew one hand from beneath the sheepskin jacket which covered him and pressed it to the top of his head. Something had happened last night. His chest ached. He felt as if someone had attempted to lift his scalp.

"Hell, yes!" His voice was so gravelly that he could scarcely speak.

"Where is the injury?" She came up onto her knees and started to examine him.

"Lady—uh, ma'am—whatever on the west side of hell you are, keep your hands off me."

She ignored him, slipping her fingertips beneath his jacket and his flannel shirt and through the buttons of his underwear to the bruised skin over his rib cage. As she touched him he jerked away, stunned more by his reaction to the beautiful woman than the pain caused by her fingertips.

"I can't be certain that you are all right unless I touch you. What's wrong? I don't understand," she said, looking at her hands in surprise.

"Hell if I understand, either," he cut her off. "Who are you and what are you doing here?"

"I'm Raven Alexander." Confusion filled her eyes. "And I, too, seem to have fallen." She leaned back, turning her head from side to side as if waiting for some unseen presence to give her answers.

Tucker closed his eyes again. His frustration was due not only to the roaring pain in his head, but also the hot liquid quality of her voice. He took in her woman smell like an animal scenting danger and reacted just as strongly. "You don't remember?"

"I was on the trail. Then—I'm sorry."

"Yeah, we seem to have wandered into the same place last night." He took a deep breath and winced.

"If you will tell me where you hurt," she offered, "I'll try to help."

"Whoa! Listen, lady, you're the one who's hurt. There's a hole in your head I could put a gun barrel in. I don't even know how you're sitting up."

"There is no pain," she said softly.

"And you're offering help to a stranger. Aren't you the least bit afraid?"

She looked around, considering his question. "Afraid? No. I knew you would come. But I didn't understand that I would feel so odd—so shivery."

This time, Tucker couldn't hold back a scoff of disbelief. She felt shivery? He didn't want to know what that might mean. "Who told you? *I* didn't even know I was coming."

"You came to me in a dream. I saw a cougar and a raven in a barren place. When the raven was trapped, the cougar freed it."

"Ravens," he repeated, remembering the flock of black birds. "After what I've been through, I can believe anything. Why this is happening is what I don't understand."

"It was foretold by the spirits that we should come together. I started on a journey and then I—I must have fallen. When I woke up, I saw you. Please, let me help you."

The imprint of her hands on his chest still burned, sending ripples of heat downward. The last thing he needed was more examination from this woman who turned cold into hot.

"I don't think you want to know what hurts, lady. And I'm sure as hell not in the mood for you to fix it. You just be still and let me see if I can figure out where we are."

She gave him a curious look. "Of course."

The woman moved away, gingerly touching the place behind her ear. He could tell she'd discovered the wound there, but, surprisingly, her expression showed no evidence of pain.

She seemed undisturbed by the situation, and Tucker sensed no fear. She seemed to accept his presence as ordinary. There were no birds, no fluttering wings, but something just as unreal was happening here.

"Is someone pursuing you?" she asked.

The bandits. Of course. They had to be, unless the birds had spooked them. At the shock of seeing her, he'd forgotten what had happened. Now upright, leaning against the cave wall, Tucker forced himself to remember.

Carefully he rotated his shoulders and moved his legs. The only pain he had came from the lump on his head, a few bruises on his back, and a rib that cut through him when he breathed. He hadn't been attacked and nobody had shot him. He must have dozed off and fallen from his horse. That explanation didn't make much sense, but it was the only one he had for now. But what about the woman?

Now that he was in reasonable control of himself, he turned to face her. She was young, slender, her skin a warm color, not from the fire but from being kissed by the sun, her voice soft and mysterious. Her hair was as dark as the night, her eyes as brilliant as the black stones he'd seen once in a necklace worn by a woman riding in a fancy carriage. He'd never seen anyone who could sit so still or be so quiet.

She wore her thick hair in a single braid that fell across her chest. The woman had an elegant beauty about her, a mystical way of tilting her head as if she heard unspoken words. But more compelling than any of these was the feeling of power that radiated from every part of her. He felt as if he were in the presence of the gods, and he didn't like the awareness that she pulled from inside him. Everything about her left him even more dazed.

All of this he knew without her speaking a word.

"You're an Indian."

"I'm part Indian." She looked down at her dress. "Does that bother you?"

He could have told her that it was the feel of her body against him for most of the night that bothered him. Indians weren't his favorite people, but something about her trusting nature made him keep that to himself.

"Just tell me you're not a Comanche. I've heard the women take male prisoners and turn them into slaves."

"I'm Arapaho and you're much too big for one woman to hold you as a slave."

He couldn't hold back a smile. "I don't know. You seem to have strange powers." That statement was certainly true. "I've managed to travel alone for thirty-two years. This is the first time I can remember waking up with a woman I didn't go to bed with."

"Don't try to understand. Just accept what has happened. We were meant to come together. Have you had no dreams of birds?"

He gave her an odd look. "Dreams? No, but hundreds of them saved my life yesterday. Black birds. I never saw such a flock of black birds before. They got me out of a pretty bad mess. Did you have anything to do with that?"

"No," she answered simply.

This was all too much for Tucker. He licked his dry lips. "Don't suppose you happened to bring a canteen with you?"

She shook her head. "I have this. An earlier occupant must have left it here on the ledge. The rain filled it with water." She reached for a piece of broken pottery and handed it to him.

He swallowed the liquid as if it were the tonic once made by his mother, the one he'd had to hold his nose to swallow every spring. To his surprise the water was sweet and cool, and in a few minutes his head began to clear.

"It's been a long time since a drink of water had that effect on me," he said, beginning to consider the possibility that this woman might not be what she seemed.

She was studying him quizzically. "One cannot understand the workings of Mother Earth. She sends many gifts that we accept without question."

"If you're telling me that Mother Earth sent those birds to save my neck, don't. I don't understand and I don't want to. Right now all I want to do is get back up there and check on my horse. Don't guess you saw any sign of a ladder, did you?"

"No, but while you were sleeping I looked around. There appears to be a kind of path around the wall heading up. Whoever used this cave in the past had to have a way to get down and back. I didn't follow it because I didn't want to leave you. It's very narrow."

Tucker groaned. No point in telling her that he'd likely look down and pass out cold. If he didn't fall, the height would paralyze him and he'd end up a mummified corpse stuck to the side of this godforsaken cliff.

"I think we should hurry," she said suddenly, tilting her head. "Riders approach from the south." Too quickly she tried to stand, swayed unsteadily, and caught Tucker's arm.

"Whoa there!" He grabbed her, sliding his arm around her as he had last night when he'd pulled her into the cave. It all came flashing back, the feel of the woman against him, the way she nestled close. He groaned and would have let her go had she not looked up at him with such trust in her eyes.

Damn! What was he going to do with her? He couldn't leave her there, yet he couldn't be sure he could get his own self back to the trail. "Riders? How can you tell?"

"I hear the horses' hoofbeats in the rock. Listen, you can hear them too."

"Riders? Hell!" Tucker listened, but all he could hear was the pounding in his head. Could it be the bandits? Why weren't they following the old miner? Tucker didn't know where the treasure was. If they discovered Tucker instead of the prospector, they were going to be even madder. A second escape was unlikely, especially now that he was not alone.

Tucker picked up his jacket, offered it to the Indian girl. When she refused, he threaded his arms through the sleeves. Wearing it was easier than carrying it.

Taking one final deep breath, he whistled and waited for Yank's answering neigh. A second horse echoed Yank's reply, and as Tucker closed his eyes and stepped out on the lip of the rock, he heard the two animals moving above them.

"I hope that second horse is yours."

"Yes, Onawa follows us. Do we go?"

"We try." Taking a chance, he looked down and swore.

This was not going to be easy. He had to find a way to think about something other than his body bouncing off the rocks below.

"*Onawa.* What does it mean?"

He delayed. She trusted him to get her out of this mess when his feet refused to move. How in hell was he going to force himself out onto that ledge?

"*Onawa* means wide-awake," she said. "Don't look down. Just stick close to the wall and I'll be beside you."

She gave him a nudge and tried to find something to take his mind off his fear. "Do you have a name?"

"Several."

"Which of them shall I call you?"

He finally took a step, a deep breath, then another step.

"The name I was born with is Tucker, Tucker Farrell."

For a long minute, he hugged the cliff, his arm still supporting her, his nose pressed against the hard rock wall. Then his foot hit a loose pebble, which rolled to the narrow edge and fell. There was no sound of it hitting bottom.

He froze again.

"Tucker Farrell," the woman said softly. "I like that name. A proud defender."

He would have argued that the only thing he defended was his own life, but he had a sudden flash of the miner back in the cantina. Coming to his aid had been a temporary aberration. He wondered if the old man had gotten away, how badly he'd been shot. For a moment, Tucker allowed himself to admit that he'd done a good deed. Then he remembered the necktie party and what had almost happened.

"Don't count on me, ma'am. I'm just a drifter, a misfit. Nothing valiant about me."

"Your animal power comes from the cougar, Mr. Farrell. You are, or you will become, that proud creature. I know. I have dreamed it."

As Tucker stewed over that bizarre observation, he

forgot his fear and took a step, then another. "Where'd you get a name like Raven?" he asked.

"That was my mother's name. It is tradition. I am considered a spirit woman."

"Spirit woman. Of course. I should have known that." As he considered that revelation, they reached the top of the trail.

"Onawa! My friend." The Indian woman laid her head against the neck of the small black-and-white horse for a moment before climbing on. She rode without a saddle.

Yank looked from Tucker to the filly and back again, his great nostrils blowing air, his head held high as if to say, *I'm the protector here.* Tucker gave the horse a disgusted look and patted his saddlebags to make sure his supplies were still there. Satisfied that they'd weathered the storm, he climbed on the horse and prepared to bid his unusual companion farewell.

"Which way do we go?" Raven asked. "Do we continue along the trail, or do we make our way to the canyon floor below?"

"Now wait just a minute, ma'am. There is no 'we.' I've got a gang of Mexican bandits behind me who think I separated them from the location of a lost treasure. You'd better find yourself another traveling companion."

"Lost treasure?"

Hell, he'd done it now. Not only was there a treasure-crazed band of outlaws behind him, the woman beside him had that same glaze of recognition in her eye. Had she followed him? Did she know about the treasure and expect him to lead her to it?

At that moment, Raven led the way, nudging Onawa into a trot.

Tucker swallowed his protest and followed. "Don't expect me to take you to any treasure. I don't know a thing about it. I just helped an old prospector who bragged about finding it."

"The treasure will wait. We must hurry," Raven said. "Your pursuers ride hard. They mean you harm."

Damn, he didn't want to have to kill anybody. He'd done enough of that as a soldier, fighting first his own kind, then the Indians. For the last few years, he'd managed to avoid trouble. The only time he used his gun now was in self-defense or to kill for food. Yet he was beginning to feel a kind of tension settle over him. Even Yank didn't have to be urged.

"All right. The horses need water. We'll make our way to the river. We can find better hiding places there."

Raven nodded.

Tucker peered over the edge of the trail and winced. "I don't suppose you know the way down, do you?"

"No, but it doesn't matter. We'll find it." *The spirits will guide you*, a voice said as clearly as if someone had spoken.

Raven glanced at Tucker, who was studying the trail behind them. She could feel the urgency building inside her, but she didn't know if it came from their pursuers or the man beside her.

As the horses moved along, Raven emptied her thoughts. She could almost feel the earth tremble, as if she were riding across the plains, a herd of buffalo coming toward her, a herd of cattle behind, the cliff on one side and the mountain on the other. Sometimes, if she waited, she'd hear the sounds of drumbeats and chanting, signaling the coming of a vision.

She glanced up and caught sight of a single black bird over her, flying along as if it were some kind of totem, protecting her.

Nah'ni chita-ini. Look, O maid, behold me.

And Raven understood she was to follow. There

would be no vision. Instead the spirits had sent a visible guide to lead them.

The trail came to the intersection. The bird overhead flew straight, following the trail that had begun to drop. It let out an urgent squawk and dipped over the edge of the canyon rim before disappearing from sight

The sun went behind a cloud, and the earth turned cool for a moment as the mountain cast its shadow across the trail.

Tucker swore.

Raven shivered and wondered what lay ahead.

The bird gave a final cry from somewhere in the canyon below.

3

More than an hour passed before Tucker reined Yank to a stop and measured their progress.

Between his headache, his sore ribs, and the woman riding in front of him, he was having difficulty focusing on the task at hand.

A fine pair they made. Both had been on the trail and both had fallen, yet she didn't even seem alarmed. It was almost as if she'd expected him. If he were a superstitious man, he'd be looking over his shoulder. The one thing he did know was that being with him put her in danger. More than that, he was entirely too conscious of her as a woman. What in hell was she really doing here and where were they going?

The treasure had to be the answer. She must be looking for it too. If she didn't know about it, he couldn't for the life of himself figure out why she'd want to ride with him.

Tucker had no illusions about himself. He was a black sheep, a man who'd deserted his country's army because he'd disagreed with the orders he'd been given. He had no future and a past that not even he liked to dwell on.

He'd done nothing to impress her with his kindness. He was hot, thirsty, and hungry, and his rib cage ached unmercifully. The crowning insult was the unmistakable smell of spilled whiskey.

She stopped.

"What's wrong?" Tucker asked, expecting to hear her say that she was leaving him on his own. He was shocked to realize he'd be disappointed to see her go. That was the last thing he wanted to feel, but he liked riding with her. For the first time in a long time, he felt like sharing himself with another person—something he'd never thought he'd do again. He concentrated on the set of her shoulders.

Raven, feeling the intensity of his gaze, didn't allow herself to look at him. Until she knew what to do, the less connection between them, the better. She understood he was part of her quest, but she wasn't yet comfortable with him or the feelings he provoked in her.

He was such an imposing figure, strong and powerful. Though he was gruff and distant, and clearly had been on the trail for days, she couldn't stop her uncomfortable awareness of him as a man.

Raven had aways been aware of the special feelings that existed between a man and a woman. First she'd seen her sisters fall in love. Then, in the Arapaho camp, she'd watched her Indian sisters and brothers express their interest in each other, openly and joyfully.

But Raven had never experienced such thoughts before. The sensation was not only disconcerting but unwanted. She was on a mission for the good of her people. Nothing, not even this man who was to show her the way, could be allowed to distract her.

"We go down here."

Tucker looked at the space in the rocks to which she directed her horse and shook his head. "The hell you say.

I've been known to climb down a few ravines on foot, but to ride off the side of a cliff is something even Yank won't do."

But Yank, who always did what Yank wanted to do, followed Onawa, carefully planting his feet between the huge rocks as he stepped off the side of the mountain. If asked, Tucker would never have admitted that he closed his eyes, but he did. Then, realizing that Yank was moving steadily downward with little effort, Tucker chanced a look.

Miraculously, they were on a trail, narrow but open. It twisted back and forth so that at any given time the only view was of the boulders ahead or the rocks beside. Unless a person knew the trail was there, it would never be seen. With any luck the bandits, if they were behind him, would ride on by.

For the first time, Tucker began to breathe easier.

"How did you know about this trail?" he asked.

"I didn't know. The spirits sent a guide. Onawa simply followed."

Tucker didn't argue, but he didn't believe her either. She'd been here before. Why didn't she admit it? Because she shared information only when she felt it necessary, otherwise Onawa's knowledge was a convenient answer for anything she didn't want to divulge. So? He'd go along. Believing that the horse was leading them made as much sense as spirit messages.

She was dressed like an Arapaho. He recognized the designs along the neckline of the garment. But now, in the sunlight, he could see that her background was as much white as Indian. The combination made her look exotic. Everything about her was different from any woman he'd ever known. Her dark hair was tied with a strip of soft leather that seemed to match the fringe on her dress. He could see the wound beginning to scab over.

She seemed at ease riding bareback, allowing herself to roll with the horse's gait. He took an appreciative glance at her long, shapely legs that she made no attempt to hide—unlike the women he'd known in the more civilized societies in which he'd traveled long ago.

Tucker would like to have seen Lucinda, the woman he'd once thought to marry, in a buckskin dress with a fringe at the bottom.

That thought was too much and he let out a silent chuckle. Hell, Lucinda's skin had never been exposed to the open air. He took another look at the woman who called herself Raven, and the thought of bare skin sent an arrow of need piercing through him. Even his rib hurt as he drew in a long, ragged breath.

Whoa, Tuck! This is not the time for fantasies, and a woman who calls herself a spirit woman sure as hell isn't the one to fantasize about. He had no explanation for the birds that had come to his rescue, but he wasn't ready to believe in spirits. Still, his companion was giving him second thoughts.

"How much farther to the bottom?" he asked.

"From the sound of the water, I'd say we're close."

Tucker inclined his head and listened. The only sound he could hear was the pounding in his head. Whatever the sweet-tasting water had taken away, the sun and the uneven ground had started up again. A dull roar sounded, growing louder. He could even feel it shake the earth beneath them.

"Wait a minute. That's not a river."

"Shush! Don't talk," the woman whispered.

Both horses stilled, and Tucker waited. He wouldn't have been surprised to see Geronimo lift his head from beyond the boulders. Then he realized what he heard. Horses. Many horses, passing along the trail overhead. The riders stopped and began to argue. One group wanted to go back, the other forward.

"The old half-breed wouldn't have disappeared without a trace."

Tucker recognized that voice. It was the bandit leader from the cantina, the one with the crossed bandoliers full of shiny bullets.

"But Porfiro, what about his partner, the one with the gold hair who was rescued by the birds?"

Tucker cringed. *Partner?* If they truly believed the old miner was his partner, they'd be on his trail forever. The bandits saw him as some kind of supernatural being. He might have laughed had it not been for the woman with the dark eyes who came from nowhere to ride beside him. It was too strange. He was just a cowboy, trying to stay alive. He didn't believe in any spirit world.

Yet the woman with him called him a cougar. She saw him as some kind of primitive creature. And she seemed to care. For too long there'd been nobody to care what he was. He'd become a faceless drifter who came and went with the seasons.

All his family were gone. All except Lucinda. The woman he'd been engaged to marry was now the wife of the mayor of Cinderville, South Carolina. The Yankee who'd come there after the war had claimed the spoils of victory: the Farrell farm, the future Mrs. Farrell, and—Tucker allowed himself a silent laugh—the pigs that were the one part of the farm Lucinda had despised. Tucker had gotten past losing his family. He'd even gotten over Lucinda. Knowing that her new husband had turned the horse farm into nothing but a pig farm made up for it somehow.

Yank moved restlessly.

Raven looked up the trail at him and put a finger of silence to her mouth.

"What was that, Porfiro?" the sidekick asked anxiously.

"Some kind of bird, Juan. Let's go on."

"A bird?" The fear in the first man's voice was contagious. The others began to whisper.

"Just a little hummingbird, you fool. Are you going to let a sound stop us from finding the treasure? Not Porfiro. I will be rich."

"I do not fear the hummingbird," Juan answered. "It is the black birds. Look, one follows us. I am worried. Let us leave this place before dark."

More animated discussion followed, then the men moved off down the trail, quietly now, as if listening.

Raven held Onawa still for a long time. The sound of a loose pebble could travel in the canyon, sometimes bouncing off the walls in an echo that was louder than the original. Finally she nudged the horse forward, making sure Tucker followed.

The Mexican bandits had clearly been in search of another man besides Tucker. In fact, they'd made it sound as if the two men were partners. And they'd mentioned a treasure. That thought filled Raven's heart with dread. She knew that Tucker was meant to take her to the keeper of the mountain, but now someone else seemed to know it too.

Another half hour passed before the sound of rushing water reached Tucker's ears. Never a man to make trouble where there was none, he'd hidden his anxiety by focusing on the mysterious woman in front of him, wondering how she'd taste, how she'd feel in his arms. He had lulled himself into a dreamlike state by the time Yank threaded his way through the rocks and stepped out onto the sandy bar along the river.

The horses moved swiftly toward the water. "No! Wait!" Raven drew Onawa to a sudden stop. Yank, close behind her, lowered his head and halted abruptly in his favorite trick of trying to dislodge Tucker.

"Not this time, you bag of bones." Tucker slid off the horse to the ground. But he hadn't counted on Yank's continued obstinacy. The Reb might try, but the big horse, determined to have the last word, lowered his head and butted Tucker forward, depositing him in the shallow waters of the Rio Grande.

"Christ!" he roared, reaching for his hat as it skittered out of reach and started a merry rush downstream. "What in the west side of hell is wrong with you, horse?"

The animal merely tossed his head and waited.

Raven smothered a grin as she climbed down and led both animals to the water. She knelt down to drink, then sat back and studied the soft sand. She had to remain calm and give her mind a chance to understand. Sooner or later the spirits would speak to her. Uncertain, she started up the canyon, feeling the vibrant aura of the ground.

She concentrated on the power that propelled her, stronger now. Someone had been there before them, perhaps the night before. Someone who'd been wounded. The path of his blood was only just visible in the slightly pink sand. Was that how the bandits had followed the trail? No, if the rain had washed most of the blood from the sand, it would have cleansed the rocky surface they had traveled.

She heard Tucker splash out of the water behind her. She turned and watched him plant his wet Stetson on his head. He wiped the beads of water streaming down his face with the bandanna he'd worn around his neck.

"Where is he?" she asked.

"Who? Where's who?"

"The man you were traveling with."

Tucker blinked, then with an exaggerated motion,

wiped the water from his ears. "What man? I may have hit my head, but I know I was alone—that is, until you came along."

"Whoever he is, he's hurt." She studied the shadows along the eastern side of the canyon. "And he's hiding somewhere nearby, I think."

"How can you tell?" Tucker asked, but he wasn't certain he wanted to know. The only man he knew to be hurt was the old prospector, and being in the same place with a man holding the secret to a treasure was not a healthy place to be at that moment.

What he ought to do was get some rest, follow the river back to Colorado, and keep on going west. He'd heard that Oregon was opening up. Good horse country there. If he could come up with a stake, he could raise horses, cattle maybe.

Cattle were a damned sight better than the pigs being raised on his father's plantation back home. And it was time he stopped drifting.

"Tucker, the men who were following us went on past, but we don't know that the trail won't lead them to a place where we can be seen. I think we'd better find your partner before they come back."

"He's not my partner." Tucker picked up Yank's reins and followed the woman, who seemed to be reading some kind of map in the sand. "I never saw him before he came into the cantina yesterday to play poker."

"I see. And what about the treasure those men are after?"

"Don't know a thing about a treasure. Don't know who the old man was or where he came from. I just didn't like those *pistoleros* shooting somebody who was just reaching for a piece of paper."

She reached the canyon wall and stood, closing her

eyes, as if waiting for something to direct her steps, until they heard a low moan.

"Here, Tucker, he's in here."

Behind a boulder in a shallow recess lay the old man, crumpled, pale, afraid.

Until he saw Tucker.

"Señor." He smiled in recognition. "The sunlight you bring with you is bright. For a moment I could not see."

"It's you." Tucker knelt beside him. "I thought you got away."

"No. In spite of your help, I'm afraid the bullet was more lethal than I thought. I have lost much blood. I was a foolish old man and now I will die."

"Nonsense. You just got a nick in the shoulder. I've had worse. Let me have a look."

"Luce," he reminded Tucker again. "My name is Luce Santiago."

Tucker glanced at the wound and confirmed what he already suspected. It was bad. If the man weren't so old, if he hadn't ridden all night, maybe the story would be different.

Tucker glanced around the harsh confines of the area with a sinking heart. The old man was going to die. Tucker couldn't see a damned thing they could do about it. He looked at Raven, but she was staring at the old miner as if she'd seen a ghost.

"We'll build a fire and get you warm," he began.

"No—no, you must take me home. I must not die before I reach the place where I am to be buried." He turned to Raven as if he'd just noticed her presence. "Yes," he whispered. "It is you for whom I have waited. You must see that I am properly buried, daughter of the moon."

Raven nodded slowly. She could see the smoky veil of death surrounding him. And she understood that he was the guardian she'd been sent to find. Tucker had brought her to him. Three wounded strangers had come together. Each had their part to play.

"Where are you to be buried, old man?" Tucker asked.

"At the barren base of the sacred mountain where the sun and the moon meet."

"Where the light of the moon meets the light of the sun," she whispered. Grandfather's words to her, the location of the treasure.

But Luce didn't answer. He'd closed his eyes.

Raven turned to Tucker, this time with a stern expression on her face that boded no good. "Do you, too, look for the sacred mountain that hides the treasure?"

"Lady, I don't know anything about any treasure."

"Then how do you account for this?" She slipped her fingers beneath her dress and drew out the gold watch fob and the nuggets.

"I forgot about them. I'll be damned."

"Most likely," Raven agreed, skepticism written across her stoic face.

"The old man bet with them in the poker game." That's what had started all the trouble, Tucker thought. "I was going to return them."

"Don't deny that you would like to share in the treasure. I wouldn't believe you."

Tucker turned guilty eyes toward his Indian companion. He hadn't considered it before, not consciously, but he could use the gold to buy land, to start his ranch. "This is where you were coming all along, isn't it?"

"Yes," she admitted. "I was sent by the Grandfather, Flying Cloud, to find the sacred treasure of the Arapaho."

"And what makes you think it belongs to your people?" Tucker asked.

"It belongs to the Ancient Ones," the injured man said without opening his eyes. "You will be the keepers of the treasure. But know this, Mother Earth jealously guards that which has been entrusted to her. Your hearts must be pure."

Raven nodded. "Yes, Tucker. It was meant to be. You will help me find my people's treasure, and I will share it with you. Will you do it?"

Here it was, commitment, the future he'd avoided, the tomorrow he'd never expected to have, being offered to him. It was time to see the bet or fold. And suddenly he knew he couldn't drift anymore. Spirit woman or not, some power stronger than he had stepped in and forced his hand.

He gave a wry laugh. "What else do I have to do? It's a deal." Tucker almost reached for her. He had a strong desire to seal their bargain with a kiss. But he knew the occasion was much too solemn for that. A cowboy didn't kiss a spirit woman. He only returned her nod of acceptance.

From behind them came the weak voice of Luce. "I pray you, beware the bronze man. Beware the dagger!"

4

Treasure.

Tucker studied the woman and Luce, wondering what in hell he had gotten himself into. If there actually was a treasure, and if they found it, the possibilities were endless. But he'd never been much of a gambler. What he could be holding here was the Dead Man's Hand. Thieves, a spirit woman, a dying old man, and he had to add himself, a fool. He could end up dead, just like Wild Bill Hickok had in Deadwood last year.

The other cardplayers never knew what Wild Bill's mystery card was. He had been shot before it could be revealed. But Tucker knew his; it was his spirit woman. And the cause of his death wouldn't be a shot in the back, like Hickok. His cause was staring straight at him.

"Listen, Raven," he began. "I don't know if you really believe all this treasure business, but you've put your life in danger by teaming up with me and Luce. I'd take you back to the nearest American settlement, but I don't think the old man would make it. And I'm not sure we'd get past the bandits."

"Thank you, but I can't go back. If I die, then it was meant to be."

"Why is it that every time you speak, I wait for thunder to roll and lightning to flash?" His question came out more like a threat, and he knew his tightly leashed fury frightened her. But she straightened her shoulders and jutted out her chin.

"I don't know what you mean," she said. "I'm sorry I make you angry."

"You don't make me angry. You make me—" *crazy, wild,* he would have said. "Damn it, Raven, you shouldn't go around trusting strangers."

"But you're not a stranger. You're part of my—my totem. You're the cougar in my dream. Your animal power is one with mine. Grandfather said it would be so."

Tucker reached out and caught her arm before he realized what he was doing. "I'd like to speak with your grandfather. It seems to me that he did a whole lot of talking without knowing what he was setting you up for."

Raven's face went white. "Grandfather is dead. Just like the rest of the Arapaho if I don't find the treasure."

"And suppose you do, what then?"

"I'll buy land so that they won't have to live on a reservation. So they won't have to depend on the government."

Tucker didn't know what to say to that. He had his doubts that the American government would allow the Indians to buy land, but then, they would probably find a way to stop him from getting his ranch too. "This whole treasure-hunting idea is dangerous," he said. "Don't you understand that bandits are chasing this old man, *pistoleros* who will torture him for his knowledge? Then they'll kill you, but only after they've done—terrible things to you."

She shook her head slowly. "No. You will protect me—and Luce."

Tucker groaned. He had to get through to her. He

was no saint, even if he wanted to be. "Raven, even I'm not that good a fighter."

"Please." She laid her hand over his. "You're wrong about yourself. This is the way it is meant to be. Alone we are weak, at the mercy of evil. But we've come together here, in this place, to accomplish our goals—together."

Together? This time Tucker swallowed his oath. Long ago, when he'd returned from the war and found the life he'd fought for gone, he'd accepted that fate played interesting games with a man's life. If he hadn't been certain then, he'd had that knowledge brought to life forever when he'd watched soldiers call innocent women and children savages and slaughter them in the name of good.

But all this was too much for a drifter like him. He didn't understand what was happening, and he didn't want to. If it meant dying, Tucker didn't want the treasure; the ranch was only a dream.

But he was a sucker for dark eyes and wounded old men. And, he told himself as he walked Yank over to Luce, he'd get Luce home to die. That was the honorable thing to do. Whether or not he wanted to admit it, he still had a tiny, stubborn sliver of honor.

Yank would have to carry both Tucker and the injured man. Tucker hoped that, for once, the stubborn animal didn't try to continue fighting the War Between the States. The horse had been on the winning side, and he seemed to delight in reminding Tucker of it as often as he could.

Had Luce been an outlaw, Tucker would have folded him over the horse's back like a sack of flour. But he wasn't. And once Tucker made up his mind to get the miner home, he wasn't going to fail.

Lifting him into the saddle was pure agony for Tucker's injured ribs. With Raven's help he finally got him up and slid in behind. Keeping Luce upright was not going to be easy for either man. Finally Tucker removed the rope the old man used to hold up his pants and tied the two of them together at the waist. Now Tucker could use his arms to support the man's head and prevent it from lolling forward. It didn't relieve the pressure of Luce's weight against his ribs, but it stopped the jostling that set off fresh waves of pain.

"Downriver," Luce gasped, and slumped forward.

The mist rising from the water burned away under the heat of the brassy morning sun. There was a quietness at the bottom of the steep cliffs through which the river had run for centuries, and an absence of animal life gave a curious empty feel to the canyon.

Only an occasional bird glided along on the brisk air currents that funneled through the slash in the earth. They came upon a solitary family of quail which had obviously flown in, hatched little ones, and apparently been unable to leave.

Raven kept a sharp eye on the edge of the cliffs, but a dozen men could be watching and she wouldn't know it. They were too close to the wall to look up and see anything but sky. And they were easy targets. Their horses' footfalls were loud in the silence, making them easy to track, easy to kill.

Finally the old man roused himself and spoke again. "Cross the river here and ride toward the cluster of black rocks with the jagged rim."

"I hope it isn't much farther, Luce. My stomach is ready for some food, and you need a bed and some rest."

"Not far" was the answer. "Behind the rock is a way up."

They crossed the water, shallow but fast moving, and made their way silently to the ebony-colored rock that took on the shape of inverted fingers, the knuckles forming the jagged edge.

Something about the formation made the hair stand up on the back of Tucker's neck. He glanced around, searching the top of the ridge. Were they being watched?

But he couldn't see anybody there.

Nothing about this made any sense to Tucker. He ought to be halfway to Oregon. How in hell had he ended up down here with a wounded man and a woman who was tying him in knots with her lush, regal presence?

The trail behind the rock was exactly where the old man had said. Once they located it, Raven directed Onawa back to the river and along the bank for a short distance, then rode the filly into the water and doubled back. She climbed down, looked around, and finally asked for Tucker's bandanna.

"What are you going to do with that?"

"Cover our tracks," she said.

Puzzled, he removed it and handed it to her.

"Now your hat."

The bandanna was one thing, his hat was something else. It was only beginning to dry after its trip down the river.

"Hurry." Her voice forced him into action. Sooner or later he was going to have to explain that he didn't take orders from a woman, Indian or white.

Quickly she filled his bandanna with river-smooth pebbles and his hat with fine dry sand. After dragging the bandanna weighted down with rocks to smooth out the hoofprints, she covered the area with a layer of sand, then returned the handkerchief and the hat to Tucker.

He studied the grains of sand clinging inside the band and frowned. "Hell! You could have used your moccasin instead of my hat, Spirit Woman."

She grinned unexpectedly as he whacked the Stetson against his thigh. "I could. But my feet are clean. I didn't think you'd notice any more dirt."

He scowled back at her. She was right. He was a mess, travel weary—he didn't know how long it had been since he'd shaved. To add to the picture, there was a tear in the knee of his denim trousers. Now, on top of it all, he had sand down his neck.

As quickly as it had come, the grin was gone, and once more Raven took the lead. She'd been injured and had ridden a long time without food, yet she seemed to grow stronger with every mile. She sat erect, proud, as if she knew exactly where she was going.

Maybe she did. Maybe this was some kind of elaborate hoax to use him. But for what? If there was a treasure, only the old man knew its location for certain. He'd never seen Raven before; he couldn't have missed her back in the village. Unless she was really some kind of medicine woman, there was no way she could have known about him and the old man and the treasure.

Why was she doing this, tagging along with a stranger and an old man, when she'd been the one to know they were being stalked? There was something about her that he couldn't explain, and Tucker didn't like things he didn't understand. He didn't trust women under the best of circumstances, and these were certainly not the best of circumstances. This one would either offer him everything he ever wanted, or she'd cost him his life.

The only thing he knew for sure right now was that his earlier observation about cheap whiskey, bad food, and needing a woman was turning out to be more prophetic than he'd known. Except that following Raven down the trail made him rapidly eliminate finding food and whiskey as the needs most urgent on his list.

Finally, just as Tucker was beginning to think they were on the mother of all wild goose chases, a cabin came into view. It was so inaccessible that it appeared to be stuck to the side of the mountain, ready to tumble off in the next strong wind. Beside the crude structure was a small lean-to with a water trough and a burro still wearing a saddle blanket and bridle and munching on a bale of hay.

"Now I get it," Tucker said, relieved to find an explanation he could understand. "You followed the burro's tracks."

Raven shook her head. "Let's get Luce inside. Then you can see to the horses."

Carrying the old man was his only option, for Luce was barely breathing now. Tucker's ribs complained, but the half-breed prospector's small stature made lifting him easy. Still, laying him down on the filthy cornshuck mattress inside stopped Tucker cold. Nobody could lie on that.

"I brought your bedroll," Raven said, behind him.

"Sure you did." That's all Tucker needed, the old man bleeding all over his bedroll while Tucker, the fool who'd rescued him, slept on the dirt floor. He no sooner had that thought than he remembered sleeping on the ground the night before, holding the woman. He felt his body stir in a recollection of its own. From where he stood, he could see the outline of the curve of her breasts against the soft skin of her dress.

As if she sensed his thoughts, her body tensed. She swept him with a stern frown before she turned to the old man. Moments later she was peeling back his blood-matted poncho and examining the wound again.

"The bullet passed through, but he lost a lot of blood on the way here."

"So, what are you going to do?" Tucker forced his attention away from the girl and studied the inside of the cabin. Though it was small and dark, it seemed more solid than he'd first thought. A table, one chair, a bench, and the cot filled the room. In one corner was a beehive-shaped adobe fireplace with a supply of wood beside it.

"First you make a fire," she directed, "then get me some fresh water."

"Then I suppose you'll tell me to sweep the floor and cook some food."

Tucker was having a lot of trouble with this woman who thought she was the boss. He had quit taking orders when he'd left the army. Even the ranchers he worked for soon learned that the work got done better when he was left alone than when he was ordered.

Raven knew she had challenged her protector's authority. Over the years, she'd become used to having her instructions followed without question. But this man was different. He rattled her, reaching in and challenging more than her words, questioning the woman part of her that she'd closed off in her quest to seek her life-vision.

"I'm sorry, Tucker," she offered. "I do not mean to assume the authority meant for you. I'll get the water if you will stay with Luce."

"Forget it, Raven. I'll build the fire. Then I'll get the water. But you'll cook the food. Unless you want me to kill us before the bandits do."

She swallowed her smile. He didn't sing or cry like the cougar, but he roared in his own taciturn way. Once she heard the big man stacking the wood inside the fireplace, Raven turned to the wounded miner. She placed her hand on Luce's chest and forced herself to erase all thought from her mind. She hadn't yet mastered total control of her visions, but sometimes she could find answers.

I don't know what to do. Help me. This man's life depends on me.

At first she heard nothing but the sound of Tucker behind her and the old man's flurry of breathing. Then, slowly, she could see a light, like silver smoke that twisted and curled around itself as if it were a whirlwind behind her eyelids, struggling to build power. Then it disappeared. Silence came, followed by the chanting of unspoken words and finally—knowledge.

Your medicine bag, Raven. Around your neck. Use your knowledge.

"Did you say something?" Tucker asked, using the third of his five matches to start the fire.

"No, I—I was merely praying that I would do the right thing. Please, go outside and bring in whatever we have in our saddlebags. Check his burro or—" She stopped, recalling his bristling at her directions. She changed her phrasing to a more suggestive manner. "Perhaps he bought supplies before he joined your game."

"There is a small amount of water in the kettle," Tucker replied. "I'll get a fresh bucket and our saddlebags. After that I—we can . . ."

His words faded away. The door to her mind closed, and Raven might as well have been alone. The need to keep Tucker close was so strong that she almost rose and walked to him. For a moment she felt fear. Suppose he left?

All her energy needed to be directed to healing this man. Yet for once, her inner power failed her. She felt tethered to the cabin, unable to soar to that place from which her knowledge came. As the fire crackled she listened for the sound of drums in the distance.

Then she realized that what she heard was the beat of her own heart. As the minutes passed she understood that there was to be no answer to this question. Luce's fate was out of her hands. Luce would not be blessed with the healing spirit. Opening her eyes, she saw Tucker, still watching her as if he expected her to grow an extra head.

"Supplies?" She returned to her usual stern voice. He swore and left the cabin, the door slamming behind him.

Raven reached inside her dress and pulled out the soft leather pouch that hung from a cord around her neck. It was warm to her touch, a living thing that seemed to pulse against her palm.

Almost afraid, she opened it, slipped her fingertips inside, and examined the contents. Small stones, a piece of smooth wood, several roots, berries, leaves, and a black feather. As she held the feather the vision of a little girl sitting at an old man's knee slipped into her mind.

The child was she. But the man she thought was an Indian had become a big, red-haired laughing man who was singing an Irish song. Then, as she continued to hold the feather, the child became a bird and flew away, taking the vision with it.

With a surety that came from her past, Raven broke off a piece of the root and removed a berry from the pouch. The kettle of water inside the fireplace was already growing hot. She crushed the berry in a tin cup, which she then filled with a small amount of the water.

"Open your mouth and drink, guardian of the past." She held up his head while she forced the liquid into his mouth. A sip at a time, he swallowed. She dropped the root into the kettle and let it boil with the remainder of the water while she searched for a rag and something to make a bandage.

She found nothing.

The door opened and Tucker entered, the bucket in his hand and the two saddlebags over his shoulder. He put the bucket by the fire and laid the pouches on the floor. Quickly Raven opened the one from Onawa's back, drew out a fancy ladies' petticoat, and stared at it in disbelief. Her travel dress. It seemed almost foreign to her here. Savagely she ripped the ruffle from the bottom.

"Not only did you fill my head with sand," Tucker grumbled as he rimmed his collar with his finger, "but you used my bandanna when you had an entire wardrobe of your own you could have destroyed."

"I forgot it was there." She poured hot water into a tin pan she'd found by the fireplace. She should have known. That thought racked her. It was as if she'd been born the morning she awoke in Tucker's arms.

They'd been lying like spoons, her bottom pressed to him, her head on one arm, her knees bent slightly so that his thighs were planted against her own. She couldn't see his face, but she could feel the warmth of his breath against her hair. For a long time she'd lain there, the wind singing a lullaby in her ear. Like a child, she'd felt safe. She'd grown drowsy and slept.

Now her blood stirred. She shook off the intruding presence of Tucker as she had for most of the morning. If the old man had any chance to live, she had to invoke all her healing powers. She ripped a swatch from the ruffle, dipped it in the bowl of water boiled with the root, and began cleaning the old man's wound. Finally satisfied that she'd washed away all the dirt, she poured out the dirty water and filled the bowl with that remaining in the kettle. Soaking a second piece of cloth in the mixture, she squeezed the water into the wound, then pressed a sliver of the soft root into the hole and bound it with the remaining strip.

"What's that?" Tucker asked.

"A root which takes away the infection."

"Where'd it come from?"

"I had it with me."

Tucker walked over to where she knelt by the bed and studied the old man. "He looks quieter."

"It was the juice of the red berry. It takes away the pain and brings restful peace."

"Where did you gain all this knowledge, Raven?"

"My mother's people believed that I was—special. I was trained to heal." She turned to face him. "Does that bother you?"

"After what has happened so far, I don't know what to believe. I fall over a cliff and hit my head. The rain wakes me up and there you are, next to me. I don't know where you came from or how either of us got there. Everything about you is an illusion. I think you and that horse must have flown here."

"No. I'm very real. Actually, I rode the stage almost to Santa Fe before I left Raven Alexander behind and became an Indian."

"Alexander? You have a real last name? That means you have a regular family somewhere."

She didn't answer.

"You have a saddlebag full of regular clothes and you're dressed in buckskin riding alone through the mountains in search of a treasure? I don't understand."

Raven didn't know how to explain. She closed her eyes and sighed. "I'm so tired."

"I'm sorry, Raven. We were so concerned about Luce we haven't looked after your wound. Do you have any more of that brew?"

"You mean the medicine water? Yes, a little."

Holding up the dainty petticoat, Tucker gave her a look that said he liked the feel of the undergarment he was holding. She didn't have to be told that he thought she was lying about her purpose.

"What are you going to do?" she asked, her face flaming. Her skin felt hot, as if his hands were touching her instead of the cotton fabric.

"I'm going to do unto you as you've done unto others." He ripped a piece from the skirt and wet it. Next he removed the thong from her braid and let it twist free.

"You don't have to unbraid my hair," she protested.

"I know. I just want to see it loose." He threaded his fingertips into the thick black hair and worked them up her scalp until he reached the place behind her ear where she'd hit her head.

"I'll see to it." She winced as he touched the wound.

"You need stitches, but damned if I can do it."

"Please. Stop!"

"Quit sidling away from me. I'm just trying to clean it." His fingers separated her hair strand by strand.

Beneath his touch, Raven began to respond to the feel of his fingers. Like hot sand against her skin, the man was absorbing her tension and replacing it with an awareness she couldn't fight.

When he finally reached the wound, she was smoldering, drawn so tightly that she was ready to flare up like the crackling fire he'd built.

"Really, I'll be fine." Her throat was so dry that she could barely speak. She cast her eyes at the floor, afraid that if he could see them he'd recognize her confusion. Both of them knew that it wasn't the wound that had coiled her senses to a knifelike edge, but his nearness. Whenever he came close to her, her heart raced and her knees felt like trembling leaves in a desert wind. The connection between them was intensifying, and it was more than just a spiritual joining. It was physical as well.

The big tawny man didn't seem to be having an easy time of it either. She'd already determined that as strong and courageous as he was, he was a man who kept his personal feelings hidden deep inside. He was strung as taut as the skin pulled across the head of a drum, yet one fingertip caressed the curve of her cheek.

"Don't. We—I have to see to Luce." Her words told him to move away, but he had to be the one to move, for she felt as if all the resistance had drained from her body.

"Be still, Raven. Let me do this for you, please."

Gently he cleaned the wound, surprised to see that it was already beginning to heal. "Whoever you are, you're some remarkable woman. Don't try to explain now. I'm willing to wait."

"Thank you." She had no answers now. The time wasn't right. All she knew for sure was that the feeling between them was too strong. Drawing on every ounce of her strength, she reached up and removed his hand. Then, rising, she turned to him.

"Tucker Farrell, you are here for a reason, just as I am, just as Luce is. Luce has protected the treasure. I must find it and use it for my people. You're the protector and for your help you will be rewarded. Until we reach our goal, we must avoid anything that might interfere. Now, go and see to the horses while I prepare food."

"Food, yes. That's one of the things I need," he agreed, turning toward the door. But she knew that wasn't the only hunger he felt, and she wondered how long she could maintain the barrier between them, the barrier that was collapsing with every touch.

5

The horses and the burro were bedded down. Tucker returned to the cabin to tell Raven he hadn't found any food.

"It's time for us to talk," she said. "Let's step outside."

He followed her, glancing back at the man who was barely breathing. "Yeah, I guess it is."

"I don't believe that Luce will live."

"Don't suppose your spirits would give him a hand?" Tucker asked flippantly, his control being tested by the certainty of her knowledge.

"I think they may already have."

Tucker glanced around the sharp gouge in the earth in which the cabin was hidden. It was as bleak and lifeless as the old man inside. How could anybody spend their life in such a place?

"I don't know how he made it this far," Tucker said.

"He had a mission, I think, and now that it is nearly over, he's losing the breath of life. About your protecting me, I was wrong to ask it of you."

"And I was probably wrong to agree. So, what now?

You go your way and I go mine? I don't think so, Spirit Woman."

"I had to do this, Tucker. All you had to do was bring me to Luce."

"And if I leave you, you're going after that treasure, aren't you?"

"I must go."

"Even if it means dying?"

"Even if it means dying."

She was so proud, so regal, standing there beside a piece of gray rock in the sunshine. It wasn't only that she stirred his blood, it was more. In some strange way, she was the promise of the tomorrow that he'd denied himself. She might die, but she wouldn't give up. And she wouldn't allow him to give up either.

"I'm probably the biggest kind of fool, but I can't walk off and leave you. What else do I have to do, anyway? Besides, a piece of land in Oregon is worth a little gamble. What do we do now, you and me?"

"First, about last night," she said shyly. "I mean, when I awoke, you were—you'd given me your coat."

It wasn't the coat that she was remembering, and he knew it. It was what had come before. Tucker reached for her hand and held it gently, his fingers moving idly back and forth across her wrist. He glanced down at the contrast of her soft skin against his.

She, too, was watching. He could see her breath catch in her throat as if she remembered his touching her. What in hell was he doing? Tucker let her go. He was looking for a treasure, not a woman ready to depend on his staying around.

"So I gave you my coat." He strode up the trail. "I'd have done the same for Luce. We'll be partners, that's all. If we survive to find it, and I doubt that we will, I'll go to Oregon and you can go—wherever it is you plan to buy land."

"Oregon," she mused. "I've heard there is fine land in Oregon. But there is good land in Colorado also."

"Oh no! Don't get the idea that I intend to nursemaid an entire tribe of Indians."

"I'm sorry, Tucker. Of course I don't expect you to do that. I know it is dangerous, and I'll understand if you choose to leave at any time. You've brought me to Luce, and that was all you were destined to do."

"Why are you so sure that we were destined to do anything? If your grandfather was dying, he could have been hallucinating."

"No, he saw the truth. But I saw you as well, in my dreams. Your animal spirit is that of the cougar."

"What was I doing?"

"The raven was trapped. The cougar freed it from the rocks."

Birds again. He didn't want to think about that now. Every time he ran into an occurrence he couldn't understand, she dragged out something mystical to confuse him even more. Tucker reminded himself that he was far too practical to believe in the spirit world. If he couldn't touch it, taste it, or smell it, it didn't exist.

For almost ten years, he'd managed to avoid responsibility, forming any close ties, any situation that would draw him into making a commitment. He'd taken a stand three times in his life, and not once had he come out on the winning side. The first—his service for the Confederacy—was purely patriotic; the second was his engagement to a woman who didn't wait; and the third, a stint with the Federal Army as an Indian fighter, ended with the massacre at Sand Creek.

Since then he'd drifted, figuring one occupation was as good as another, so long as it didn't involve killing the innocent or righting somebody else's wrongs. And he didn't take orders from anybody.

Now he'd landed flat in the middle of a different kind of mess. He was stuck with a dying man being chased by bandits, and a woman who seemed to think that there was a treasure waiting to be found. A disaster in the making—any way he looked at it.

"Damn it, Raven. I don't understand it, but I do know there's no way you can go find this treasure without help. I'm in. Just remember when it's over, I get my cut. In the meantime we've got to eat. What do you have in your pack?"

"Nothing eatable, I'm afraid," she said, making her way back to the cabin. She picked up the twin leather pouches and spread them across the kitchen table. "Go on, open them." She stood back.

It was time he found out something about what he was facing and the woman he was facing it with. Almost reluctantly he unbuckled one of the saddlebags and reached inside, pulling out the traveling dress and petticoat. Next came soft white undergarments that made Raven wince, then, finally, a nightdress. Tucker opened the other bag and found a faded daguerreotype of five women.

Tucker studied the smeared likeness of four light-skinned, fair-haired women and a young darker one. Raven. He held it out to her. "Looks like you do have a family somewhere."

She took the likeness from him. "Sabrina," she whispered, "Lauren, Mary, and Isabella and—" For a second, in her mind, she was at the top of a ridge, looking down at a snow-blown valley, watching her sisters standing around a freshly dug grave. There were men there too. "Papa," she whispered.

"I didn't see a man." Tucker reclaimed the daguerreotype.

"He was killed in a mining accident. These are my sisters."

Tucker gave Raven a long look, then glanced back at the picture. "Not a whole lot of family resemblance between you and the others."

"We had different mothers."

He plundered her cache again, bringing out a fringed leather carrying bag, painted with white, black, and yellow symbols.

"What is this?"

"It was my mother's. It shows her family signs."

Behind them, Luce sat up and began to speak in an agitated voice. "She is the one. She has come.

Raven rushed to the old man's side. "Be still. You'll start the bleeding again."

"Aiee! The sign. It is here."

"What sign, Luce?" Tucker walked toward the old man who was staring at the object in his hand. "You mean this?" He held out the painted leather square.

"Si." He took Tucker's hand and pulled him even closer. "You must promise me—promise me . . ."

Raven knelt beside the older man, putting her hand behind his neck to help support him. "Promise you what?"

"I must be buried at the base of the rock with the matching mark."

Tucker looked from the leather pouch to Luce and back again. "I've already promised, old man. Where do I find the rock?"

"Follow the water. Wash me. Shave my head. Then the way will come clear. You must promise." He fell back to the bed.

"Of course we will," Raven reassured him. "Now you must rest while I prepare food to make you strong."

But he'd used up the last of his strength and fallen into a raspy sleep.

Raven's gaze caught Tucker's and she shook her head. "I don't know what he's talking about."

"Well, whatever this is sure set him off. And you don't know what the painting means?"

"I wish I did. Grandfather only gave it to me a few days ago." She studied the bag, fingering the beading, then held it to her bosom. Her mother's signs, her ancestors' totem, perhaps. The design was a combination of wavy lines, jagged triangular marks, a strange-looking sun, and a gold-and-black butterfly.

Nothing about the design spoke to Raven. She wished she could feel close to the woman who'd given her birth. But there was only a lonely emptiness inside.

By midafternoon a rabbit Tucker had killed was stewing in the pot, along with some wild onions and gnarled potatoes she'd found in the cabin. The old man was still sleeping, and Tucker had disappeared outside.

Raven looked around, satisfied that she'd done all she could for now. Finally she decided that she couldn't eat or relax until she washed some of the last three days of trail dust from her body. Somewhere there would be water. Follow the water, Luce had said.

Checking Luce one last time, she stood in the doorway looking out at the small clearing surrounding the cabin. Over the ridge and across the mountain to the east lay the Rio Grande and the bandits who'd followed Tucker. The cabin was in a sheltered area, protected by a scattering of red rock lined with streaks of white, like a frothy layer cake she'd seen at the hotel back in Denver.

Colorado seemed a lifetime ago. After Sabrina had married, Raven had never felt comfortable with her life in the cabin where she'd been raised. She'd spent more and more time with her mother's people, the Arapaho, and the Grandfather, Flying Cloud. She belonged with them.

Now she was in a different place, away from everything she'd known before. Luce was dying. It was only a matter of hours now. Then there'd be only Tucker.

Tucker Farrell, her cougar, the man who'd been caught up in her quest. She could understand his being tempted by the treasure. But more than that was holding him. She couldn't forget the wary, tense look in his eyes, the tender touch of his fingertips as he separated the blood-matted strands of her hair. He'd let her think that he was a hardened drifter, but beneath his stern exterior was a softness he tried to hide.

Being held in his arms had felt unmistakably safe, and that was a sensation she'd never experienced before. Even as she tried to close off the unwanted response that seemed to hover just beneath the surface, a quiver started in her thighs and moved toward the apex of her legs. Instinctively she tightened the muscles around the feminine part of her.

For a long moment, Raven stood still, clearing her mind, seeking comfort from the spirit world, some thought, some word to which she could cling. At first none came. The visions were absent. She felt suddenly uneasy. Who was she to be charged with such a mission, and how would she be able to carry it out?

Then she felt rather than heard the whispery sound of many voices, the drums and the chanting, softly at first, then growing more insistent. She couldn't understand the words, but she felt their urgency. There was no trance, no vision. Only a voice.

Follow the water to the treasure, where the light of the

moon meets the light of the sun. The command was barely a whisper.

For a moment she thought it was in her head. Then she decided that it was Luce's voice she was hearing.

She moved back to the old man's side. His eyes were closed. He was asleep. "Why?" she asked. "I don't understand."

The voice spoke again. *You will—soon. You are the key.* She waited, but there were no more words. Finally she gave in to the pull drawing her outside again, toward the back of the cabin and up a narrow path.

"Who are you?" she whispered. "What are you asking of me?"

But no answer came. Only the wind through her hair, caressing her like warm fingers, like Tucker's touch when he'd treated her wound. As she walked an urgency swept her up the path.

Then she heard it, the musical sound of water. A splash and an oath. Tucker. Planting her feet carefully, she peered around the rocks that blocked her way. High on the side of the ridge, through a smooth hole worn through a rock, a narrow stream of water plunged to a hollowed-out pool below.

Standing in the pool was Tucker Farrell, hair in wet strands that dripped water down his massive, naked chest. His clothes were draped across the rocks to dry in the sun, and he was peering into a sliver of broken mirror, raking a razor across the last patch of soap on his face.

She was acutely drawn to him. Despite her mental commands, she couldn't take her eyes off him. Everything was turning out to be so much more complicated than she'd thought. The journey, the unknown, the danger, all were things she could deal with. She hadn't counted on Tucker Farrell.

Gone was the unruly drifter he'd pretended to be. The man before her was now the sleek cougar he'd always been in her mind's eye. She'd known he was big, but his clothing was deceptive, giving him bulk when he was pure muscle. A jagged scar streaked down his back, disappearing into the water at his waist. He was spectacular.

It was all she could do not to call out to him, not to touch him, not to—

"Ouch!"

As he jerked away, his elbow caught the mirror and it narrowly missed his body as it plunged into the water. "Son of a—" He stared down at his body through the clear water. "Nothing like turning yourself into a gelding. Though you might as well be for all the chances you've had lately."

Raven let out a startled gasp, then held her breath as he looked over his shoulder. A narrow seeping of blood sliced his cheek and ran down the watery smear of soap left behind.

She ducked down, her back to the rocks, eyes closed. Maybe if she was very quiet, he'd decide that the sound he'd heard wasn't human. Maybe he wouldn't know that she'd been spying on him, that she'd had improper thoughts.

"I hope that's you, Spirit Woman. I'd rather not have to shoot an intruder, since my gun is with my pants, and as you can see, I'm not wearing them."

She continued to hold her breath, willing him to reach down for the mirror so that she could escape.

A slosh of water, followed by cold drops of it on the top of her head, said she'd been discovered.

"I'm sorry, Tucker. I—I was looking for a place to bathe. The water looks very pleasant."

"You were staring at the water?"

"Of course. I mean I wasn't staring. I just didn't expect you to be . . ."

"You were staring. I saw you in the mirror. You want a bath. Come on in. I'll even scrub your back."

She pressed her back against the rock, her face flushed and her breathing altogether too uneven.

"Raven, stand up and look at me."

"I can't." She willed her eyelids to remain closed. She wouldn't look at him. She couldn't. But it didn't matter. This time she felt it coming, the swirl of smoke that clouded even her mental sight. Powerful, different, the smoke was golden, shot with tiny points of iridescent light.

What was happening? If this was a vision, it was very different from the others.

The hot shower of mist seemed to draw into itself, forming a picture of an enormous bronze man looming over her, threatening, evil. Then, as quickly as it had formed, the shape softened and, almost as if it were protecting her, became the golden man she'd likened to a mountain lion. She didn't have to see him with open eyes. And she didn't have to touch him to feel his hands on her. He caressed her with his spirit. And she was welcoming him, reaching out to him.

His hands were on her. His lips, moving across her face, her neck, and her bare breasts.

Bare?

How could that be? She felt the rocks against her back, the weight of her deerskin garment against her skin. Yet Tucker was surrounding her with his presence. And she was reaching out to pull him close to her. Beads of perspiration slickened their skin where they met. Between her legs came a hot dampness, and she felt the taut flesh of his buttocks beneath her touch.

Yet all the while she knew that her palms were still

splayed against the rock. That Tucker was behind her, looking down. Still, she felt him, his male part swelling and caught between them, touching, sliding back and forth.

Her breath came in short pants as the coil of heat inside her expanded, sending fingers of fire shimmering along the vessels inside her skin.

They were together, this tawny man and his dark-eyed raven. Yet they were not. She was on fire now, reaching, writhing, wanting.

"Christ, Raven, what's happening here?"

Tucker's voice, tight and hoarse, came from far away. "I don't know what on the west side of hell you're doing, but if you don't stop it, I'm not going to be able to hold on to my good intentions much longer."

The droplets of water that hit her forehead were no longer cooling. They were as hot as the temperature of her blood.

Then he was physically beside her, jerking her against him, crushing her with his huge hands. "Stop this!" He shook her. Still she couldn't shake the image. It was stronger than her mind, stronger than the man now lifting her in his arms and striding toward the pool.

He put her down, ripping the buckskin dress from her body in one swipe. Then he lifted her again.

Cold! The ice of a thousand storms melted and sizzled against the heat of her body as she hit the water in the pool. From above, a continuing torrent of melted snow fell over her, quenching the firestorm in her mind.

At last, limp with exhaustion from the shock of what she'd seen and felt, Raven opened her eyes and found Tucker in the pool beside her.

"I—I'm sorry," she said.

"What the hell was that?" he asked. "I never felt anything like it."

"Neither have I. I believe it was a waking dream."

"You mean a vision strong enough to make a man—?"

She turned a troubled gaze on him. "You felt it too?"

"Felt. Experienced. Yes. At least I assume that we were in the same—vision."

Now that she was cool, Raven was totally drained. She had to move away from the intimidating presence of Tucker Farrell. As she took a step toward the edge of the pool, she looked down at her body.

"What happened to my dress?"

"I slung it into the rocks. You were burning up. I was afraid it would catch fire. I'll get it for you."

But he couldn't move. The sight of her body in the water immobilized him. He'd never seen anyone so beautiful. Her breasts seemed to float just beneath the surface of the water, their rich warm color shimmering like amber in sunlight. Nipples as full and dark as ripe cherries begged to be touched. And between her legs, the soft curls of dark hair rippled as the water moved against her.

The erect male part of him jerked involuntarily, pulling him toward her. He didn't look at her face, for he didn't want to see the fear reflected in her eyes.

She whirled around, reached the other side, and pulled herself to the ledge, ducking beneath the waterfall. And just as quickly, she was gone, leaving him bewildered and out of breath.

Tucker closed his eyes, then opened them again in time to see her disappearing through the rocks, drawing her buckskin dress over her shoulders. He moved back toward the edge of the pool and sat on the rock.

What had just happened?

He'd been aware of her. He'd caught sight of her in the mirror. Her presence had rattled him so that he'd cut himself. When he'd heard her gasp, he'd called out to her and waited for her to respond.

But she hadn't. Instead he'd felt her experiencing the incredible onset of heat that arched between them. And he'd left the pool and leaned over the rocks to reprimand her. Except he'd been caught up in whatever was happening and seared against the rock, looking down at the top of her head.

From that point on, he had no explanation. Even with the rock between them, he'd been burned by her heat, her desire, her fear, and in his mind he came to stand before her, pressing against her, feeling her body against his.

And she'd welcomed him. She'd wanted him. They were mentally making love, powerfully, erotically, almost beyond the limitations of what he could ever have imagined.

Then, as if the sun were about to explode, he'd feared for her. Too much heat. Too much need was burning her alive. Collecting his spiraling emotions, he had physically pried himself from the rock and lifted her, the heat burning his hands and his body as they plunged into the icy water.

Then they were apart. In that second he'd seen something that even while it was happening he didn't believe, a figure twice his height, a giant bronze man wearing armor. Then suddenly, as if the sun had vanished behind a cloud, the vision was gone and she'd disappeared behind the falls.

Had it all been a dream? Had the blow to his head done permanent damage, setting off some kind of hallucinations? Was she a witch with powers he didn't even want to believe in?

As he stood he caught a flash of silver at the bottom of the pool. The broken mirror caught the beams of sunlight through the shimmering water, sending out a blinding ray that held him spellbound.

Body drained, Tucker pulled himself from the pool and donned the clothes he'd left to dry on the rocks. As he started down the trail he felt as if he'd been asleep for a very long time, as if he were recovering from an illness that had taken every ounce of energy from his bones. Back at the cabin, he paused, considered for a minute that he would be well served to leave before she'd completely ensnared him with one of her spells.

Then he went inside.

She was feeding the old man, coaxing him into taking a few swallows of broth. Only the dampness of her hair reaffirmed that the past half hour hadn't been a dream.

"About what happened," he began.

"Did something happen?" She looked at him with concern.

"Of course something happened. Up at the pool. I've heard about people being hypnotized into seeing something that wasn't there, Spirit Woman. I don't know how you did it, but you made me believe it was real."

The white-fingered grip of her hand on the spoon told him that she was fooling herself about what they'd experienced. Fooling herself because she didn't understand any more than he.

"There is only a thin veil between what is real, Tucker Farrell, and what is imagined. Do not confuse the two." She put down the cracked cup she was holding and walked toward the table. "Sit and eat. Your mind will be still."

It wasn't his mind that was tortured. And it wasn't his stomach either. He thought for a moment about the food on the table. One of his needs was about to be satisfied.

He wasn't sure about the others.

• • •

Tucker climbed higher into the rocks until he reached a point near the top of the ridge overlooking the Rio Grande. From here he could see the entire canyon below and the formation of sandstone cresting the other side.

Across the river, near the top where he and Raven had spent the night in the cave, he saw them. *Damn.* Indians. Arapaho, he decided from their dress. Were they following Raven? This was Apache and Comanche country. There was no other reason for them to be here, unless they were planning to do a little treasure hunting too.

And what were they looking at? Tucker knew that the miner's cabin was totally hidden from view, unless their smoke had given them away.

No, it wasn't that. He waited and watched. He heard the sound before he saw the riders. Mexicans, on the floor of the canyon. They were still searching for Luce. If they kept snooping around, sooner or later they'd stumble onto the way up.

Making no attempt to hide their arrival, the bandits rode brazenly forward along the river, then paused to water the horses.

Tucker cut his gaze back to the top. The Indian who seemed to be in charge gestured angrily toward the trail below. The Arapaho waited in silence, watching as the horses drank nervously. Tucker thought about Raven, the old man and himself, in that same spot earlier. He felt like bait in a steel trap which was already set and ready for the animal to make a wrong move. If he was spotted, they'd find Raven. If the bandits didn't find their trail, the Indians would.

Unless he managed to get her away first.

He needed a distraction to provide cover for his

movement. Tucker searched the ground around him for a good-sized rock. He was no discus thrower, but all he had to do was get the rock to a place upriver from both groups. With any luck, if he hit granite, the echo would confuse both. Better still, a confrontation would make both the Indians and the bandits find another prey. Slipping to a place where he would have a better angle, Tucker threw the rock with all his might.

Seconds later he heard a sharp ping, then a second one. At that point all hell broke loose. The bandits caught sight of the Indians about the time the Indians got off the first volley of shots. But even in the midst of battle, one Indian kept a lookout. It was no contest. In less than a minute, five Mexicans were dead. The others had found shelter behind an outcropping of rock.

So far as Tucker could tell, the Indians hadn't lost a man. But he hadn't been able to leave either. Now he didn't dare try for fear of being seen. In the meantime his stomach seemed to reach down and tickle his knees. He was glad he didn't have to stand. Looking down into the canyon took his breath away. He couldn't have run if he'd wanted to.

To his surprise the Indians rode away. Why they'd ambushed the bandits and not followed through to take their guns and horses was a puzzle.

Unless they were after a bigger prize. Unless they were all searching for the same thing. It made sense for the bandits to be after Luce, but the Arapaho? They had to be after Raven. Somehow they must have learned about the secret treasure.

Tucker dropped to his belly and slid away from the edge until he could come to a crouch. The outcropping of rock took a turn to the left where he could make his way back to his horse and the cabin. He didn't trust either the Indians or the bandits. He needed to get Raven and Luce far enough away from the cabin that they wouldn't be trailed. And he needed to do it soon.

Raven managed to get a small amount of liquid into the old man, but not enough to keep him alive. It was almost impossible for him to swallow.

Where was Tucker? She'd heard gunshots earlier. Now he'd been gone for hours. Was he dead? Did she dare leave Luce to search for him?

As the shadows of late afternoon crept across the side of the mountain where the cabin was located, she walked toward the door and looked out over the sprawling scattering of rock.

She felt uneasy. But there were no voices, no chanting. The whole world had gone silent. Something was waiting out there.

Something threatening, hazy, just beyond her mind's eye. It was big, imposing, solid yet shadowy. She found herself looking up, narrowing her eyes so that she could find the presence that she could feel, yet not see. There was something vaguely familiar about it. Whatever it was, she'd encountered it before and it was a threat. And then she knew. The huge bronze man from her vision with Tucker. Was it real? Or was it Tucker's presence that brought her such a sense of both fear and anticipation?

No, it was more than that.

Beware the bronze dagger, the voice said. *You will know, Raven—soon.*

6

Tucker spent most of the night at the top of the canyon, watching for any sign that their trail had been discovered. But morning came without intruders.

He couldn't just sit and wait. He had to know what was happening. It took most of the next day, but he managed to cover the entire upper ridge that separated the cabin from the valley where the river flowed.

Everything seemed quiet. Too quiet. The bodies of the bandits were gone, and no campfires signaled the presence of the Arapaho. Still, there was something eerie about the silence.

One lone buzzard made low, lazy circles downriver. Heat waves shimmered in the late afternoon sun as shadows washed the red from the canyon walls, turning them gray with the loss of light.

He'd spent more time than he'd planned scouting the area, finding one excuse after another to keep himself away from the cabin, from Raven. He knew that Luce was dying. Once that happened, he'd be left alone with a woman who was reaching out to him in a way he could neither understand nor stop. His thoughts shied away from what had happened at the waterfall. He didn't want to think how close he'd come to . . .

The whole thing was downright spooky. If he were drinking, he might have passed it off to bad whiskey. But he was cold sober. It was more powerful than anything he'd ever encountered.

Once the old man was buried, they'd look for the treasure. If they found it, he'd take his part and move on. She could buy her land. No, damn it, he couldn't walk away and leave a woman alone, at the mercy of Indians and bandits. Not now and not then. As much as he talked to himself, he couldn't get away from the fact that protecting Raven Alexander had become an obsession. It was the most important thing he'd ever done. He just didn't know why.

Finally, when the light was almost gone, he started back. At least whoever had built the original cabin had done a good job of finding a place that was hidden from the world. The more he studied the surrounding area, the more Tucker decided that many others had been here before. The pathways were worn, if one knew where to look.

Even now he sensed the presence of others. That was what made him so uneasy. There were no physical signs, but he could feel the hair on the back of his neck prickle.

Christ! You're beginning to sound like Raven, hearing voices when there are none. He let out a measured sigh. The sooner they moved away from this place the better he'd feel.

As he skirted a low cluster of boulders he saw her. She stood in the doorway, watching him as he came down the ridge from the north. There was something comforting about her presence, about knowing that she waited for him.

"How's the old man?" Tucker asked her when he reached the cabin.

"He's sleeping."

"Did he say anything else?"

"Only that he's always been here. This was his father's home and his grandfather's. The family believed they were to be guardians over the sacred mountains."

Tucker stopped just short of the cabin. "Did he identify which part of the mountain he was guarding?"

She shook her head. "If you mean did he tell me where the treasure is hidden, no, he didn't. All he says is follow the water to the place where the light of the moon meets the light of the sun. If I hadn't seen the nuggets, I would say he didn't know anything."

There was something odd about her acceptance of their situation, as if she were looking past him, seeing something in the rocks in the distance. "What is it?" he asked, turning to follow her gaze.

Shaking her head, she moved back inside. "It's nothing, just something about the way the light falls on the mountain up there. Come and eat."

Tucker looked back at the mountain. The sunlight was gone now, leaving only the pale light of the rising moon. He could see nothing unusual. But the feeling of being watched still plagued him.

"If we're going to be here long, I'll have to find a better source of food," he said. "I don't know what the old man planned to eat. The burro's pack was empty."

"He had gone into town. Probably intended to buy supplies." Raven dished up some rabbit stew for Tucker. "But you're right. This area is too barren for berries and wild plants. I'll have to get back to the river."

"No!"

She looked up, puzzled at the vehemence of his word. "Why?"

"The bandits returned. And there are some new players in this game, some of your own."

"My own what?"

"People. Indians. There's a small band of Arapaho on your trail. Friends of yours?"

She sank down on the rough bench beside the table and thought about what he'd said. But she could find no connection. Only a sense of dread. "No. I don't think so. Did they see you?"

Tucker picked up a tin pan and placed it on the shelf Luce's family used for a worktable. He poured water over his hands, washed them, and splashed it over his face. Grabbing a cloth beside the jug, he dried his hands, allowing a grin to curl his lips as he realized that his towel was another part of the ruffle from his spirit woman's petticoat.

"See me? Oh, no. They were here earlier. At that time they were too busy to worry about me. But they'll be back."

"What were they doing?"

"They were watching the valley." He didn't want to tell her about the attack. "You know we aren't safe here." Tucker took his place across the table and ate vigorously.

"But we can't leave Luce and he—he—"

"I know. Three days. Tomorrow is the third day since we found him. Do you think he'll last that long?"

She shook her head. "No, I don't think so. But we must wait. Then we must bury him, according to his instructions."

"I know, shave his head. If we don't get ours shaved first."

"The Arapaho don't take scalps anymore, Tucker. And the only reason they'd attack you is if they thought you were trespassing on sacred ground."

Sacred ground. That explained their actions—maybe.

•   •   •

In the middle of the night, Tucker let himself out of the cabin and began to pace. He'd spent uncomfortable nights in his time, but in comparison, the loneliness of the prairie and the cold wind of a winter ice storm were preferable. Alone on the range, all you thought of was your own misery. Here, all he could hear was Raven's soft breathing. All he could think about was the torment of being so close to her without touching her.

The tension that had been there from the first continued to grow, twisting his gut, leaving him open-eyed and unable to be still. Like riding a devil horse, he had to hold on and he dare not let go, else he'd be trampled in the fray.

What he wanted to do was climb on Yank and hightail it out of these mountains, back to some ranch that needed a loner to ride fences. Once, he even started toward his horse.

But something stopped him. A woman who needed him. A woman he couldn't walk away from.

"Tucker?" The voice of his tormentor came through the darkness from inside the cabin. "Were you ever a soldier?"

"Yes?"

"And did you do a lot of marching?"

"Not if I could help it."

"Then why are you starting now?"

He frowned. What in hell was she talking about? "Is there something wrong in there?"

"Nothing that a little quiet can't fix. If you're having trouble sleeping, I could fix you a potion."

"If I needed a potion, I have my own." He patted the pint of whiskey he'd so carefully protected for the last two days. "Maybe," he offered with a grin, "you'd like to join me."

"Go to sleep, Tucker. You're safe tonight."

"Well, certain—damn—ly, General. Why didn't I know?"

He pretended not to hear her soft laugh as he headed away from the cabin up the trail to the waterfall. He'd sleep under the stars. At the rate they were going, he wasn't likely to get much rest until Luce either recovered or went on to his Maker. Until his spirit woman took away the spell she'd woven around him.

Ever since he'd touched her on that ledge, his senses had been simmering, desire just beneath the surface, threatening to erupt. Then, at the falls, though they were three feet apart, she'd touched him with her heat and set free the demon of need.

Tucker might be confused about many things, but his body wasn't. Raven was a woman who simmered, too, and sooner or later they were going to have to put that fire out.

All his life Tucker had operated on instinct. Instinct had saved his life during the war with the Yanks more times than he could count. Necessity made him sign up for duty in the West after that war, but instinct made him ride away from massacring Indians.

But this time he was paddling in deep water. His instincts were hazy, uncertain. He took a deep breath and released it slowly. He needed to slow down. Tucker didn't hanker to leave this life yet, even if it didn't have much to offer.

Raven settled back down on the bedroll she'd spread near the fire. The night was cool and finally quiet. She didn't know where her protector had gone, but she was glad it was far enough away that she didn't feel his physical presence.

Too much had occurred that she didn't understand.

Her head ached from the strain of trying to make sense of what they'd experienced. She'd made a promise to come, but how could she fulfill her grandfather's wishes? And did she have the right to involve Tucker in her mission?

Tucker believed the Indians were after her. Were they? She couldn't believe that Flying Cloud had sent others without telling her. She wasn't even certain they had come from the north. Part of the tribe had remained in the south. Luce, as keeper of the mountain, was part Arapaho. Perhaps they were members of his band. Now there were Mexican bandits out there after the treasure as well.

She didn't like being so uncertain. That feeling was as foreign to her as her reaction to Tucker's touch. She'd never known such a connection to a man before.

Back at the falls, she'd felt something powerful, that was both passionate and compelling. A sweeping sense of urgency inside her sprang to life at the thought of Tucker. The picture of his body flashed in her mind, sleek and lean in the water, his face shorn of whiskers, his hair trimmed. A wet heat expanded in her stomach, stealing her breath and setting off spasms that ran down her body toward the apex of her legs. Was this what it meant to feel desire for a man?

Was this meant to be, a joining of the cougar and the raven? Were the spirits preparing her for some kind of sacrifice?

She sighed and turned her face toward the blanket, forcing her mind to become clear. She waited for the spirits to speak. Slowly she felt sleep creep over her, sleep and the beginning of the dream. She stood once more on the precipice, the wind at her back, poised to fall forward into the beckoning air.

But this time something held her. This time a golden cord was attached to her wrist, holding her on the ledge.

The jeweled chains of the restraint burned hot against her skin. She tried, but she couldn't remove it. And then she knew that the cord was attached to the man—to Tucker Farrell.

Her breathing slowed as a sense of well-being stole over her. The golden cord bound them together and, for now, she was safe.

The next day Tucker decided that the waiting was getting to him. He never minded not having anything to do, but he wanted to be the one who decided that.

Luce was barely conscious now. Any hope they might have had that he would describe the hiding place was rapidly fading. "Follow the water" was too vague for Tucker. And the reference to the light of the sun and the moon was like trying to unscramble a riddle. Unless Raven was holding out on him, he saw nothing ahead but failure.

Tucker had promised to bury the man beneath the rock with the mark of the sun from the leather carrying bag. Tucker was an experienced tracker and scout, but drawings didn't leave a trail. If he were going to live up to his word, he'd better find the place, and soon.

During his search, Tucker managed to trap two more rabbits, and in spite of the danger, he gathered some wild cabbages and onions along the river. Young cattails would have finished out the meal, but his harvesting was cut short by the sound of a horse, and he'd only just managed to hide Yank when one lone bandit rode leisurely downstream.

He'd learned the Mexicans were down the Rio Grande, and the Arapaho were upriver, leaving him with a dying prospector and a mystical medicine woman boxed rather neatly in between. He understood the old saying, damned if you do and damned if you don't. This time he was double damned and he knew it.

Back at the cabin, Raven couldn't leave Luce and she couldn't be still. Until now she had been content to wait for answers, but her uneasiness grew by the hour. She felt as if she were going to explode. She had to move, to find a way to release the tension building inside of her.

She walked back to the old man and touched his forehead. Even with the fever, it was cold now, and clammy. Nothing she had done had helped. He was within hours of dying, maybe less. Where was Tucker?

Had something happened to him? Had he ridden away, leaving Luce and her alone? In desperation Raven unfolded her bedroll and sat down. She rested her hands loosely on her knees and closed her eyes.

"I speak to the spirits," she whispered. "I ask your help."

A long moment of silence followed. Then the drums began. A distant murmur of voices floated through the stillness. As if a veil had been parted, she was the raven once more, flying high over the canyon. Along the Rio Grande below were swarthy-skinned men dressed in black trousers and short jackets. They wore flat-crowned hats trimmed with red, and they were firing their guns.

Where was Tucker? Falling with the air currents, she searched, flying inside the body that had come to be the spirit part of her own.

There, on the opposite ridge, she saw him, crouching so that he could see the battle. One Indian was not watching the battle. One Indian who sat tall in his saddle. He was watching the raven fly just above the ledge where Tucker lay.

Swift Hand.

She knew this man, knew and feared him. He'd tried

to come between Raven and Flying Cloud. His jealousy was well known to the elders in the tribe, and Raven knew that he hated her and would take her life if he could.

After she'd led him to the treasure.

Then the vision was gone and Raven's breath caught in her throat as if Swift Hand had sent an evil spirit to take her breath away.

"Tucker!"

She left the cabin and ran up the path, fear following her like fog. Swift Hand would kill Tucker. Swift Hand had sworn never to go to the reservation. He would kill every white man who spoke of forcing them off their land. He was crazed with anger and desperation. Somehow he'd found her and she'd led him to Tucker and Luce.

Like the bird that had become her totem, Raven dipped and swayed, moving over rocks and around boulders until at last she reached the crest and saw Tucker moving toward her.

"Tucker, you're safe."

She hurled herself into his arms, laying her trembling body against his, sliding her arms around his massive chest.

"Whoa!" He rubbed her arms and back, tasting her fear like bile in his mouth. "What's happened?"

"The Arapaho. Their leader is Swift Hand. He will kill you if he finds us."

"Swift Hand? Who is Swift Hand?"

"He believed that my grandfather was wrong about making peace, about our people's future. He goaded those who would join with him into fighting the authorities."

"Why does he follow you?" That question disturbed Tucker almost more than his fears for his own life. He'd faced death a hundred times and laughed in its face. But Raven was still fresh and pure. Everything she did was for someone else. She didn't deserve to die.

"I don't know. How did he learn of the treasure? We must not be found. Please help me."

Tucker remained silent, comforting her with his touch, with his arms. He knew she'd draw back if she realized what she was doing.

Tucker had long ago lost any belief in innocence. Women used men for their own purposes, lying as easily as they smiled. Indians were better than most at guile, smiling, agreeing to whatever a man said at the same time they were deciding how to kill him. They'd learned this from the whites. They'd had to in order to survive. But not Raven. She was truly innocent.

Now two sets of intruders were stalking them. And Raven would be the focus of their attention once they learned that she held the key to the discovery of the treasure.

"You're safe. For now, Swift Hand doesn't know where we are," he finally said, trying to focus on her fear and not the ever growing awareness of his own body. Damn it to hell, she fit into his arms as if the space had been made for her form. He understood that she didn't know what she was doing when she rubbed her breasts against his chest, when she leaned her head back to look up at him and by that movement thrust her pelvis against him.

Tucker groaned and tightened his grip on her arms. His lips moved against her hair, drifting lower until he found her lips. They parted beneath the pressure of his touch, allowing their mouths to merge, to join, to bond.

He could hear her breathing change, feel her heart fluttering even as he told himself to pull back.

But he couldn't help himself, and in her innocence, she didn't stop him. Her lips parted, taking his tongue inside her mouth as she rocked against him.

Drawing on one last sliver of control, Tucker lightened his kiss, softly caressing her back and arms as he withdrew. Finally they were separated, standing only inches apart, staring at each other as if they were strangers.

"Tucker?"

"It's all right, Spirit Woman. I never should have kissed you. I was wrong."

"Why? It seemed right. I liked it, the way we feel together. Is this not a good thing?"

"This is *not* a good thing, my trusting one. We have a band of wild Indians looking for you and a gang of Mexican bandits looking for me. We have to get Luce and leave here."

"Luce can't be moved, Tucker. He's very near death."

She looked up at him, worry bringing moisture to her eyes. Her concern melted all the distance he'd managed to put between them.

She could only stare at him as his fingertips left her shoulders and lightly brushed her cheek. Her skin was so sensitive to his touch that he overwhelmed her. Even the soft buckskin of her dress seemed to grate against her flesh. His male scent heightened her awareness with every ragged breath she drew.

A steady thud began to pound in her temple, and Raven knew that she had to push him away. She gasped as she stepped back. But distance didn't stop the writhing of her insides.

She didn't know how she could draw strength from this man who seemed to take their journey reluctantly, or why, beneath the uncertainties, the promise of fire was there, igniting at their slightest touch.

The promise of fire. Raven trembled and pulled her gaze to the ground beneath his feet. She had to get her emotions under control. There was something more important that she must do. "Luce," she said in a low voice. "We'd better get back to him."

"Yes. We'll stay until the end. Then we'd better get out of here. All that business about finding a rock with a mark like the sun on your ceremonial bag sounded good, but if there's a mark like that around here, I haven't seen it."

"It's here," Raven insisted. "We have to find it."

"And if we don't, then what? We can't fool around here looking. The area is getting too crowded. We'll have to go. Later, maybe, we can return and search."

"But what if Swift Hand finds the treasure?"

"He won't. Whether I believe in spirits or not, it's pretty clear that you're the key to the location. If it's to be found, we'll find it. But it won't do your people much good if we die in the process."

"We will not die, Tucker."

Adroitly he turned her and, with his hand on her shoulder, pushed her ahead of him down the trail. "How can you be so sure? I'm not."

"Because it was meant to be. Because we were chosen."

Being chosen to die wasn't Tucker's idea of good fortune. If Raven's spirit world intended to make sacrifices, he didn't intend to become their lamb.

Swift Hand finished off the last of the Mexican cigarillo he'd taken off the dead man and smiled. He sat astride his horse, studying the mountains above the canyon wall.

It had taken two days, but his men had finally found the way up the ridge. Come morning they'd climb to the other side, where she'd be within his reach.

He'd force her to reveal the location of the treasure.

Or maybe he'd just let her find it and take it from her. Then he'd take his rightful place as leader of the Arapaho. Once he had gold, they could buy horses and land. No man would order them around again. Or woman.

With his fingertips he pinched off the fire and stored the remainder of the cigar in his pouch. The fat little bandit who'd provided the tobacco had been a simpering coward, but his full knapsacks redeemed his pitiful death.

A horse. A new rifle. Ammunition and a handful of the thin black cigars. A few bandits had escaped, but they knew the power of Swift Hand and his braves now. They wouldn't return.

Swift Hand glanced around. There was something about these mountains, something uneasy. He'd always known certain places were sacred, forbidden to man, but he'd never experienced such apprehension before. Leaving this place would be good.

7

They'd finished eating when Tucker heard the braying of a burro. He grabbed the rifle and waited by the door, listening to the sound of the complaining animal.

"Hello, the cabin. Are you in there, cousin?"

"I'll go," Raven said. "Better that nobody knows you are here."

The stranger standing beyond the door was another half-breed miner, younger than Luce, yet with the same physical characteristics. He had a proud nose that told Raven of his Indian ancestry and a short stature that spoke of his Mexican heritage. He was dressed in a poncho and sandals, leading his own burro, with a shovel and pickax tied to his back.

Before Tucker could stop her, she was out the door. "Good morning."

"Morning, señorita." He looked surprised. "I would speak with my cousin, Luce."

"Luce is not here." Until she knew more, it was better for the visitor to think Luce was gone instead of ill.

"I am Benito," the stranger said.

"And I am Raven Alexander, Luce's—friend. What did you want him to know?"

Benito studied the ground, shuffling his feet uncertainly. "The hills—the hills are not safe, señorita. I worry about Luce. He should leave this place and go down to the village."

"What do you know about Luce?" Raven asked, still suspicious.

"Luce is my cousin. His mother was my father's sister. We both share the blood of the Arapaho and the Spanish."

"And do you know why Luce stays here?"

"No. He only says that he must remain until someone comes to take his place. Is that you?"

"Yes," Raven said softly. "I think it is."

Nervously the man studied her, glancing toward the mountain and back toward Raven. "I would have come to warn him sooner, but I had to travel from the back side of the mountain to avoid the strangers."

"Strangers?"

"Outsiders. Bandits look for Luce, and Indians search for one of their own. A spirit woman has been stolen from their tribe. Are you the one they seek?"

Better to confront the accusation head-on. Raven let out a light laugh. "You think Luce stole me?"

The miner looked sheepish. "I do not know. I only know that his wife is dead and he is alone. But he is old and sometimes he talks crazy."

"You talked to the Indians. What did they say?"

"The leader offered me horses to find the woman. I told him I did not know of a woman in the mountains. Luce should not have taken you. I will wait until he returns."

"Come inside, Benito." He'd already seen her; there

was no taking that back. They must either change the prospector's mind or play on his decency. "Luce has been badly hurt by bandits. He is dying."

The miner followed her, his hand beneath his poncho as they went into the cabin. His eyes widened when he caught sight of Tucker holding a rifle leveled at his mid-section.

"So you've come to protect Luce?" Tucker asked.

"He would do the same for me and my family." He caught sight of the bed and moved to the side of his cousin, taking his hand. "Si, he is leaving this cursed place."

Raven watched Benito take Luce's hand. "Cursed?" she questioned.

"Luce swore the Ancient Ones made his family guardian of the mountain before our tribe was divided. That was so long ago that we no longer knew which tribe we were."

"The Arapaho," Raven whispered. "Half of the tribe remained in these mountains, and half journeyed to the north. Your tribe was guardian of the treasure. My mother's tribe was charged with claiming it when the time came."

Benito shook his head. "I've searched the hills all my life, señorita, and I've never found anything. There is no treasure. Luce was my cousin, but he was a fool."

Tucker could have produced the gold nugget and the watch fob, but he didn't. If Luce had wanted his cousin to know what he'd found, he'd have shown him. Though Benito's affection for Luce was obvious, Tucker sensed that for now, the less said the better.

After sharing their meager supplies, Benito sat by Luce's side. When night came, he made his bed outside the cabin beside the lean-to. During the night, Tucker was aware of every time Raven tried to force rabbit broth and water down Luce. But he refused to swallow and finally she gave up.

Tucker worried for the first part of the night about how he could ensure the prospector's silence. Finally he decided that one of the nuggets could be sacrificed. The next morning, he'd give Benito the gold and promise him more if he would conceal Raven's presence.

But the next morning, Benito was gone.

When Tucker returned to the cabin to warn Raven, she met him at the door, her eyes washed with tears.

"I think he must have known. Luce is dead."

"And we still don't know where we're supposed to bury him."

"We will be shown," Raven said with more confidence than she felt. "First we bathe him."

"I know, and shave his head. Though for the life of me, I can't see why. Most Indians associate losing their hair with losing their power."

"He was insistent." Raven turned back to the cabin to gather their supplies. "Give me your razor. And bring the bedroll."

Tucker, who was following, came to an abrupt stop. "Why?"

"How else are we to shave his head?"

"I didn't mean the razor. Why bring the bedroll?"

"We have to have something to cover him with."

Tucker groaned. "I was afraid of that." He handed Raven the straight razor and wrapped the old man in the blanket. The pain in Tucker's ribs was less now as he carried Luce up the trail to the waterfall.

On reaching the spring, Tucker laid the old man down and started back down the path.

"Where are you going?"

"Back to the cabin. Just to be on the safe side, I'm

going to pack the saddlebags and bring the horses and the burro to the spring. They can drink and graze on what little grass they can find while we give Luce his last rites."

Raven didn't have to be told that Tucker was worried. She was worried as well. Benito had disappeared. No telling what he would do. If Swift Hand was still in the area, they could be in even more danger. Because of her, Tucker's life would be threatened.

Tucker was right. The sooner they buried Luce, the better. She'd figure out a way to convince Tucker to move on. Then she'd find the treasure herself.

She quickly shed her buckskin dress and slid into the water, pulling Luce's head over the edge of the pool. By the time she heard Tucker returning, she was lathering Luce's hair with the root of a plant that was sometimes used as a poor man's soap.

Tucker rounded the boulder and stopped short. He hadn't thought ahead to what would happen at the spring. He certainly hadn't expected to find Raven in the water, without her clothes. Nudity was natural for Indian women, but it wasn't natural for Tucker, and he didn't welcome his body's response.

"You'll have to help me, Tucker. I will hold him while you remove his hair."

"Yes, ma'am!" he said, covering his confusion with his sharp reply and snappy salute. "Do I remove my clothes, too, or just jump right in?"

"I'm sorry, Tucker. I don't mean to take charge, it just seems to happen. What would you like me to do?"

"Put on your clothes," he snapped. "Get on your horse and ride back to wherever you came from."

She stood, supporting Luce's head in the icy water. "You know we must do what we promised. Then you can go, if you choose."

"And if the Mexicans and the Arapaho come, you'll

dig a tunnel and haul off the treasure. And if there are any wild animals, you'll kill them with your bare hands."

Tucker saw the wounded expression on her face and realized how he'd sounded. He was worried, very worried, and he didn't want to think that most of his concern was for this woman. Not because of her possible enemies, but because of what he was feeling.

"I'm sorry," he said. "You're right. I gave my word." Determined to put her nudity out of his mind, he hobbled the two horses and the burro. Taking a deep breath, Tucker pulled off his shirt and removed his boots. Still wearing his trousers, he picked up the razor from the bank and slid into the pool.

This woman was changing the patterns of his life. He'd already slept with her without making love to her. Now for the second time, he was about to try to ignore her lush nude body while he stood hip to hip with it.

He began to shave away Luce's hair, catching it as it fell and slinging it toward the rocks on the bank. Having the horses drink from the pool and bathing in it seemed natural. But Luce's long, unwashed hair felt wrong.

As Tucker shaved, a series of black marks were revealed.

"Look, body painting," Raven said. "The design must be some kind of tribal symbols."

Tucker frowned. "You probably know more than me, but I've never heard of them being applied to the head."

"Neither have I, unless someone wanted to keep the design secret." She raised her gaze to Tucker. "Do you suppose this means something?"

"The only thing I'm sure of, Spirit Woman, is that you're turning into a prune and my razor is getting dull. Let's get him bathed and get out of here."

Moments later Tucker had finished the job and pulled Luce back into the shade of a boulder. Squatting beside the body, he studied Luce's head. Something about the design looked familiar. Following a hunch, he removed the tin pan from Yank's saddlebags and, with his knife, transferred the pattern etched on Luce's scalp to the bottom of the pan. He was beginning to get an idea.

"What are you doing?" Raven asked as she pulled her dress over her bare body and came to kneel beside him.

"Bring your mother's carrying bag."

Raven handed it to him.

Tucker looked at both the pan and the drawing, then nodded. "They're the same, or almost. Except for the butterfly."

"Why a butterfly?" Raven asked curiously.

"I have no idea. On your drawing there are little jagged marks between the dots and wavy lines. I think both of these sketches are maps."

In the bright morning sunlight, Raven squinted her eyes, trying to see a map in the pinpoint holes Tucker had made with his knife.

She couldn't make any sense of either. Surely they hadn't come this far to fail. Flying Cloud had said the spirits would protect her. Maybe, if she concentrated, they'd show her the way.

As she looked her heart rate decreased and she felt very cold. A bright blue-white glow settled over her, but the glow was not warm.

From some far place, she heard the low, mournful sound of drums beating in a curious marching rhythm. This time the chanting spoke of the sun and the moon, of water. She saw the drawing in her mind. Lines radiated outward from the sun. As she watched they rippled like the waves of a mirage on the desert floor. The sun rolled and began to move. Behind it, like thunderheads in a storm, lines curled into round half-circles.

Then came water, a great flood of water that lifted

and swept her along. *Follow the water*, the voices said. Then came darkness and great pain.

"Raven! What's wrong?"

Tucker lunged toward her, catching her as she fell, pale and lifeless, onto the rock beside the pool. With his hat Tucker scooped the icy water and splashed it across her cold face.

Too cold. She felt like Luce, like death. Quickly Tucker carried her away from the pool, wrapped her in her own blanket, and cradled her to him. To hell with the treasure, with burying an old man who meant nothing to him. All he cared about now was the woman in his arms.

There was something ethereal about her pale skin, about the dark, lush lashes that lay still on her cheeks. Shell-like pink lips closed, barely moving as she breathed. She lay still against him, as trusting as a sleeping child. Was she dying? Was he responsible for this terrible thing?

His heart hurt. After the painful war years, Tucker had managed to separate himself from caring about anything. Now this woman had split him open and forced him to care.

"Open your eyes, sweetheart," he pleaded. "Smile at me like you did that night on the ledge when we kept each other warm."

Her eyes fluttered for a moment. He leaned closer to hear the words she was whispering. "Promise me you'll bury Luce."

"Luce is dead. I can't do anything for him now. But I'm not going to let anything happen to you."

But she remained still. She appeared to be in some kind of state halfway between sleep and death. She didn't get any better, but she was no worse either. He had the feeling that she was waiting.

Finally Tucker got to his feet. He had to get Raven

to a doctor, no matter the risk. But first he was honor bound to bury Luce. But where?

He'd give it one last shot. He'd climb up the cliff beyond the rock where the water fell into the pool. If the rock with the mark didn't present itself, he'd just dig a temporary hole. Then when he'd gotten Raven to safety, he'd come back and look some more. Tucker covered Raven and returned the pan to the burro's saddlebags.

Tucking Raven's map inside his shirt, he laid Luce across the burro, secured the pick and shovel in the small animal's pack, and started up. Constantly watching for Indians, or bandits, or even Benito, Tucker climbed. The trail was nonexistent. The burro complained. They climbed over boulders, the stream disappearing for long stretches, only to reappear just as Tucker was ready to give up and dig.

As if it were playing a child's game, it led Tucker on. Finally, as the sun began to fall lower in the sky, its rays slanted across the rocks, temporarily blinding Tucker. What in hell was he doing up here in the mountains looking for some secret mark on a rock when Raven was in trouble?

A loud squawk broke the silence. Tucker swore, then blinked and blinked again. A quick picture of Raven came to mind and he groaned. How long had he been gone now? What kind of man walked away from a woman who needed him?

No answer came. What kind of man went back on his word to a dying man? Besides, he'd promised Raven. Tucker took a deep breath and hazarded one last attempt to open his eyes.

Suddenly, as if it hadn't been there moments before, he saw it. There, on the rock, was a drawing, red against the dazzling white limestone. Stick men held bows and arrows, and crudely drawn figures were dressed in armor.

But the drawing that caught and held his gaze was that of a crude circle with rays radiating outward overlaying the same pattern of dots.

Luce's sign. He'd found the spot.

Like a man possessed, Tucker began to dig. He didn't know how long he'd been digging when he realized that he was standing in the hole. "Deep enough." He climbed out and pulled Luce into the hole, then covered him with dirt. Finally, his promise satisfied, he staggered back down the trail.

The descent was easier. He was so tired that he could barely walk by the time he got back to the pool. Late afternoon shadows fell across the pool. Tucker took a deep breath and focused his gaze on the spot where he'd left Raven. She was gone. There was no sign she'd ever been there. Even the horses were missing.

Every thought left his mind as the truth registered. Either Raven had left of her own accord, or she'd been kidnapped. Either way, she was gone.

For a long minute, Tucker simply stood. Then, like the mountain lion she'd likened him to, he let out a roar of pain that echoed through the rocks and was carried away by the wind.

At almost the same time Tucker was smoothing out the earth over Luce's grave, Raven was seated on Onawa as Swift Hand tied her hands together and looped the reins around them.

"You will tell us the location of the treasure, Raven," Swift Hand threatened, "or your man will die."

"I say once again, I have no man."

"Then who belongs to the black stallion?"

"He is a stranger, following an old miner who boasts

of finding a mountain of gold. Did you not see that I had been drugged and bound?"

Swift Hand looked uneasy. He still couldn't make sense out of what he and his men had stumbled on. Two horses were hobbled near the pool of water. Raven had lain under her blanket in a deep sleep, and there was no sign of anyone else. Only the drying strands of body hair flung against the rocks signified some kind of sacrifice.

"Perhaps. But I saw no sign of restraints. Where is this man?"

"I do not know. All I can tell you is that he found me on the trail, injured. For three days," she improvised, "he kept me prisoner while he went into the mountains."

"Looking for the treasure," Little Eagle said. "She probably already told him where it was. Now he's gone."

Swift Hand gave a last vicious tug to the knot, almost pulling Raven from Onawa's back. "Flying Cloud had no right to give the secret to you. Rightfully, I should have been sent to bring back that which is ours."

Raven's head ached. Her mouth was dry, as if she'd crossed the desert without water. She was having great difficulty understanding what had happened. The last thing she remembered was studying the tin pan with the holes punched in it. Only when she began to wake did she realize that she'd been captured.

"Please understand. I am only following the Grand-father's wishes. I do not know where the treasure is. I would take you with me if you promise to honor my pledge to buy land for our people."

"Hah!" Swift Hand swore and lapsed into the Arap-aho language, gesturing wildly as he spoke.

Raven straightened her back and held her head high. "Then we will not agree. And I tell you again, I cannot guide you to the treasure, for I do not know where it is hidden."

Swift Hand paced back and forth, pausing to stare off into the distance, then pacing again. Finally he stopped, squatted, and conferred with Little Eagle. Then he stood.

"We will leave this place for now. No man abandons his horse. Your man will come for it, and we will just let him tell us where the treasure can be found."

Raven was afraid that Swift Hand was right. Tucker might not care about her, but he'd not give up Yank easily. Once more she'd put her rescuer in danger.

Oh, Grandfather, why is this happening? I cannot believe that you wanted this.

Swift Hand vaulted onto his horse and led the procession of braves back down the trail to the cabin. Any hope Raven had of stopping there quickly vanished when he rode past, taking the hazardous trail back toward the gorge where the Rio Grande flowed.

Already shadows filled the crevices of rock. It was the time of night just past sunset, before the moon's faint rays ventured across the blackness. More than once Swift Hand stopped his pony and listened. Even Raven was beginning to feel a curious unease.

When they reached the ridge, the leader came to a stop. "We will camp here." Swift Hand threw his leg over his pony and slid to the ground.

He pulled Raven from her horse and shoved her to the ground near a yellow pine growing at the center of the rocky ledge. As his men built a fire Swift Hand searched the saddlebags, finding Tucker's bottle of whiskey. The Indians argued about who would keep watch and who would share their find. Soon they forgot about her. All but Swift Hand.

Though she was both hungry and thirsty, she ignored her discomfort, concentrating instead on trying to reach Tucker. She emptied her head of all thoughts, allowing

her spirit to wander free. She smelled the earth, felt the
rough bark of the tree against her back.

Her mind seemed in tune with the very air. She
waited, as if she expected at any moment to hear someone
speak to her. The wind turned brisk, yet the night sky
remained clear. Closing her eyes, Raven remained totally
still.

Hours passed. She couldn't see Swift Hand, but she
knew he was there, in the darkness behind her. The fire
burned down and the braves stretched out to sleep, leaving
only Swift Hand and the one called Little Eagle to watch.

Still Raven waited.

The night was silent, disturbed only by the occasional
howl of a wild animal and the wind. Like a whisper it
came, softly but insistently, the sound of wings, brushing
the night with flutters. Raven felt the touch of something
mystical.

Then suddenly, in one ice-drenched moment, she felt
an intrusion, a presence. No face, no flesh to touch, but
she could feel him. And silent words—unbidden yet welcome.

"Where are you, Spirit Woman? I feel you, but I cannot see you."

Tucker, she whispered. *Be still and I will come to you.*

Beyond her skin. Beyond the night she reached, her
mind probing, searching for the golden cord that linked
them. And she knew that she had changed. Whatever she
had been before, she was different now. Her past remained, her future was uncertain. But she could examine
both from a far distance. This man, Tucker Farrell, was
her link, her bridge from one to the other.

She brought his face into view, focusing on his blue
eyes, his golden hair, and his weathered skin. He was
strong but human. Her reluctant self-appointed protector

was willing to risk his life to protect hers. And he searched for her now.

She could see him, sense him, but for now the elusive golden cord floated in the unknown realm of her mind, unjoined.

Still, her heart filled with joy. He was alive. And he searched for her. She would wait.

8

Tucker moved steadily through the night, arguing now
and then with Luce's burro, who saw no reason to travel
at such a speed. Swift Hand and his braves had made no
effort to conceal their shoeless pony tracks. It was obvious
they wanted to be found.

After his forays into the mountains, Tucker found it
easy to trail them. He was able to move swiftly, for he
knew the way.

By the time the eastern sky began to lighten, pearly
wisps of clouds swirled around the mountaintop where
Tucker walked. There was an eerie quiet. No birds sang.
No wind. Only silence.

Tucker paused, closed his eyes, and tried to concentrate on Raven. *Where are you, Spirit Woman? I know
you're here somewhere but I can't find you. I still don't believe
in all this spirit stuff, but I'd welcome a sign about now.*

Nothing. No squawking birds, no pictures drawn on
rocks, no visions. He hadn't expected anything, yet as he
waited he felt a presence, a commanding sense of connection. He could neither see her nor hear her, but somehow
they touched.

It was the altitude, he decided, shaking off the eerie feeling that had settled over him. He emptied the last sip of water from Luce's canteen and rested for a few minutes. With new purpose he went forward, making his footsteps as soft as the pads of the mountain lion to which Raven had likened him.

Around the next outcropping of rock, he saw their fire. Swift Hand and his braves. They were sleeping, even the guard. It was too easy. Swift Hand might be confident, but he was no fool. Unless he wanted Tucker to take Raven. Unless he'd been drawn into a false sense of security.

He counted seventeen Arapaho. Their ponies had been hobbled and left to move awkwardly beyond their camp on the small flat ridge where they'd stopped for sleep. He could see Yank's huge silhouette in the light, and the pinto mare who stood beside him. But where was Raven?

His gaze traveled around the smoldering campfire, counting sleeping forms in the shadowy light. Then he saw her. In the middle, leaning against a rock, she sat, looking straight at him as if she could see him through the darkness.

No, not yet. Beware.

Her warning came to him as clearly as if she'd spoken. It was only a slight sound of movement that gave Swift Hand away, a sound so faint that it might have been caused by a leaf falling. But Tucker knew instinctively. The Indian was there, beyond the circle, waiting.

Did he know that Tucker had caught up with them? Tucker didn't come any closer. He could see the camp, yet he was still too far away to be seen. But Luce's burro had other ideas. He sensed the presence of the other horses and began to strain to free himself to reach them.

Then it came to Tucker. Use the distraction, not to

rescue Raven as they expected, but to take Yank. Raven's importance was not lost on Swift Hand. He wouldn't hurt her, and Yank's disappearance could be explained as natural, particularly if he arranged for some of the other horses to escape as well. With a horse to ride, when he took Raven, they would have the means to escape.

But as logical as his thoughts were, Tucker didn't know if he could walk away and leave her behind. Would she understand what he was doing and why? Could he do it? Perhaps he wouldn't have to.

Tucker tied the burro to a bush, loosely enough so that he could eventually free himself. Then, drawing down behind the boulders, he backtracked and moved higher into the rocks, working his way around the camp to the other side where the horses were.

Moments later the squealing burro raced down the trail, through the camp. The Indians reacted automatically, reaching for their rifles and positioning themselves for an attack. Swift Hand closed the distance between him and Raven, standing boldly beside his captive.

But it was the Indian horses that foiled Tucker's plan. One scent of Tucker and they reacted with fear and agitation. He had to act quickly or they would give him away. As he cut the rawhide from its hooves, Tucker grabbed a packet of food from the saddlebag of one of the Indian ponies and stuck it into Yank's saddlebag. He then unshackled a second pony and Yank. He would have freed Onawa, but Raven would need a safe mount until she could be rescued. The best Tucker could hope for was that the Indians would believe the burro had followed them on his own and in the confusion the horses had escaped.

He had intended to lead Yank away and turn him in the direction of Luce's cabin. The big horse would eventually stop and wait. But in the melee of the burro's disturbance, Yank pulled away and ran with the Indian ponies to the north. Tucker hadn't counted on Onawa's determination to follow, even with her legs hobbled. He had to cut her free or run the risk of injury to the young horse. So be it. He cut the cord, flicked the mare on her rump, and watched her escape into the darkness.

Tucker quickly made his way back to a place above the site so that he could monitor the Indians' movements. He had to move carefully now, else he'd let loose one of the boulders behind which he hid.

Boulders. The perfect answer. If there was a way to make certain that the falling rubble missed Raven. He poked his head around the rock he used for shelter and took a quick look.

The sun, rising across the canyon to the east, cast a pallor over the campsite. The Indians were trying to calm their horses. Two braves raced down the trail after the escaping ponies. Swift Hand had jerked Raven to her feet and was dragging her toward the largest horse, unleashing a furious tirade in Arapaho.

"What makes you think anybody directed the burro? He's just used to being with the horses," Raven said. "I already told you that Tucker went hunting yesterday and never returned. My guess is that the Mexicans got him."

Swift Hand looked around uneasily. It was obvious that he wasn't buying her explanation, but since Tucker hadn't tried to rescue Raven, the Indian was confused.

"Where's Onawa?" Raven asked.

Swift Hand jerked around, noting for the first time that, along with the big black, the painted mare was also gone. The loss of four horses meant that some of the braves would walk, and none wanted that assignment

"Let's go," Swift Hand ordered. "You can ride double."

"Why would you want to leave when the treasure is behind us?" Raven asked shrewdly.

Swift Hand glanced back up the trail warily. "The spirits are restless," he said. "They do not welcome the Arapaho."

"This is because they do not wish you to invade their sacred mountains. Let me go, and I will share whatever wealth I find with all the Arapaho people. I give you my word."

"No, it is a trick. I do not trust you, Medicine Woman. Bring my pony." He let go of Raven for a moment to cut the tethers from his horse.

At that moment Raven glanced up in the rocks. She saw the boulder begin to shimmy, slightly at first, then wildly. Loose gravel began to slide down the mountain. Then with a great creak, the boulder toppled over and began to fall toward the spot where Swift Hand stood.

He heard the commotion and looked up, let out a yell, and started after Raven. But she had already plunged into the rocks out of the boulder's path and started climbing upward.

"Get back here, Medicine Woman!"

The boulder suddenly veered, hit a larger rock, and bounced, breaking into three pieces and rolling in opposite directions, one piece splitting Swift Hand from his braves, another separating him from Raven. By the time the dust settled, she had vanished.

"Spread out," Swift Hand called to his men. "Find her!"

But they only stared. It was obvious to Tucker that none wanted to risk rousing the wrath of the mountain. In order to save his dignity, Swift Hand must counter the interference of the elements.

His quick search of the area proved unsuccessful. Swift Hand's expression was perplexed at first, then uneasy.

"She is nowhere," Little Eagle said.

"She is somewhere," Swift Hand insisted. "Look again."

But this time Little Eagle seemed even more reluctant to follow orders. "She is a spirit woman; maybe while we were not looking, she turned into a raven and flew away."

"You are right, my brothers," Swift Hand agreed, "we must not act too quickly and anger the spirits. We will wait until the time is right. Then the treasure will be ours." He turned, threw his leg across his pony, and rode away, his men following without even a backward glance.

Once he was certain that Swift Hand hadn't doubled back, Tucker called out, "Raven, where are you?"

But there was no answer. He was beginning to get a bad feeling. Where was she?

He moved quickly down the mountain, being careful not to dislodge any more loose rock. He went to the place where he'd last seen her.

Then he found her, hidden beneath debris and brush. The third rock had found its mark. Raven lay white-faced and still, with the rock resting on her leg.

"Damn it to hell! I thought your spirits would protect one of their own."

"I'm all right, Tucker. I won't do any marching, but then, you have the more experience at that. Call Onawa."

He found a limb to use as a wedge and moved the rock, grimacing at the nasty cut just below her knee. "Onawa's gone. I set Yank free and she insisted on tagging along."

"She'll return, when it's safe."

"I hope so." He was beginning to wonder if safety was something they could ever look forward to. "Can you stand?"

"You mean can I walk?" She gave him her hands and allowed him to lift her. Standing was possible, but she winced, and blood began to flow from the wound.

"Take a step."

She let out an agonizing cry and nearly crumpled as she put her weight on her injured leg. "Well, I guess that takes care of walking," she said with a grimace. "I think I sprained my ankle."

Tucker looked about anxiously. Swift Hand may have ridden away, but there was no guarantee that he wouldn't double back. In fact, all of this could be an elaborate hoax to draw him out. With Tucker out of the way, Raven would be forced to rely on Swift Hand's help.

Walking back to Luce's cabin under the best of circumstances would be risky. Now it would be impossible. Without horses they couldn't make any kind of time.

"Well, I guess I'll have to carry you." He lifted her in his arms and stoically refused to show any evidence of the pain her weight caused his sore ribs.

"You can't carry me," Raven protested. "You're still injured."

"I'm fine. Have I complained?"

"No, but no man heals that quick."

"But I'm a cougar, remember?"

His warm breath fluttered her hair. Then he pulled back, his blue eyes teasing as he smiled, erasing for a moment the seriousness of their situation. Her breath caught in her throat as she glimpsed a side of Tucker Farrell she hadn't seen. She was aware of the feel of his hard, sinewy chest pressed against her, of the beat of his heart and the pressure of his fingertips against her thighs. His nearness took away her fears, replacing them with a mad surge of something she couldn't put a name to.

For a second his fingers dug into her rib cage, and she knew that he was feeling the same flash of awareness. "I know that I'm heavy," she said in a breathless voice. "Even for a cougar."

"You're—you're just right."

She let go of one hand and traced the tiny scab left from where he'd cut his face shaving. "You're very strong."

"And I'm also very much a man, Raven Alexander. Stop rubbing yourself against me unless you want me to find a cave and—"

She gasped. "And what?"

"Well, let's put it this way. Cougars aren't solitary animals. And it's spring."

She gave his face one last touch and replaced her hand around his neck. She felt the tight resistance in his body and the tension in her own as it brushed against him.

"I may not have any personal experience with men, Tucker, but I know the danger we are in and I know you could get away and go back to find the treasure for yourself. Why are you doing this?"

"Damned if I know. Because you put some kind of witch's spell on me, I suppose."

She paid little heed to his warning. She wasn't afraid of her cougar, whether it was spring or not. Like his animal spirit, he was a magnificent specimen of a male, and she couldn't stop herself from pulling his head down to hers. He'd kissed her once and the memory of those lips against hers was driving her to distraction.

Her lips parted sweetly beneath his, her tongue sweeping past them and finding the essence of the man she was learning to need more than life. There was a moan. She didn't know whether it was her or Tucker, but as the fire caught, she gave in to the incredible need to fold herself around him.

She kneaded the back of his neck, saying with her hands and mouth what she couldn't put into words. Because of their situation, this might be all she'd ever have of this man who was becoming so important to her.

His hand beneath her bottom clenched and unclenched, moving up and down as if he couldn't be still.

Finally, with a gasp, he pulled away and went down on one knee.

"Don't do this, Raven. Suppose Swift Hand returns?"

She was breathing so hard that she could barely talk. She burned everywhere they touched. "I don't think that's going to happen. He knows now that these mountains are sacred. He'll have to find more courage before he can return."

"That's what I mean. We only have a few hours to put some distance between us. We can't do this."

Roughly he lifted her and stood once more, heading not up the trail as she expected but in the same direction as the Indians had gone. He was going to return her to Swift Hand. She'd pushed him too far.

"I'm sorry, Tucker. I didn't mean to make you angry."

"Angry? Spirit Woman, I'm a lot of things right now, but angry isn't one of them. Just keep quiet and let me think."

She complied, trying to hold herself away from him, from the continuing heat of his touch.

"I think we'll confuse him a bit," he said.

"Isn't this a bit like the tortoise chasing the hare?"

"Not exactly. The tortoise is going to take a short cut." With that he left the trail and started upward, carefully threading his way through the rocks.

"Where are you going?"

"Benito talked about a village in the valley beyond the mountain. If we go there, we can find shelter and help. Relax, Raven. I'm not saying no to your offer, I'm saying wait."

Patience was a trait Raven had never developed. But Tucker's implied yes was intriguing enough for her to contemplate. As they made their way up, the sun followed them, moving higher in the sky. Its light erased the wispy patches of clouds, turning the glistening rocks of gray granite a silvery color. The climb was exhausting and hot, and they had no food or water.

Tucker was strong, and after her initial worry, Raven relaxed against him, her arms around his neck, her forehead tucked into the hollow beneath his chin. Once again, even in the midst of danger, he'd made her feel safe.

As they climbed he grew winded and had to stop frequently. Finally, as the sun sprang into the space directly overhead, he reached a stand of stubby mesquite trees and laid her down in the patch of shade they provided.

"I'm going to leave you here for a bit and double back."

"Why?"

"I want to find a place where I can see behind us." He needed to make certain they weren't being followed. He also knew that in spite of her calm demeanor, the constant movement of her ankle caused her a great deal of pain. And sooner or later, they had to find water. With water he could clean her wound, maybe even brew up some of that red berry liquid that would ease her pain.

Raven watched him go, swallowing hard, fighting the urge to call him back. Tucker was right to be concerned, for she knew that Swift Hand wouldn't give up. She had sensed his fear of the mountains, his uncertainty of her powers, but greed and the need to be a hero in the eyes of their people would soon override his anxiety.

She stretched out her leg and winced as she caught sight of the swelling. Being carried was pleasant, but Tucker couldn't hold out for long. As he climbed back down the mountain, she saw that he leaned slightly to the side and carried his elbow flat against his rib cage, tribute to the pain that his efforts must have caused. She didn't have to test her ankle to know that walking was something she wouldn't be doing for a while. But Tucker was not invincible.

Laying her head back, she closed her eyes. Tucker couldn't carry her forever; they'd have to find somewhere to hide before night came again. They'd wrapped Luce in Tucker's bedroll for burial. Now with the horses gone, so was her blanket, and all their food and water.

She tried to evaluate their options. Tucker still had his pistol and she still had—she touched her neck—yes. Her medicine bag was still there. Once she took a little rest, she might be able to fashion some kind of crutch or splint so that she could manage on her own. If only she had some water, she could treat her wound. Food she could do without.

But beyond that, the question of locating the treasure still loomed large. After finding Luce and coming so close to her goal, they appeared to be heading in a totally different direction. She and Tucker had become a kind of team, but now their personal survival stood in the way of their mission, and she couldn't let that happen. The government would soon gather her people and force them farther west. She didn't have a lot of time.

She dozed for a while, fitfully, and when she woke she discovered that Tucker was still gone.

Despair swept over her. The pain in her leg rolled through her empty stomach toward her chest like an avalanche. She felt such loss, such pain. She'd always spent time alone, but that was before Tucker Farrell, before the raven had met her mountain lion.

"The dream was right, Grandfather. The raven was the injured one. The cougar saved her."

Raven lay, freeing her mind. This time she consciously willed a vision. She needed direction. She needed some kind of confirmation that all was not lost. Slowly at first, the drums came, growing louder as she waited. Then the chanting began, familiar words, a children's song about games. But the chanting became louder and she joined in repeating the words.

> *Natinachabena!*
> [Now I go to seek my horses!]
> *Ni nananaechana!*
> [So here I stand and look about me!]
> *Ni nananaechana!*
> [So here I stand and look about me!]
> *Natinachabena!*
> [Now I go to seek my horses!]

The sound grew and grew until she felt her body begin to flutter. Her feet left the earth and she began to rise. Soon she was high in the sky, looking down at the woman sleeping beneath the mesquite trees below.

Feeling the wind beneath her wings, she soared, leaving pain and uncertainty behind, allowing the earth and the sky to cleanse her, free her to fly.

Still the song echoed in her mind. *Seek the horses! Seek the horses!* Then she saw them, Yank and Onawa racing through the rocks and scrub as if they, too, felt the wind against their chests, their manes flying in the breeze that swept them along.

Through the eyes of the raven, she searched the terrain until she saw Tucker, leaning against a boulder, pressing his hand against his ribs. He was tired, in pain, but he only stopped for a moment, then forced himself to turn and head back up the mountain toward the spot where he'd left her.

The flying black bird could see no sign of Swift Hand and his warriors. Dipping her wing, she allowed the current to sweep her toward the horses. *Hear my words, On-awa, follow the raven.*

The small mare lifted her head and snorted, studying the sky, pawing at the earth anxiously.

Come, faithful friend. Bring Yank and follow me.

After several moments of indecision, the horse began to move, slinging her head often to keep the black bird in sight. The travel for the horses was slow and often dangerous, for they had to forge through steep areas where there was no trail. A false step could have meant death. Yet Onawa kept coming. And Yank followed nervously behind.

The raven began to tire. She was thirsty and there was no water close enough for her to drink. The horses were thirsty, too, and unsettled. Never before had they followed a spirit guide.

The winds dropped. The raven's wings grew heavy, and, like a leaf falling from the tree, the bird came slowly back to earth, disappearing as if it had never been. The drums hushed. The voices quieted. Raven slept.

Swift Hand reined in his horse and brought his men to a stop.

"Why did we flee?" Little Eagle asked.

"The spirits were not happy. They moved the mountain to show their displeasure. We will wait until the medicine woman finds the treasure. Then we will take it from her."

"Our bellies are empty now. What shall we do?"

"There is a ranch near Santa Fe. It covers all the land that once belonged to our people." Swift Hand thought for a moment, then whirled and rode away. "We ride down from the mountain and take what we want from those who took from our forefathers. Aieee!"

9

When Tucker returned, he carried a shovel with a broken handle. Somewhere along the way, he'd removed his bandanna from around his neck, tying it around his forehead like the wild Apache he'd accused Raven of being.

The tear in the knee of his pants had widened, allowing almost his entire kneecap to poke through. Perspiration stained the denim of his shirt. A cowboy he might be, but becoming a mountain man in hiding wore uneasily on the big, tawny man.

"Raven," he said, relieved to see that she was watching him as he came to her side. "How is the leg?"

"Swollen and painful. We're both in pretty sad shape, I'd say. Did you see any sign of Swift Hand?"

"No. I think they must have kept riding." He didn't tell her that the Indian was probably smart enough to figure out that the best way to find the treasure was to let Raven lead them to it. Why risk losing the location by confrontation?

There was no sign of her captor now, but with his skills, Swift Hand would be able to track a wounded woman and a man on foot. Somebody would be watching, sooner or later.

He tried to erase the frown of concern from his face. He knew that her endurance was being tested as much as his own.

"It's all right, Tucker. I understand how bad the situation is. But our horses will be here soon, and we can ride over the ridge to Benito's village."

Tucker hadn't seen any sign of the horses either, but he was too whipped to argue. He'd been moving all night and he was tired and thirsty. "First things first." He started to dig at the base of the mesquite tree.

"What are you doing?"

"Surely you know about the mesquite tree's roots seeking water. An old rancher told me once, the only way they can survive out here is if there's water. We just have to go deep enough to find it."

"I know about mesquite trees, Tucker, but you can't dig deep enough up here to find water. This ground is almost solid rock. We'd do better to get moving. Onawa will soon be here and we'll make better time."

"And how do you know that?"

"I just know that she and Yank are near."

Tucker's argument was cut off by the sound of movement behind them. Seconds later Onawa picked her way across the loose boulders and came into sight, followed by Yank and a complaining burro.

"Christ, how do you do that?" His voice was cross. He'd had as much mysticism as he could stand. "Do you and the horse share some kind of mental connection?"

"I do not know. It has always been so."

It might have been, but the idea unnerved Tucker. At least he didn't have to dig halfway to China. "Now we have the horses, who also need water," Tucker said, hoping their canteens were still in the burro's pack. They were. They could drink from the tin cup in the saddlebag, but his hat was gone, and damned if he intended to fill his boot with water so that the animals could drink.

Searching further, he pulled out the tin pan. "Too bad I put holes in this. They never made any sense and now it's worthless. I ought to throw it away."

"No. I'm certain we'll find a use for your map. Look again. The cup should be there."

It was. Tucker uncapped one of the canteens and poured a small amount of the liquid into it. He first offered it to Raven, who refused to take more than a sip. Next he drank, sparingly, but more deeply than Raven. He allowed each horse a small amount of the precious liquid, then recapped the container and packed it in the saddle-bags once more.

"I don't suppose you'd like to dream us up a nice stream and a fat rabbit, would you?"

"I wish I could, Tucker. But I don't always have control over my visions. They come from the spirit world."

"Well, maybe we'll get lucky. Let's keep moving."

By now the sun had slipped over the rim of the ridge behind them. They needed to move quickly since they could more easily be tracked in the daytime. Delaying the treatment of Raven's injury, Tucker set her on Onawa's bare back. Then he mounted Yank, who for once didn't protest, and rode the big horse toward the summit.

"Just let the horses choose," he instructed Raven. "They'll find the way better than you or I."

They reached the top of the ridge by late afternoon and started down. The horses were tentative at first, then moved more eagerly. Suddenly Onawa came to a stop, forcing Yank to do the same.

In the twilight's dead quiet, Tucker heard the sound of the wind sweeping down the draw. The leaves of the cottonwood trees rustled below, faintly at first, then louder. Someone was moving there.

Tucker slowly drew his pistol from its holster. He narrowed his eyes, studying the shadows. If Swift Hand lay in wait, there was little Tucker could do. They were all exhausted. The ridge was behind them and the intruder was waiting below.

Then Tucker let out a chuckle and a deep breath. "It's okay, Raven. It's just a wild animal. Maybe a deer. If I dared fire this pistol, we'd have supper."

"How can you be sure?"

He didn't have to show her. The burro, untethered, bounded down the trail. His screams of pleasure frightened a small mountain goat, who ran from the trees, scrambled up the rocks, and disappeared into the shadows.

"I think we can be sure that we're alone." Tucker relaxed for the first time since they'd crested the ridge. "Otherwise that goat wouldn't have been grazing down there. From the burro's behavior, I'd say there is water beyond those trees. That's where the horses have been heading all along."

Yank and Onawa moved quickly down the draw, into the stand of cottonwood and piñon. Tucker climbed down. He heard the soft ripple of a stream rolling over stones and hitting a pool below. Soon the animals were drinking noisily.

He could tell from the slump of Raven's shoulders that she'd gone as far as she could go. "I'll help you down."

"Yes. Can we have a fire? I'm suddenly getting very cold."

" 'Can we have a fire?' Is the general abdicating her post?" he asked with a smile.

"The general is too weary to worry."

Tucker put his arms around her waist and swung her down, being careful not to touch her swollen leg to the ground. He held her, for just a moment, then chastised himself for his thoughtlessness. She was hungry, thirsty, and exhausted, and here he was acting like some randy cowboy with nothing but lust on his mind. Looking around, he settled her on a tree stump by the water.

"I'll lay out your bedroll. I guess we're fortunate that Swift Hand decided to make you sleep sitting up. Otherwise we'd have left it behind."

She didn't answer, but seemed content to watch him make camp.

As quickly as he could, Tucker cleared the ground and unrolled the mat. Once more he moved Raven, placing her on the blanket. He removed his vest and folded it, sliding it beneath her head as a pillow. For just a second, he allowed himself to look at her, then reluctantly moved away to gather dry wood for a fire. Using one of his precious matches, he lit the moss and watched it blaze up. Soon the fire licked red tongues around the dry branches.

"Isn't it dangerous to build a fire?" Raven asked wearily.

"I don't think it matters. We're over the ridge in a low place, in the trees. If Swift Hand is following us, he already knows where we are. We'll have to make do with cold tortillas I took from one of the Indians' ponies."

Raven licked her dry lips. "We wouldn't have that, except his braves were more interested in the whiskey they found than the food."

Whiskey. His whiskey. He fumbled through his saddlebag. "Damn!"

"What's wrong?"

"Nothing. I guess it was too much to hope that they wouldn't find it. At least our escape makes more sense."

"Sorry about your whiskey. Guess you'll just have to drink water," she said.

The cornmeal fritters were hard and dry, but after being dipped into the cup of spring water, they were eatable. After they'd finished the meal, Tucker filled the tin cup once again and set it in the fire to boil.

"Do you have any more of that root and berry medicine?"

Raven pulled her medicine bag out from beneath her buckskin dress and pulled it open. "Yes, a small amount."

"The berry concoction takes away the pain?"

"Yes, but I don't think I'll need it." She handed him the last piece of the healing root. "Place this in the water and boil it."

He followed her directions, then muttered, "I wish I still had the whiskey."

"Well, I could probably find some bark and make you a nice tea," Raven said.

"I didn't intend to drink it. I was going to treat your wound with it." Wetting his bandanna in the stream, he sat down beside Raven.

Her sun-kissed legs were long and supple, used to walking, but not to a man's touch. At first she started, then let out a deep breath and visibly forced herself to relax as he lifted her foot with one hand and her knee with the other. Carefully he washed the cut, pleased that so far as he could see in the lengthening shadows, it didn't look angry.

He continued to wash and touch her long after his need to treat the wound was done. She was a beautiful woman, openly showing her trust in him. He couldn't justify or restrain his growing reaction to her body.

Forget it, Tucker. This woman is hurt. Put your mind out of its misery and get to the job of treating her wound.

After he'd poured the root liquid into the cut, he put the cup back on the fire and heated more water. Then, dipping his bandanna into the water, he applied the hot cloth to the wound. Over and over, he repeated this until he was satisfied that the leg was totally warmed. Finally he stood.

"I hope Swift Hand's braves didn't get a hankering to take a lady's petticoat back to the village." He removed their packs from the horses, opened hers, and drew out the soft white cotton garment. "Nope, it's still here."

Ripping the rest of the ruffle away, he bandaged the wound, then bound the ankle, splitting the end of the strand of material and tying it to hold the fabric tight. By the time he'd finished, Raven was half asleep.

He covered her with her blanket, then piled more wood on the fire and lay down on the ground beside her, but far enough away to keep from touching. "I'm sorry you had to use your bedroll to bury Luce," she whispered drowsily.

"Don't worry about it. I've slept on the ground plenty of nights."

She pulled back her blanket. "Don't be silly, Tucker. Come here."

"I'm not sure that's a good idea, Raven."

"My protector," she teased. "We've come too far to worry about good and evil. Besides, I'm cold."

Tucker unbuckled his gunbelt and laid it at the top of the blanket, then slid into the bedroll. As naturally as if they'd always slept together, she snuggled against him, pulling his arms around her, one beneath her head and the other around her waist.

"Tucker?"

"Yes, what's wrong? Does your leg hurt?"

"No, it isn't my leg. It's my stomach. It feels very strange. Does your stomach ache?"

Not my stomach, darling. "No. Maybe it was the tortillas."

"I don't think so. I had the same kind of pain that

night in Luce's cabin. It seems to come at the strangest times."

She moaned slightly and wiggled her bottom over and over as if she were tightening and letting go of her muscles.

"Don't do that, Raven."

"All right, it doesn't seem to help anyway."

"Go to sleep, woman. You're just tired."

"I suppose—Tucker?"

"Now what?"

"Will you kiss me?"

He had no business even touching her, certainly not responding when she rolled over in his arms, threw her leg over his thigh, and lifted her face up to his. But there was just so much any man could take, and Tucker had passed that point long minutes ago.

He kissed her, not because she asked, but because he needed to. "Just a minute, Spirit Woman," he whispered and tugged the thong from her braid, loosing her hair across her shoulders.

"What are you doing?" she asked.

"I just have a great urge to feel your hair," he whispered. "Besides," he lied, "that rope was cutting into my shoulder. That and those beads on that dress you're wearing."

"Oh, I'm sorry. I didn't think." She pushed herself up, and before he realized what she was doing, she'd pulled the dress over her shoulders and pitched it across the tree stump. "I never liked sleeping on them either," she said and leaned over him, ready for his kiss.

"What are you doing, Raven? We can't sleep like this."

"Why not? Would you like to remove your shirt and boots?"

He groaned. "Your leg," he mumbled, threading his

fingertips into her hair and pulling it over her bare breasts in a halfhearted attempt to cover the beauty of her body.

"You're right, it would be more comfortable lying flat. Let's turn over." Before he could tell her to stop, she'd rolled back over, pulling him with her. Now his face was over hers and his hand, still tangled in her hair, was resting on her breast.

"Oh, Raven, what in the west side of hell are we going to do?"

"I truly don't know, but you're a man and I thought you might show me."

"Under other circumstances I might," he admitted, feeling his fingers disregard any sane command from his mind and begin to tease the nipple already beaded hard and erect. "But you're tired and hurt."

"I don't seem to feel the hurt now, and I think something has given me energy. Maybe it was the root medicine. Kiss me, Tucker, or I shall die."

He was lost. He'd been lost from the moment he'd awoken on that ledge to find Raven Alexander staring at him. He'd fought his desire for her, but with her scent filling his nostrils, her supple body beneath his, her silky hair and smooth skin caressing him, he knew he was losing the battle.

Her fingers ran rampant, sliding between the buttons of his shirt, touching, examining, brushing him with fire.

"No, Raven. Stop this. You don't understand what you're asking for."

She grew still. "No, I don't, but I've seen my Indian sisters with their sweethearts. Am I so awful that you don't wish to have me?" She was having as much trouble controlling her desire as he was. Unless he could curb that need, he'd never be able to hold back.

"Perhaps," he whispered, "there is something I can do. Just don't touch me, Raven. Try not to touch me."

"Why? I like touching you. It gives me great pleasure."

He groaned. "That's the problem. Pleasure is most intense when it's shared. But it's also more lethal. Just lie back, Raven, and let me make you feel very good."

For once she took orders, relaxing her fingertips and allowing them to be freed from his shirt. He took both her hands and lifted them above her head as he kissed her. Beginning with a soft brush of his lips against hers, he was rewarded with gentle response. From there he deepened the kiss, increasing his pressure as well as his urgency. She followed.

When she began to undulate her body beneath his, he pulled away. "Oh, will you remove your clothing too?" she asked.

"No," he gasped, before clasping her breast with one hand. "This is for you, darling, not me."

"But would it not be better if we were both naked?"

Tucker blanched, his entire body shuddering at the innocence of her remark. He didn't answer. For all the angels in heaven, he couldn't think of a reply that wouldn't make him completely lose control. Instead he used his other hand to caress her skin, skimming, kneading, moving ever downward as she writhed beneath his touch.

Finally he reached the soft hair at the source of her heat.

"Tucker?"

"It's all right, sweetheart. Just trust me. I'll take care of you." He let go of her breast and found her mouth once more.

As her lips opened beneath his he slipped his tongue inside, matching those movements with his fingers as he slid inside the tunnel of moisture between her legs. Slowly at first, he played with the tiny nub at the crest of the opening, then moved in and out, never pushing past the barrier he felt inside.

God, he wanted her. He might not even have to enter her to find release. As he moved against her thigh he felt himself swell, harden, and throb.

Raven's breath began to come fast and frantically. She was holding his head now between her hands as she sucked and plunged into his mouth in rhythm to his movements. Then he felt it, the ripple that suddenly became a wave of release.

She let go of his head and broke away from his lips, crying out in unrestrained passion of release. As she trembled, Tucker marshaled every ounce of control he had and forced himself to be still. So close, too close, he didn't dare breathe, or else everything would be lost and he'd roll over and plunge himself inside her.

Finally she was still.

"My mountain lion," she whispered. "He has every right to roar in the night."

Roar, maybe, Tucker thought. But it would be in frustration, not triumph. He realized that she didn't understand what agony he was suffering. But she would, one day, by heavens. The right man would come into her life and she'd know. He was sorry it wouldn't be him, but that could never be. Sometime in the last three days, he'd come to understand that she was to be the savior of an Indian nation. He was just a drifter. What was he doing with a savior?

He couldn't interfere with her mission. And he had no part in it, beyond helping her find the treasure. Then he'd take his share and buy land for a ranch. Raven could never be his; he wasn't good enough.

"Did I do something wrong?" Raven asked, creeping back into the safety of his embrace.

"No, ma'am. You did everything just right."

"But you—I don't know much, but I thought that men were the ones who felt the pleasure."

"They do. Don't ever think you don't bring a man pleasure, Raven Alexander, for you do. Great pleasure and the promise of more. Now sleep. We can't rest too long. The Indians are still out there and maybe the bandits as well."

"I'm not worried, Tucker Farrell. I'm safe here with you. I know."

"I wish I were sure, Spirit Woman. I wish I were."

Raven turned to her side, swallowed back a yawn, and let out a deep satisfied sigh. "I feel very good. This is much better than the juice of the red berry."

As the light of the sun gave way to the light of the moon, Tucker lay listening to Raven breathe, taking in the sweet woman smell of her. A few arrows of sunlight shot through the patches of foliage overhead. Onawa, Yank, and the burro moved along the stream, feeding. And the evening was quiet.

10

Raven opened her eyes to find a brown-frocked priest sitting on the tree stump watching her.

"Good morning, señorita," he said, smiling broadly. "I didn't mean to wake you, but I didn't want to take Jonah without telling you. I expect you'd like to dress, so we'll just be on our way."

Raven pulled the blanket higher and cut her eyes to the empty place by her side. She was alone in the bedroll where last night she'd— She blushed. Where was Tucker and why wasn't he saying anything?

"Jonah?" she managed to whisper.

"A sorry excuse for a burro, he's forever running away from home. He likes to visit people he meets when he accompanies me on my rounds. Gets himself into some terrible predicaments. That's why I named him Jonah. Thank the Holy Father that we have no whales in the territory."

The odd little man stood up, smoothed the skirt of his robe, and turned to lead the burro away.

"Wait." Raven sat up, clutched the falling blanket, and reached for her buckskin dress.

"Yes?"

"The tin pan, in the saddlebags. It belongs to me."

"Forgive me, I should have asked." He turned his back and opened the pack.

Taking advantage of his move, Raven pulled her dress on and started to stand. In her haste she forgot about her ankle and attempted to put her weight on the injured foot.

"Ahhh!" That wouldn't work. She dropped to her knees, throwing all her weight on her good leg.

"Is there something wrong, señorita?" The priest hurried to her side and looked down at the bandaged limb. "Oh, forgive me, you are hurt."

"No. I mean yes. I fell."

He looked curiously around. "Are you alone here?"

"My . . . husband is out—hunting." She hoped that her words spoke the truth. Onawa stood munching grass beside the creek. But Yank was gone. She didn't want to think that Tucker had abandoned her. But where could he be?

"I do not like to leave you here alone," the priest said. "I am Father Francis. I see to the spiritual needs of the village below."

"Village below? Benito's village?" she asked eagerly.

"Si, señorita. You know Benito?"

"Yes, he said he was Luce's cousin."

"Luce. Yes, I know Luce." The priest pursed his lips. "Was? You speak of him as though he were in the past. Is something wrong?"

"I'm afraid that Luce was shot by bandits. We found him wounded. I did the best I could for him, but he died."

"I will say a prayer for his soul," Father Francis said somberly, then glanced around once more. "Bandits?" he questioned softly, as if he thought they might be listening. "Would that be Porfiro and his gang of outlaws?"

"Why yes, how did you know?"

"For days they've combed these mountains, searching for a cowboy traveling alone. They stayed for one night in the village, stirring up much mischief before they rode out."

"Then they've gone? Did they say where they were going?"

"No, señorita, but now that I know what you did for poor Luce, I cannot in good conscience leave you here. Where were you heading?"

"To Benito's village," she answered. "You see, we have to buy supplies—we were attacked by Indians and lost ours. We'd hoped that Benito would help us get more."

"I will take you there, señorita. Then I will send someone to look for your husband."

"But Tucker isn't—" She stopped. It would serve their purpose better to let the priest continue to believe that they were man and wife. "—isn't lost. He'll be here soon."

"I'm here now, sweetheart," Tucker said as he stepped into the clearing, his face and hair beaded with water, his hand resting casually on his pistol. "Thank you, Father, for allowing us to accompany you."

"I didn't see you when I came," Father Francis said suspiciously.

"Nor I you," Tucker answered. "I was downstream. When I heard a man speaking, it seemed more prudent to find out what you wanted before I revealed myself. Would you like to wash your face before we go, Mrs. Farrell?"

He couldn't conceal the twinkle in his eye as he lifted her and carried her toward the creek bank nearby. "Father Francis and I will pack up, then I'll come back for you."

Raven nodded, her heart thumping from both gratitude and his nearness. As soon as Tucker was gone she took care of her morning ablutions and braided her hair, tying it with a piece of the fringe torn from her dress. When he returned, she felt better, though she doubted that she looked any different.

When she called out that she was ready, Tucker lifted her, whispering impishly in her ear, "Mrs. Farrell. You look beautiful this morning."

"I didn't know what else to tell him," she said, placing her lips close to his ear.

"You did exactly right. Now, if you'll just come up with some reason why we were traveling up here in the first place, we just might get away from our enemies."

"We tell the truth. We were traveling north and encountered Luce on the trail. He was wounded and we brought him home. Then the Indians attacked us. Why wouldn't he believe that?"

"I can't imagine," he said, thinking of a hundred reasons why the truth sounded like a lie.

He placed her on Onawa, rolled up their bedding, and tied it on Yank. He glanced around their hidden glade. It had been like a secret garden for just a while. Leaving it behind was leaving another of the memories Raven had helped him make, memories he didn't want to cherish.

Their trip to the village was uneventful. After rounding a sandstone outcropping of rocks, they were on a well-worn path that led steadily down the valley. Soon Raven could hear the sounds of children and see the adobe walls of the village houses and, at the end of the street, Father Francis's church.

"Welcome to Santa de Miguel," Father Francis said. "We are a poor village, but we will share what we have with you."

On seeing the priest, the children ran forward, curious about the guests, whispering about the woman wearing the Indian dress.

Father Francis walked with them to his church,

opened the gate, and led the burro into a small fenced area where a herd of goats, a bony horse, and a milk cow were penned. "The village corral," he explained. "You are welcome to stable your horses here."

Tucker quickly decided that the sooner they moved on, the safer it would be for a village obviously too poor to welcome outsiders. "Thank you, Father, but we really can't stay. If you'd just let us buy another blanket, a shovel, and some food, we'll be on our way."

"I am afraid we have no extra blankets, and the only shovels we have are needed to tend our crops. But we'll share our food with you. It is little, for the winter was rough and the spring has not yet blessed our fields."

Tucker took another look around at the children and the adults coming toward them and confirmed the reality of the priest's words. Anything they took here would be at the expense of the village. They couldn't do that.

"At least share our breakfast," Father Francis said, "and fill your canteens, but if you are seeking Luce's treasure, let me tell you that it would be a foolish dream."

"Luce's treasure?" Raven echoed with feigned ignorance.

"There is a legend that his family were guardians of a treasure hidden high in the mountains. They never left their cabin because of this belief, and in the end, they all perished."

Raven nodded and waited for Tucker to help her down. "And you don't believe there was such a treasure?" Raven asked as she tested her leg by leaning on Tucker.

Father Francis led Onawa into the corral. "I don't know. I only know that the mountains protect what is theirs and God sends us what we are to have. I would not want you to come to grief. Come inside the church and we will get you some food."

"Let me walk, Tucker," Raven said, disturbed at Father Francis's warning. "I'll rest my weight on you, but I must test the ankle."

He slid his arm around her waist and pulled her arm around the back of his neck. Slowly they made their way inside the little church. The priest ordered three of the children to fetch bread and goat cheese for their guests. The others were to fill their canteens with water.

"Señor! Señorita!" It was Benito, hurrying to greet them. "You honor us with your presence. How is Luce?"

If the priest noticed Benito's greeting to the "señorita," he didn't show it. Raven was already beginning to wish they'd been more honest with the little friar in the rough brown robe. She dropped her eyes. "Luce is dead, Benito. We buried him where he asked us to."

"Then why are you here?" Benito asked.

He looked to Tucker to give the explanation. "Swift Hand and his Arapaho followers kidnapped Raven."

"The Arapaho attacked one of their own?" Benito was shocked. "Why would they do that?"

"They are desperate. The troubles of our people weigh heavily on Swift Hand's head," Raven answered. "Though we share the same past he would do me harm."

"My goodness," Father Francis said. "The Arapaho are your people also, aren't they, Benito?"

"Si, it is said they were once, long ago. But those of us still left in the south are just simple village people, and they do not recognize us as blood brothers any longer. Are you all right?"

"Yes, except for—my wife. She sprained her ankle."

"Can you direct us to the nearest settlement where we can buy supplies?" Tucker was beginning to feel uneasy. It was time for them to move on.

Father Francis answered. "That would be San Felipe.

If you follow the trail past the church and through the mountain pass, you will come to the village. They will have what you need."

San Felipe. Tucker started. He'd come full circle. San Felipe was the last place he wanted to go. The bandits were more than likely there, at the cantina. Still, with Raven hurt, their blankets lost, and their food gone, they had little choice. "Is there someone trustworthy there?" he asked.

"Trustworthy?" the priest echoed. "Oh, you are thinking of the thieves that often occupy the plazas. Yes, you should seek out Gomez Hidalgo, the mayor. Though he is ambitious, he is an honorable man who will see that no harm comes to you."

From what he'd seen of San Felipe, Tucker doubted that anybody would cross Porfiro and his bandits. Tucker had little money, and so far as he could tell, Raven had none. They'd have to sell at least one of their nuggets. If they could trade one of them for goods without arousing suspicions, they might be able to get away.

They bade Benito, Father Francis, and the villagers goodbye. Once out of sight, Tucker voiced his plan. "I think you should put on your traveling dress, Raven."

"Why would I do that?"

"With your sprained ankle and your dress, the villagers will think you're a traveler in distress."

"And what will they think you are?"

"They'll think I'm your husband, of course."

Raven grinned. "I think I might like that."

As they neared the village Tucker became increasingly cautious. If they were caught on the flat open road, they'd have no place to hide. Raven had wounds on her head and knee and a sprained ankle. She'd been through so much already, he didn't want her to suffer any more pain. Reluctant though he might have been to act as her protector, he'd taken the role seriously. He didn't want her hurt while she was in his charge. He cared too much for her, though that fact was difficult to admit.

He claimed a quick look at the woman riding next to him. If she had the proper clothing, her composure might make her look like a grand Spanish lady, but now, in her buckskin garment, she was every inch a spirit woman.

"Do you want me to change now, before we get into town?" she asked.

"I think so. The road looks like it widens up ahead. Maybe we'd better stop while there are still trees to shield you." He took Yank from the road into a stand of cottonwood. Tying him to a tree limb, he helped Raven dismount. She opened her saddlebag and pulled out the badly wrinkled travel dress.

"I hope nobody sees me lift my skirt," she said, eying the petticoat with only half a ruffle left. "With this petticoat and the wrinkles, they'll never believe I'm any kind of lady."

Tucker pretended not to see the knit stockings she was holding, nor the dainty blue leather slippers with the tiny spool heels. He'd thought she couldn't be more appealing than in her Indian clothing, but the idea of her as a fine lady made his heart pound.

She limped behind some low-growing brush and pulled on her stockings, tying them at her thigh, then donned her petticoat. She didn't know what had happened to her chemise, but it was missing from the bag. For all she knew, she might have left it back along the trail outside Santa Fe.

Finally she was dressed, all but the tiny buttons on the back of the garment. She'd slid it around her front to unbutton them when she'd removed the dress, but now she couldn't manage alone.

"Tucker? I need some help with my buttons."

Tucker groaned. He'd had the devil's own time keeping himself from rounding the brush to begin with. "Damn it, Raven, don't do this," he said, heading toward her.

"Do what?" She lifted dark feathery eyebrows in question, totally unaware of the appealing picture she made in her blue traveling dress.

"Give me an excuse to put my hands on you."

She blushed, as if remembering what had happened, and her hands dropped from the back of her dress and fluttered against her thighs. "I—you don't have to touch me, just my buttons. I'm afraid I'm going to look pretty silly. The dress is wrinkled and I can wear only one shoe."

"You're beautiful. But there's no way we're going to get into the village and out again without calling attention to ourselves. Let's just hope the mayor is a trusting soul." He moved behind her and began awkwardly to close the buttons up her dress. Tiny black things, they fought with his attempts. Uttering an oath, he finally reached the top.

"I don't know why any woman would want such a garment. Your buckskin dress is much more sensible."

"Yes," she admitted, tugging at the skirt and trying to cover her own confusion over the intimacy of the moment. "I prefer it also."

She hobbled toward her horse, stepped on a loose pebble, and stumbled. Tucker lunged forward and caught her. Then, unable to help himself, he pulled her into his arms and kissed her. He'd sworn he wouldn't do it. He'd told himself that they'd been caught up in the moment before, in the out-of-control heat that sizzled between them constantly. He hadn't been with a woman in a long time. He was an honorable man, but he was incredibly weak.

She was incredibly willing, and before he knew it, he was plundering her mouth, pressing his body against hers, reacting to her willingness to mold her body to his.

Raven's face flushed, her breath came fast and shallow, and she cried out at the invasion of his tongue in her mouth, and the force of her response fired every part of him.

It was Yank who interrupted them, butting his head squarely against Tucker's back. Tucker didn't know whether to shoot the big horse or thank him. Raven almost fell again, and as Tucker reached to steady her he heard the sound of horses, many horses.

"Raven, you must stop tempting me," Tucker gasped. "You're going to get yourself into deep trouble and maybe get us killed."

"From being kissed?" she said in a breathless voice.

"No, from distracting me. Quick, let's hide Onawa and Yank." They moved the mare inside the thicket and watched as a band of Mexican riders passed by, heading in the direction from which they'd just come.

"That was close," Tucker said.

"It was," she agreed. "I am sorry that I distracted you. I watched my sisters and their . . . their future husbands kiss before. I'm sorry if I don't do it right."

"I'm not your future husband, Raven. And you do it very right. It's just that we can't be together like that."

"Why? Do you not like me?"

Tucker groaned. Here he was in the middle of the biggest mess he'd faced in years, with the first woman he'd ever really cared about, and he had to give lessons in propriety.

"I like you—too much. But we have a mission. Remember? We have to find the treasure, rescue your people, buy land in Oregon."

"And kissing will interfere with that? I don't understand why."

"Because you make me lose my edge. I'm thinking

about you instead of our enemies. We must focus on first things first."

"I'm so sorry, Tucker," Raven admitted, guilt filling her eyes with moisture. "I'm being selfish. It's just that I've never been kissed the way you kiss me before. But you're right. We'll find the treasure first, then you'll teach me more about kissing. Was that Porfiro?"

It took Tucker a minute to direct his focus on Porfiro and the matters at hand. Kissing was infinitely more powerful and more appealing. But there would be none of that if they ended up dead.

"Yes," he said. "At least he's left the village. Maybe we can get in and out before he returns. Let's ride."

Quickly they mounted their horses and rode into San Felipe. It was very warm. Perspiration beaded Tucker's forehead and darkened his collar.

The square was almost empty. Tucker felt a ripple of unease run down his back as he remembered how close he'd come to becoming a permanent resident of the area. If it hadn't been for the birds—

"It looks peaceful," Raven said. "Where will we find the mayor?"

"I'll ask." Tucker hoped that none of the shopkeepers recalled his near demise. Reaching one of the small trading posts, he slid from his horse and went inside.

In broken Spanish he asked, "Do you know where I can find Señor Gomez Hidalgo?"

"Si," the shopkeeper answered, nodding his head. "The mayor is also our banker. He is a very successful man in our village."

"Perfect." Tucker relayed the information to Raven. "We can exchange the gold for money and nobody will be the wiser."

Moments later Raven hobbled into the bank, where Tucker introduced them as Mr. and Mrs. Farrell. "We have come to do some business with you. We'd like to open an account with these gold nuggets. Would it be possible?"

"You wife is injured?"

"Just a sprained ankle. We were attacked by Indians and we're lucky to be alive. Now, about the account."

"Of course, señor. I will be happy to open an account for you. Will you be staying in our little settlement?"

"Only for a few days this time," Tucker said.

"Oh?"

"We are looking for land to buy—later."

The banker examined the nugget. "I see. And have you any special place in mind? I am also the land surveyor. I'd be glad to help you there as well."

It didn't take Tucker long to figure out that Hidalgo thought they'd discovered the gold nearby. He thought they were going to buy land all right, the land where the gold vein was located. Now they'd have the Mexican bandits, the Indians, and the townspeople after the treasure.

"No," he quickly corrected, "the señorita's father recently died, leaving their ranch to her brother. To my wife he only left a small inheritance of jewels and these nuggets. With her father gone, we have decided to find land of our own in New Mexico."

So far Raven had held back, allowing Tucker to do the talking. Now she leaned forward, an earnest look on her face. "Do you think you can advise us about such matters?"

Señor Hidalgo quickly fell victim to her charms. "Certainly, Señora Farrell. There is much good land farther south along the Rio Grande. I will be happy to introduce you to some of the landowners. Many of them will be at my house this evening, for fiesta. Will you do me the honor of joining us?"

Raven had little choice but to agree. "I'm afraid that

the run-in with the band of Indians cost us our wagon and my trunk," she confessed. "I trust that you will advance funds so that I can buy some suitable clothing."

"Of course," he agreed. "And you will stay with my wife and me. I'll arrange for credit at the store, and when you're finished I'll escort you to my hacienda, where you may refresh yourself."

Tucker considered the invitation and came to the conclusion that staying with the banker would serve two purposes. Raven would have a place to rest, and they would be away from town, where he might be recognized. Perhaps it would be good to have the implied protection of those in power. If they were dressed as successful land buyers, they wouldn't be recognized as the fugitives being hunted by outlaws and renegade Indians.

"Thank you, Señor Hildalgo. We accept your invitation with pleasure."

An hour later, planting Raven on a barrel inside the store, Tucker purchased the supplies they needed, including proper clothing, a saddle, and more ammunition. He made arrangements to have everything but the clothing stored at the livery stable, then assisted the limping Raven outside the store, where Señor Hidalgo arrived shortly with a smart little two-seater black buggy.

Helping Raven into the carriage, the mayor indicated that Tucker could follow on the horse tied to the back of the conveyance.

Concealing his annoyance from the mayor, Tucker complied. To his chagrin, the creaking of the carriage wheels and the sound of hoofbeats effectively drowned out the conversation between Raven and Señor Hidalgo. An occasional light trill of laughter only served to further inflame his fury.

They headed east, toward the Blood of Christ Mountains. Being on the open prairie made Tucker uneasy. It was unlikely that Swift Hand's braves would venture out here. And they'd seen Porfiro headed in the opposite direction. But there was something about the wide open spaces that made him uncomfortable. Everything was too quiet. Except for the conversation occurring inside the carriage.

His stomach was protesting the length of time since they'd shared the bread and cheese of Father Francis's and Benito's village. The sun was overhead now. High noon. How far was the hacienda? Could they trust Gomez? Suppose he was tied in with the bandits?

Raven Alexander was his responsibility, and he'd do what he had to in order to take care of her. By the time they reached the ranch, he was ready to throw Raven over his horse and ride away. He was willing to forget about the treasure, the Indians, and land in Oregon. All he wanted was—

Damn it! Tucker pulled off the new felt hat he'd bought and ran his fingers through his hair. He needed a bath and a shave. He needed to get his mind back on track. He couldn't admit the truth.

But the truth was, all he really wanted was Raven Alexander.

11

The hacienda was small but elegant. Señora Hildalgo came hustling to the door to meet them. "Welcome, welcome, Señora Farrell. Come inside and rest your sore ankle. I have your quarters ready."

Tucker gave her a startled look.

"Gomez sent word that you were coming," she explained. "Welcome to our home."

"Thank you." Raven stiffened her spine, becoming every inch the wealthy land buyer she pretended to be. "We are pleased to accept your kind invitation."

"Let me get you to your room, where you can bathe and have a nice long rest before the fiesta begins at dusk. Did my husband tell you that we are celebrating our daughter's engagement?"

"No, I'm sorry, we would not have intruded on a family affair," Raven said.

"Do not worry. Everybody in the territory will be here. Come, let me show you to the guest room."

"The guest room?" Raven repeated with a shy smile.

Tucker gave the lady of the house a dazzling smile calculated to cover his consternation. "Perhaps my wife would be more comfortable if I found other quarters for this evening."

Raven shot Tucker a stern look. "Don't be silly, Tucker. A sprained ankle is no reason for you to sleep in the barn. I'll be just fine."

Señora Hildalgo looked uncomfortable. "If you're certain. We are very short of space, due to the other guests."

"I insist," Raven said.

"In the meantime, Señor Farrell," the banker said, "will you join me in the study for a glass of my special Spanish wine? We'd like you to feel our house is your house."

"Don't spoil your lunch, Gomez. I'll have it brought in to you momentarily. Señora Farrell would probably like to have something light in her room."

"That would be very nice," Raven agreed, hoping it wasn't too light and didn't take too long in arriving. The food they'd shared with Father Francis this morning had been filling, but not enough and not for long. "But I'm afraid that I'm not yet confident in climbing the stairs. Tucker, would you . . ."

As Señora Hildalgo and the servants began mounting the stairs, Raven held up her arms prettily, settling against him in a way that was designed to tease. She was rather enjoying the game they were playing. Besides, she'd never been in such a luxurious home, and she intended, just for now, to allow herself to be pampered, both by her hostess and by her husband.

"Stop it, witch," Tucker whispered as he carried her, ignoring the protests of his healing ribs. "You're carrying our pretense a little too far. Behave yourself!"

"Of course, darling," she said coyly, taking a lesson in flirting from her sister Isabella. "I just like being married."

"You're going to be sorry," he said gruffly. "I'll make you walk up on your own."

She pressed her breast against his hand for one quick moment. "But I need you to protect me. I'm still weak with fear from our near fatal attack. Suppose the Indians come back?"

She'd become less mystical and more womanly. He liked that—too much. "The Indians won't come here. What you'd better worry about is the bandits and whether or not the mayor is in cahoots with them."

She went still and her face paled, making him sorry he'd said anything. She needed rest and food and a few days to get herself ready for the ordeal ahead. Now he'd made her worry.

"Oh, dear. I'm not very good at flirting, am I?"

He planted a light kiss on her lips. "No, you're not," he lied. "And I like it that way. Just go on pretending to be afraid and let me do the talking."

Señora Hildalgo stopped at a bedroom door at the end of the corridor. "Rosalita will bring hot water for your tub. It will help your foot to soak it. A nice nap with pillows beneath your leg should make you feel much better."

Tucker let her down just inside the door and looked around with approval. The simple white room was stark but comfortable. There was an outside door leading to a balcony overlooking the courtyard below.

"Through here is a small room normally used by one of the ladies' maids. For now, Mr. Farrell can use it to clean up and dress for the evening. That way you won't be disturbed. Later one of our guests will sleep there."

"I'm afraid we are becoming an inconvenience for you," Raven observed. "Perhaps we ought to go back to town. Surely there is an inn or a hotel?"

"Oh, no," Señora Hildalgo said in horror. "The only rooms to be had are those over the cantina, and I don't think you'd be comfortable there. You'll stay here. It will be fine, I promise."

"The room is lovely, Señora Hildalgo. We thank you for your hospitality. I'm sure Raven will feel better after a good rest."

"Raven? That's an unusual name."

"Yes, it was my mother's." Raven debated whether or not to announce her Indian heritage, then decided that for now she'd keep that to herself. "I wish you'd call me that."

"Of course. I'll have the hot water and your clothing sent up."

She walked to the door and waited, making no effort to leave the room. Finally Tucker realized that she was waiting for him.

"Are you ready, Mr. Farrell?" their hostess inquired, opening the door.

"Of course. Get some rest, darling." He smiled and kissed her lightly on the lips. "No dreams of mountain lions this afternoon. You're in good hands here."

"I'll try," she admitted, feeling the rush of emotion that swept over her every time this man touched her. She shivered. What if she really were Mrs. Farrell? A real home, a ranch, children? She'd never considered any of those things.

Clutching the pillow close to her, she thought about children, a baby. Could she truly be a mother? As the door closed and she heard footsteps moving down the hall, she felt tears well up in her eyes.

Enough of that, Raven Alexander, she chastised herself. You promised the Grandfather that you'd find the treasure. You don't have time to think like a woman.

All she needed was food, sleep, and getting her ankle well. A few days might not make that much difference in what happened, but she had no way of knowing that. She'd already allowed too much time to come between her and her mission. Now she was a potential land buyer pretending to be a wife, when she ought to be climbing the sacred mountain.

Raven stood in the middle of the room and cleared her churning mind. It had been too long since she'd felt the presence of the spirit world. She'd lost sight of her goal and allowed herself to become involved in a relationship that was becoming too personal. Tucker Farrell had been sent only to get her to Luce, not become her husband.

But later, maybe after they'd found the treasure, a husband might be nice.

The tub was made of shiny copper and filled with steaming hot water. Once Raven settled for a long, soothing soak, the servant girl named Rosalita, who'd filled the tub, continued to dip out the cooling water and replace it with more kettles of hot.

Raven lay for as long as she dared, then came reluctantly to her feet and with help from Rosalita hobbled to a chair by the window, where a small table had been set up. After settling her charge in the chair and planting Raven's injured ankle on a stool stacked with pillows, Rosalita poured liquid from a jar into her hand and began to massage the ankle. The medication had the scent of wintergreen and some other pungent herb Raven couldn't identify. Soon Rosalita's firm application of the medication brought a healthy blush and a tingle to the skin of Raven's injured ankle.

"Rosalita, tell me about the fiesta."

"It is to announce the engagement of the señora's only daughter. Everyone will come."

"A wedding. A new beginning." For a moment Raven thought of her grandfather. He had left this world to be reborn in the spiritual one. She knew that his people had seen to the burial customs, but she regretted not being there. And she knew that she would always miss him.

"You are sad, señora?" Rosalita questioned.

"Yes. But it will pass. I plan to enjoy the fiesta tonight. I suppose Señor Hildalgo and his wife are pleased to be gaining a son-in-law."

"He is a fine young man and this will be a glorious event." Rosalita told her how everyone for miles would come. Neighbors, townspeople, and every man, woman, and child on the ranchero. "Señora Hildalgo is very generous," she confided as she kneaded Raven's ankle.

"And the groom, what does he do?"

"He is the son of the largest landowner in the area. They have been promised since childhood."

"When will they marry?"

"The banns will be posted soon, and the wedding will take place in late summer."

"And do they love each other?"

Rosalita looked at her in surprise. "Of course. Why would they not?"

Raven didn't answer. She'd have to think about that. Her own four sisters had never been promised to anyone. There had been no eligible men in the Front Mountains of Colorado where they'd lived, not until Sabrina had rescued the four Confederate soldiers captured by the army at Fort Collins and brought them home to work in her papa's mine.

They hadn't known these men since childhood, but they quickly fell in love with each other. And there was Tucker. She hadn't known him since childhood, but she'd always known that there was something, someone out there waiting for her. Now she knew that it was Tucker, her cougar.

Finally Rosalita stood up, washed her hands in the tub, and removed the cloth from the table, revealing a plate of broiled chicken, cheese, and fruit.

Washed down with cool milk, the food was quickly gone, and Raven's attention was drawn to the courtyard outside the hacienda window. In the mountains the air was still cold; snow still lay in the crevices. But here the spring flowers were in full bloom. Tables were set up around a tinkling fountain, and servants were covering them with colorful cloths. Musicians were already tuning up on a raised platform at the end of the patio.

Fiesta, the banker had said. She hadn't thought too much about it then, so anxious was she to convince him to advance funds against their nuggets. Everybody in the territory would be here. Now Raven wondered how wise they'd been to take part. Surely Tucker would see the potential problems. They'd better discuss the possibilities.

Just then she saw a half-familiar male figure cut through the courtyard and disappear beneath the balcony. Who was the man? She'd seen him before, but she couldn't remember when.

Moments later she heard footsteps in the corridor and finally sounds inside the maid's room Señora Hildalgo had offered to Tucker.

Raven badly wanted to speak with him, but she couldn't be certain when Rosalita would return for the tray. She'd better wait until she had a better sense of what was happening.

A soft knock and the opening door admitted Rosalie. As she cleared away the tray she inclined her head toward the huge bed and smiled.

"Yes," Raven eagerly agreed, "that is a good idea. A nap. I'll take a nap before the fiesta."

Rosalita immediately put down the tray and turned to assist Raven to the bed. Gently testing the ankle, Raven was pleased that it was much better; she could even walk on it. The hot water and medicinal rub had been very effective.

Raven leaned back and stretched. She was used to sleeping on the ground, but a soft bed was nice too. Moments later Rosalita left the room, closing the door gently behind her. At almost that same moment, Tucker walked in from the other room.

"Are you all right?" he asked, pleased to see that her color was quite good and the welcome in her eyes was undisguised.

"The ankle is almost well. I'm glad you came. I needed to talk to you. Do you think that Señora Hildalgo believes that we are married?"

"Of course. Why shouldn't she?" Tucker took one look at Raven's hair curling damply against her face and at the delicate sleeping gown she was wearing and wished he'd waited until later to see her.

The bed in which Raven lay had a brightly embroidered canopy and gauzy hangings that were tied to the posts. His gaze wandered to the tub, still filled with soapy bathwater. On the floor was a colorful woven rug, and flowers graced the table by the window. Raven was such a contrast, sleeping beneath the stars one night and occupying a Spanish hacienda the next. She was magnificent on a horse, but she was just as appealing here.

"Are you feeling better?" Tucker asked.

"I'm stronger. By morning I should be able to travel."

"Good. We'll ride out, let them think we're looking at land and that we'll return."

"Aren't we taking a big risk attending a fiesta here? Suppose there is somebody who saw you in the cantina?"

"One of the bandits?" he asked in surprise. "Why would they be guests here?"

"I don't know. I just thought I recognized a man I saw earlier."

"Who was he?" Tucker asked, puzzled at the revelation.

"I'm sorry. I just don't know. Rosalita said that everybody in the territory will be here. I only caught a glimpse of him. But I'm worried. I just don't want anything to happen to you."

"Look, Raven, I escaped a necktie party the last time I was here. I'm not a bit worried this trip. I'm a respectable married man now."

"Yes, you are," she said shyly, holding out her hand. "You've never said, Tucker. Have you ever been married?"

Tucker took her hand, allowing her to draw him down to the bed. "Not likely. I never stayed in one place long enough."

"Indians travel from place to place, moving their camp to find food and water, but they marry."

"But I'm not an Indian."

She gave him a long, searching look, then, as if satisfied at what she saw, she slipped her fingers inside his and brought his hand to her lips. "Does it matter that I am part Indian, Tucker?"

When she kissed his knuckles, he blanched, unable to believe the intense wave of need that swept over him. "Don't be foolish." He drew his hand away.

"Good."

"Now," he continued, taking charge of the situation, "don't worry about the party tonight. I think we deserve a night of fun before we look for the treasure again. We'll eat too much and dance too—"

Raven let out a wistful sigh. "I don't think so, Tucker. I'll attend the fiesta and I'll watch you and all the eager young señoritas, but I doubt I'll do much dancing."

"Then neither will I," he said with firm resolve. "But you won't be going if you don't get some rest. The evening doesn't begin until late, so I want you to take a nice long nap."

He stood up and turned purposefully toward the door, then retraced his steps. "Raven," he whispered. Then he kissed her, lightly, tenderly, before he left the room.

Once Tucker shut the door, Raven wanted to jump out of bed and go after him. Then, just as quickly, she wanted to cry. Tucker might be reassured, but everything about her usual calm demeanor was unsettled. To her surprise, being alone was just as bad as having him beside her. The ache of wanting him was like an annoying catch in her side that refused to go away.

She didn't expect to sleep, but she did. When she was finally awakened by a knock on the door, the afternoon sun was low in the sky.

"Are you ready to dress, señora?" Rosalita entered the room with some brightly colored fabric draped over her arm. "The señora thought you might like to borrow a Spanish dress for the fiesta. This belongs to her daughter."

Raven fingered the red blouse that matched the bold designs of the skirt. A pair of matching sandals, a fringed shawl, and combs and ribbons for her hair completed the ensemble.

"I don't know. Are you certain that the other guests will be dressed like this?" She hoped her question didn't give away her ignorance. She'd never worn such colorful garments.

"Oh yes, señora. You will be beautiful."

Before Raven could change her mind, Rosalita had produced a ruffled petticoat and undergarments. With the young servant's assistance, Raven donned the bright garments. The banker was right. She no longer looked like an Arapaho. She looked like a Spanish lady.

"Let me arrange your hair," Rosalita insisted, drawing up the front sections and anchoring them firmly with the Spanish comb. "Now, some color for your cheeks and lips, and a fan."

Raven looked at herself in the mirror and gasped. The face looking back at her was nothing like the Alexander sister who'd left Denver and even less familiar than the Indian girl who'd left the train for Santa Fe.

With Rosalita to lean on, Raven started toward the door. At the head of the stairs, she caught sight of Tucker looking up at her, his face frozen in surprise.

"Is something wrong?" she asked.

"Uh—no. It's just that you're—you're even more lovely than before, and I didn't think that was possible."

If he thought she looked different, her transformation was nothing compared to the change in him. He was wearing a short black jacket, trousers with a red stripe down the side, and a matching red silk shirt. His hair, still damp from his bath, was drying in curls across his forehead and around his face. The blue of his eyes had heightened, catching the light of the candles in the corridor and reflecting them like stars.

"You can walk?" he asked.

"I can hobble," she admitted, trying to conceal the pain of her weight against the bad ankle.

"Not tonight." He climbed the stairs, lifting her in his arms as easily as if he'd never been hurt.

"Your ribs?" she whispered.

"Didn't bother you before, when you were tormenting me on the upward climb. Besides," he countered and walked down the stairs, "they've missed you."

Outside, the sound of horns and guitars broke across

the courtyard, followed by laughter, a clicking in rhythm with the music, and the clapping of hands.

"Señora Farrell." Mayor Hildalgo came forward to take her hand and plant a kiss across her knuckles. "You are truly a Spanish lady now. Come and watch our daughter and her fiancé dance for our guests."

Candles graced every surface of the courtyard, including the outer walls. Colorful paper animals hung from the trees, and blindfolded children with long sticks were poking at them.

"Who are the children?"

"They belong to our friends and the workers on the ranchero. Everybody is welcome at a fiesta."

Raven wanted to ask what they were doing, but held back for fear of revealing her deception. Fascinated with the picture of color and movement everywhere, she commented instead, "They look as if they are having a grand time."

"My wife makes certain that the animals contain many toys and candies. Once the children break through the paper shell and the candies fall to the ground, you'll really see them scrambling."

From the back of the house, brightly dressed servants, led by Rosalita, brought great trays of food and drink to every table. Suddenly the music stopped and two dancers burst into the center of the courtyard. The woman was petite, very young, and beautiful in her ruffled yellow and red satin dress and Spanish combs. The man, also small in stature, was dark skinned and handsome. He was dressed like Tucker, except his clothing was solid black.

The man and woman positioned themselves before Señor and Señora Hildalgo's table, as if waiting for a signal to begin.

"Good evening, Padre," the young woman said, her eyes full of joy.

"You will honor us with a dance, my *querida?*" he asked, pride bursting from his face.

"Si, if you permit."

"Then dance, Evita."

Moments later the slow staccato music and the sultry movements of the dancers began. Teasing, rejecting, showing their desire with their bodies and their faces, the young couple moved their feet in time with the click of something the woman was holding between her fingers.

As if they were enacting the mating game of two wild creatures, she tempted and tantalized the man until at last he caught her and jerked her to him. The tempo increased, pulling Raven along. She didn't move. She didn't have to. Her inner spirit embraced the feeling and the rhythm. At the height of the dance, she realized she was holding her breath. Letting it out in a long stream, she glanced at Tucker, who wasn't even pretending to watch the dancers. His gaze melded to hers.

He was such a glorious man, every inch of him male, every inch of him caught up in the mood of the occasion. He would never tease as the dancer was doing. He'd take what he wanted with the force of his desire and make the woman want it just as badly.

Raven's heart raced. Her blood pounded in her ears and suddenly it was happening again. Though there was a space between them, she could feel his touch. The music grew wilder. The other guests watching began to blur, and she could feel Tucker's breath against her hair, the heat of his body hot against her.

And she knew as she looked at him that he felt it too. His lips parted and he drew in a long heated breath. Then he smiled and she felt her heart lurch.

"Not now, Spirit Woman," he said, though he never moved his lips. "Our time will come, but not yet."

And she felt the response of her body. The quick, hot

pulsing of her blood seared under her skin and made her feel as if she were on fire.

The music and the dancing made normal conversation impossible. Raven leaned closer to Tucker. "What is it called?" she asked, not so much to know the answer, but to hear his voice.

"The fandango," he answered, his mouth only inches from her ear.

They were talking about the dance, but Raven knew that their thoughts were on each other. She wanted this man in a way that she'd never known. And he wanted her as well. Tonight she couldn't think about the future. She could only think about being here, with Tucker.

She shivered.

He moved his chair closer to prevent others from hearing their conversation. "It's the dance of courtship."

"And seduction," she added in a breathless voice.

Tucker's eyes, now black as midnight, never blinked. "They're the same, aren't they?"

"No. One is for the moment. The other is forever."

Then the frenzy of the music came to a climactic ending when the dancer dropped to his knee. His partner haughtily slapped him across his cheek with her fan and dramatically turned her back.

"Not always," Tucker said, his expression turning dark and dangerous. "Sometimes it leads to rejection."

12

Tucker and Raven met the bride, who was polite and gracious but who only had eyes for the man she was to marry. Her fiancé was pleasant to Raven, but seemed particularly interested in Tucker, though he didn't linger to talk. Tucker and Raven shared in the rich, spicy food and the wine, which flowed generously, signifying the banker's prosperity and position.

Raven knew she was out of her element here. She resented being diverted from her mission. She would have preferred to remain in her room, but it was impossible to watch the dancers and listen to the lively music without being drawn into the joy of the young couple. Their happiness set off an odd kind of longing in Raven.

Now that she understood what they were feeling, it was even harder to ignore the smoldering excitement that arced between her and the handsome blond man who was so attentive to her needs. He towered over every other man there. Both his size and his coloring set him apart.

He was simply looking at her now, a sappy smile plastered across his lips.

"You don't act like a husband," she hissed.

"I don't know what a husband acts like," he countered, "but from what I can see of the ones here, you're right, I don't."

"What does that mean?" She opened her fan and hid her smile behind it as she leaned forward.

"They seem to be talking with other husbands instead of their wives."

"Maybe you'd better do that," Raven suggested, leaning even closer.

"Not when you're dressed like this." He put his hand on her arm and slid it behind her neck, her closeness allowing him to glance down the top of her blouse. "They must all be blind."

This time Raven blushed and moved the fan to cover her breasts. "Are you always so honest?"

He shook his head. "I rarely say what I think. Especially with a woman. That gets you into hot water." He moved his chair closer to her so that he could whisper in her ear.

"But tonight I'll be honest. You're the most beautiful woman here."

"Stop that, Tucker!"

He brushed his lips against her cheek and moved down to her neck.

"I'm sorry," he apologized, "but the music is so loud I can't hear you."

He pulled one of the flowers from her hair, kissed it, and tucked it between her breasts. He didn't have to say that he wished his lips could be there instead. It was like being in a waking dream, except this was no dream. She felt as if every eye in the courtyard were on her. She couldn't be still.

"The bride is lovely," she said, trying to force his attention elsewhere.

"Not as lovely as you."

"Tucker, don't do this. I can hardly breathe."

"It's your fault for wearing that dress. You're laced up like a Christmas goose. Every man here is practically overheating. Didn't you know what would happen?"

She hadn't known. Not until he looked at her. He'd been practically devouring her with his eyes ever since. Nervously she tugged at the top, pulling it higher, only to take a breath and see it slide down again.

"Please, don't talk like that. I don't know what to say. You're making me feel so strange." She fanned herself. "I'm getting very warm. Would you get me something cool to drink, a cup of punch perhaps?"

"Of course. But that won't cool you, Mrs. Farrell." Lazily, as if he knew she was watching every move, he came to his feet and started across to the refreshment table.

All eyes shifted from Raven to Tucker, all except one man's. Raven spotted him again, the stranger she'd seen before. And he was looking at her as if she had two heads. He was leaning awkwardly against one of the posts supporting the balcony outside Raven's room, looking very uncomfortable.

She studied him, trying to remember where she'd seen him before. The stranger talked with the future bridegroom for a moment. Then, as if he knew that he was being watched, he turned his gaze back to Raven.

He smiled and started toward her.

"Excuse me, Señora," he said, "but you seem very familiar. Have we met before?"

"I don't think so," she began. Then, suddenly, she remembered. He was the journalist she'd shared the stage with on leaving Denver. What on earth was he doing here? And would he be able to place her on that stage? If so, he'd certainly remember her changing into her Indian buckskin and leaving the stage. Frantically she searched for Tucker.

Behind the cover of her fan, she tugged at the neckline of her blouse and frowned. "I'm certain I'd remember."

"Larry—no, Lawrence Small." He held out his hand in introduction.

"And this is my husband," she said as Tucker appeared by her side, carrying two ornate glasses of wine.

He placed them on the table, then leaned forward just at the right moment to intercept the journalist's hand. "I'm Tucker Farrell."

But the reporter wasn't about to be pushed aside. He continued studying Raven.

"Señora Farrell? No, I don't know that name. But I'm certain that we've crossed paths."

"What are you doing here in New Mexico?" Tucker smoothly slid into the chair beside Raven and pushed her glass toward her.

"Looking for stories about the West for my newspaper." He was like an eager child, trying to make his case. "Easterners are frantic to read about outlaws, bandits, Indians. . . . Indians—"

Then he stopped, and she knew he recognized her. "Please," Raven whispered. "Don't."

"You were on the stage out of Denver. Weren't you? Until—"

"Until I left it and rode out alone," she admitted, her voice filled with misery.

"You understand," Tucker interrupted. "My wife would prefer to keep that information private. May we count on your discretion?"

The reporter smiled and slowly nodded his head. "Of course. I'm very interested in feature stories about unusual people and events for my newspaper back East. Names are unimportant. If you'll let me interview you, I'll be glad to keep your identity secret."

"In other words," Tucker growled, "if we give you a story, you'll forget that you saw Raven on the stage?"

"I will."

"Then this is the story." he said. "We are running away from—"

"Oh, Tucker, don't do it. No more tall tales. He's no bandit and he couldn't be tied in with Swift Hand. He already knows too much. We might as well tell him the truth."

Tucker couldn't decide whether she was being sincere, or whether she had a different objective in mind. For the moment he'd go along. "How do we know what this man is really doing here?"

Lawrence moved closer. "I heard a story in town about a man, a big American in a poker game."

"There are about as many famous poker games as there are tales of lost treasure in the area."

"Then you do know about the treasure," Raven said.

Tucker swore. "There's always treasure down here. There's the Lost Devil Mine, the Friars' Cave, even the Holy Mother's Hole in the Desert. Treasures have been lost and found since the time of the Spanish invasion."

"I don't think that's what the villagers are talking about," Lawrence insisted. "I'm referring to an old miner who came into the cantina several nights ago. He bet two gold nuggets the size of hen eggs and a ruby-set watch fob. Said he'd found a lost treasure."

"How'd you hear about that?" Raven asked, suddenly concerned for Tucker's safety. What happened to her was up to the spirits, but she'd been lulled into a false sense of security about Tucker. She mustn't make that mistake again. She flipped open her fan and leaned closer. "And what happened?"

"It seems that the American managed to create a diversion while the old man got away. Then the American was captured by the Mexican bandits. He was about to be strung up when a flock of giant ravens assaulted the courtyard, helping him to escape."

The newspaperman took a long, pointed look at Tucker. "A big golden man, an American," he said slowly. "And your name is Raven. Coincidence?"

"All right," Tucker agreed. "So I was in the game. I'll give you the story, but not here and not now. Can I ask you to give me your word that you won't let this go any further than the three of us?"

"What's to tell? Everybody at the fiesta knows about the birds."

"Then you'll keep my secret?" Tucker asked.

"I could be persuaded. But I need to know what's in it for me."

"The story of a lifetime," Raven answered, "and maybe more."

Lawrence pulled a thin black cigar from his pocket and lit it from the candle on the table. "I agree. You cannot know how important this story is for me. My future depends on it. I give you my word."

Hidalgo approached them. "Ah, Señor Small, I see you've met Señora Farrell and her husband. They're looking to buy land in our area, to raise cattle."

"Really?" Lawrence said. "My readers would be very interested in such a project. Have you already picked out the section you wish to settle?"

"Yes," Raven said.

"No," Tucker said at the same time.

"What we mean," Raven explained, "is that we want

to buy land along the Rio Grande, probably north, toward Santa Fe."

"But we haven't settled definitely on the piece," Tucker added.

"Perhaps you'd let me tag along as you look," Lawrence said enthusiastically.

"I think that is a splendid idea," Señor Hildalgo agreed. "Just think of what it would do for the village of San Felipe. Your article would attract a great deal of interest."

Attracting interest was the last thing Tucker wanted. But short of being rude or calling attention to themselves even more, he could see no way out. "All right, Mr. Small. Let us drink a toast to our new partnership. We'll take you along, provided you can ride a horse and take care of yourself."

"I'll manage," the slightly built young man pledged. "I won't be a problem, I assure you."

Tucker wasn't reassured. Inviting a newspaperman to accompany them on the journey he and Raven were about to take was plain folly. But leaving him behind might be worse.

Now they'd have the bandits, the Indians, the banker, and the press in tow. He hoped that Raven's spirit animals were short-tempered and liked their privacy. Maybe they'd intervene and clear out the intruders. Even if he didn't believe, Tucker would welcome a little help from Mother Nature.

But first they had to get through the fiesta. The dancing had broken out in earnest now, and the courtyard was packed with guests. He noticed Raven swaying to the music, and suddenly he wanted to dance. When the music turned soft and romantic, Tucker held out his hand. "Would you care to dance, Raven?"

"But my ankle," she protested, more nervous that she didn't know how. The only dancing she'd ever done was around the campfire. Still, for just a moment she was tempted. She'd be in Tucker's arms.

"Don't worry." He stood and slid his arm around her waist so that he could support her weight. He led her to the edge of the garden, into the shadows beneath a flower-covered trellis. "You stand still and I'll do the work."

As soon as he put his arm around her waist, he knew he'd made a mistake. There was no way in hell he could hold her, touch her, and not kiss her.

"Just hold me, Tucker," she whispered, concentrating on the music.

He felt the very air around them becoming charged, like the afternoon at Luce's pool. Though he was standing at a respectable distance, he could feel her body touching his, her bare body, with nothing between them. His clothes were gone. They were alone in the sweetly scented garden, swaying to the music of the night. He didn't kiss her. Their lips never touched, but he felt her hot, urgent mouth pressed against his, her hand touching him, moving down to caress the most intimate part of him.

"Raven, don't to this."

"I do nothing, Tucker," she whispered.

And then he understood. They were caught in a "waking dream" so powerful that he was about to explode. At the same time he was touching her breast, he could see the dancers beyond the trellis, moving to the music as if nothing was happening. Then came showers of stars, and Tucker felt his body turn into a burst of light.

The music ended and Lawrence Small's voice came from out of the darkness. "Señora, your ankle is improved."

"No," she said in a shaky voice, bringing herself and

Tucker back to the present. "I'd thought it was, but I'm afraid that it is still too painful. Will you take me to my room, Tucker?"

"Of course, darling," he managed to say, and forced his own legs to move her slowly back to the table. Ignoring Lawrence, Tucker sought out their host and hostess and, using Raven's ankle as their excuse, bade them good night.

"My wife needs to rest for our land-buying journey in a few days," he explained to Lawrence. "Her ankle is still too weak for immediate travel."

"I'm sorry to hear that. I'd hoped that it was better."

"I'm afraid not. But if you'll wait here for me, I'll return and we'll share another glass of wine in celebration of our new partnership."

"I'd be pleased to do so," the eager journalist said and followed them inside the house, ignoring Tucker's protests. He waited at the foot of the steps under the pretense of offering his help in assisting Mrs. Farrell upstairs, but Tucker wasn't fooled. He simply wanted to know the location of their room, and Tucker had no means to conceal it. Sooner or later he'd learn the truth.

They had too many people watching them, interested in what they were doing. Somebody was bound to follow them when they left. Now Lawrence Small was determined to accompany them. But that didn't have to happen. Not if they left in the midst of the party, while everybody was still celebrating.

Not if they left right away.

Once inside the room, Tucker set Raven down, allowing himself a moment to hold her, to feel her against him, to remember the moment they'd shared when they danced.

"What will you do about Mr. Small?" she asked.

"I think I'll introduce him to the artificial benefits of

Dr. Tucker's Feel Good Tonic. Do you have more of the red berries?"

She smiled. "Of course, but only a small amount."

"I don't need much." He took the last of the berries, kissed her with sweet restraint, and started toward the door.

"Will you be long?" she asked shyly.

His answer was the one she wanted to hear, but she couldn't know that his meaning was not the same as hers. "Not long at all."

Taking seriously Gomez Hildalgo's invitation to make himself at home, Tucker asked Lawrence Small to join him in the study for a glass of the señor's special wine. The red berry he'd taken from Raven's medicine bag was easily concealed in the glass he poured for the toast.

"I have to tell you, Mr. Small, that I'll help you with your story if I can, but I'm nobody's partner."

"Of course. Why don't you start by telling me how you really got away from those bandits."

"You don't believe the ravens rescued me?" Tucker asked in amusement.

"Of course not. They just made up that story to cover up your escape. But the story makes good copy, don't you think?"

"You're probably right. But you promised to keep my identity a secret."

"So I did. I'll respect your privacy if that's what you wish." The reporter nodded as he drank deeply of his wine. "But your wife promised me the story of a lifetime and maybe more."

"Well, as I mentioned before, my wife and I are going to buy land . . ."

"Buy land? Mr. Farrell, that's hardly the story of a lifetime. I think I ought to tell you I know that you and Miss Alexander deposited two gold nuggets and a ruby in Señor Hildalgo's bank. Let's not play games."

Tucker sipped his wine. So much for any hope of keeping the true purpose of their journey secret. Raven had been right to begin with. They'd be better off making the man think they were including him rather than letting him make wild speculations in the press.

Tucker casually closed the open door, then went to the window and peered out. "All right, then. Suppose, just suppose, there is the possibility of a treasure. Are you up to the danger of the expedition?"

The first trace of worry colored the reporter's voice. "Danger?"

Tucker put a concerned expression on his face. "Of course. The journey will be difficult. We must go into a mountainous area filled with peril."

"Peril?"

"Yes. In addition to the wild animals—mountain lions, bears, snakes—those Mexican bandits from the cantina also seek the treasure. And the Indians who consider themselves the protectors of the sacred mountains where it is hidden."

"Indians? I didn't know about them. Do you really think they're a threat to us?"

"Of course we have to search for the treasure. The old miner who knew the location has already been killed, and nobody else knows for sure where the treasure is hidden. Then there is the bronze dagger."

"What about the bronze dagger?"

"According to the legend," Tucker said in a low, serious voice, making up the story as he went, "any outsider must get past the bronze dagger. Even knowing about the dagger puts a person in danger. But the risk is worth it, don't you agree?"

"Risk?"

"Yes. Just think, a mountain filled with Spanish gold and jewels. Now, you must swear on your mother's grave to keep the secret, else you will die."

Lawrence Small seemed to shrink. "Do you really believe that?"

"Look what happened to the miner when he told the secret of the treasure."

Suddenly the reporter yawned. "Yes, I . . . swear."

He could barely pronounce his words, and his eyes were glazing over.

"I'm glad you're coming along," Tucker said conspiratorially. "We were worried with only two of us. It will be good to have another gun, someone we can trust who has as much at stake as us. The odds of survival aren't much better, once you learn about the dagger, but three is still better than two."

But Tucker's last statement came too late for a reply. Lawrence Small's head lolled back against the sofa, and his glass of wine teetered wildly as Tucker grabbed it. He lifted the newspaperman, laying him out on the couch in the shadows, then blew out the lamp on the desk. With any luck the man would sleep until morning. Hopefully he'd be too scared to talk about the treasure. By that time he and Raven would be long gone.

The only truthful thing he'd said was that having another gun along would have been an advantage. But one last look at the man belied that idea. Mr. Small was a writer, not a fighter. He wasn't armed and Tucker doubted he'd ever fired anything more dangerous than a slingshot.

Quickly Tucker closed the study door and started up the steps. But he hadn't counted on Rosalita, whose voice he could hear beyond Raven's door. She was insisting that Raven get undressed and into bed. Raven was arguing but Tucker could see that she'd have to comply. He only hoped that she didn't take long.

He listened to the low lyrical sound of her voice. She seemed so different tonight, nothing at all like the serious spirit woman she'd been on the trail. He liked this woman who laughed and wanted to dance the fandango. He suspected that he was seeing a side of her that no one else had ever known. That made him unexpectedly happy. If only they had the time to stop and enjoy that new Raven. But that couldn't happen—yet.

"Get undressed, Raven," he whispered.

"If that's what you want," he imagined her saying in return.

But Tucker couldn't lurk around in the corridor waiting for Rosalita to leave. That would be awkward. He'd check out the party with an eye to making their escape unobserved.

Señor Hildalgo intercepted Tucker as he entered the courtyard. "I think you ought to know that there is a great deal of interest in an old miner who took part in a poker game a few days ago."

"I heard about it," Tucker said casually. "There must be many tales like that circulating about."

"Of course. And there are many lost treasures in the hills. But once such a treasure is found, not many people have the means to dispose of it discreetly. I do."

The gauntlet was thrown, the challenge issued. Tucker considered his options. First the reporter, now the banker. "If there was such a treasure, and it was found, a man like you would be an asset to the finder."

"Then we understand each other?" the banker asked.

"I think we do," Tucker said, then turned away and disappeared on the pretense of having another glass of wine. For the next half hour, he mingled with the guests, making certain that those present knew that Raven was already in bed and that they would be leaving late in the morning to view local lands for sale.

Then he slipped to the stables, where he staked out a carriage and a horse drawn up to the outer ring of conveyances. Traveling by buggy would be slower, but unharnessing the carriage or separating and saddling horses might draw attention.

Satisfied that their means of escape was set, he stole around the wall to the outer staircase leading up to the balcony overlooking the courtyard. Once he reached Raven's darkened room, he found it a simple matter to enter from the outside.

"Where have you been?" She slid her arms around his neck and lifted her lips for a kiss. "I got undressed as you wanted."

Christ! She'd heard his whisper.

Rosalita might have convinced Raven to don her nightdress, but she wasn't wearing it now.

"I've been toasting our new partnership with Mr. Small," he stammered. "Where are your clothes?"

"I don't know. Did you satisfy Mr. Small's questions?"

Tucker opened his mouth to answer and groaned instead as she placed one of his hands on her bottom and pulled the other around her waist.

"Let's just say he's feeling very good about things. Raven—"

"Tucker, I'm feeling very good too," she whispered. "Or I will be when you stop being so—" she laughed lightly, "stiff, and kiss me back." She didn't know how to flirt; she'd never had any reason to before.

But tonight she wanted Tucker to see her as a woman.

"Kiss me, Tucker, please?"

Tucker groaned. "Raven, there is no way a man could

touch you and not be completely and totally aroused. But we can't do this now. We have to go."

"Go?" she said in disbelief. "You mean leave tonight—now?"

"Yes. Mr. Small won't sleep forever. Our trustworthy banker is entirely too interested in the possibility of lost treasure. I don't think we should stay here any longer. We have everything we need. Plus, we have the element of surprise."

"Are you sure?" she asked in a voice filled with disappointment. "Couldn't we wait, just a little while? I thought . . ."

"I know what you thought, and yes, I'm sure. The celebration will continue all night. We'll never have a better time to escape than while the fiesta is in full force."

Raven, pleasantly tipsy on wine and desire, knew that what he said made sense. She understood the logic in Tucker's thinking, but the logical side of her nature seemed to have disappeared. Tonight she was a woman possessed. She had found the man she wanted. She'd never imagined that she would feel like this, never even wished for it. But it had come like a hot storm and encircled her, filling her mind with physical yearnings, destroying her control. She was lost, caught up in the moment, for one night putting her own desire above her mission.

"Please, Tucker. Before we go, just one kiss—one kiss."

"Raven, please," Tucker growled. "There's just so much a man can take. Remember your promise to Flying Cloud."

Flying Cloud. Raven felt a curtain of ice fall over her. Stunned by her behavior, she pulled away, a small part of her hurt by Tucker's inability to understand how much she needed him to comfort and hold her, the other ashamed of her loss of purpose. For once she hadn't wanted him to be her strong and wise protector. She'd wanted him as a woman wants a man. And she was just beginning to understand that kind of power.

But he was right. She had given herself to a greater cause. She had no choice, she'd let him go, but first—

She kissed him one last time, a punishing, hard kiss that told him what he'd missed, what might not be offered again.

For just a moment, Tucker allowed himself to give in. He returned her kiss, tightening his arm around her waist possessively, pulling her against him. It was time he showed her that he could feel and return her desire. That she couldn't shut off his feelings as she did her own. That when the time came, they'd face this fire between them and there would be no going back.

His fingers tore through her hair, savagely pulling her head closer, capturing her mouth, delving inside the hot sweetness with his tongue. His hand cupped her breast, tweaking her nipple as he pressed his stiff manhood against her, finding the crease between her legs where he most wanted to be.

At first she gave as good as she got, using her own hands to explore, sliding lower until she found the object of her search. His neck muscles strained beneath one hand as the other encircled him intimately.

"Raven!"

"Yes?"

"Stop that, now!"

"Of course." She let him go and, using every ounce of her self-control, stepped away. "You see, Tucker Farrell, we are bound together, all parts of us, for now. This I know, though I do not yet understand all that it means. But we will dance to the music of the spirits. Sooner or later you'll understand."

She turned away and pulled on her buckskin dress, leaving her colorful fiesta clothes behind. "I'm know I'm not Mrs. Tucker Farrell and I never will be. No matter how much I've let myself pretend tonight, there is no place in my life for love."

Raven the spirit woman was back.

It was Tucker who was confused and uncertain.

Love? Where in hell had that come from? He didn't know anything about love, didn't want to, refused to consider that possibility. Even the word scared him silly. He was a man who'd been given a responsibility that offered the means to realize a long-forgotten dream. Love didn't, couldn't, enter into it. Love guaranteed failure.

He'd see that this woman found her treasure, for which he'd be rewarded. Then he'd go to Oregon and find the life he'd turned his back on so many years ago.

And Raven? What lay in store for her? Would she follow her dream alone?

That thought lay heavy on his heart, along with unexpected pain.

13

Shame—and guilt, that's what Raven felt as they slipped through the darkness past the open gate and toward the carriages beyond.

For one night she'd put herself and her feelings above her sworn oath, something she'd never thought she'd do. Her people were depending on her, and she'd almost allowed herself to be caught up in her desire for this man.

Tucker had never faltered.

She'd been the one to fail.

The cougar and the raven were two different species; they didn't belong together. She was a spirit woman, charged with the future of the Arapaho people. Tucker was a drifter with no past and no future. Why he'd been chosen to accompany her, she couldn't know. But she did know that in some way she had been tested.

Once they reached the carriage, she climbed in, ignoring Tucker's caution to be quiet. She couldn't have spoken if she'd wanted to, so deep had she sunk in her misery. At every turn they'd encountered danger, possible failure, ever relentless enemies ready to take what she was charged to find. And at every turn, Tucker had found a way to free them and move them closer to her objective.

Tucker was the strength; she was the vision. But she'd become a willow in the wind, unstable, fragile. How could the Grandfather have chosen her? Swift Hand, though still finding his way, was stronger. Even he understood the power of their quest and the spirit world that commanded it.

"You know that what you are experiencing is desire, and it is the most powerful emotion on earth," Tucker finally said.

She didn't answer.

"Few people ever truly understand what it is for two bodies to be perfectly in tune with each other. Women sometimes give their love to a man who doesn't appreciate the gift."

"I don't wish to discuss it," she said. "It was the wine. It won't happen again."

"It wasn't the wine, Raven, and under other circumstances I would have taken what you offered and given you what you need."

"I said, I don't wish to discuss it."

"All right, but it is still there and it's not going to go away."

Something about her stern countenance worried him. What she might have felt back at the fiesta was gone. The passion of her kisses in their room might never have been. The woman riding beside him as they reached the outskirts of San Felipe seemed to have turned to stone.

Still dressed in his black Spanish clothing, Tucker climbed down from the carriage and helped Raven dismount. He released the horse and watched as it wandered off and began to graze on the thick prairie grass nearby. On foot they slowly made their way into the square and quietly across the darkened plaza toward the livery stable.

A few coins to the proprietor was the best Tucker could do to ensure his silence. It wouldn't last long, but at least they'd have a head start on anyone asking after them.

Gathering their newly purchased supplies, Tucker packed them on a skittish Yank and Onawa. They would have been better served with a burro, but there was none to be had. Soon they were traveling down the same road they'd watched the bandits ride out on when they arrived.

Raven would have asked about his plans, but she'd made up her mind that Tucker's instincts were trustworthy. He understood many practical things that she did not. As much as she would have liked to go on alone, she understood that was not meant to be.

"Do you intend to remain silent for the rest of our journey?" he finally asked.

"No. Do you think it is wise to talk when we might be heard?"

"If anybody listening doesn't hear our horses, they won't hear our conversation."

"All right, then, I'll listen to whatever you have to say."

Tucker wanted to shake her, to arouse some emotion in her, to bring back the woman he'd traveled with up to now. But he had no choice but to wait for her to get past what had happened and her reaction to it. They'd both been loners for too long. Sooner or later they had to become a team again, or their mission was doomed to failure.

Perhaps that was to be their fate. If the treasure was never found, there would be no saving the Arapaho. There would be no land in Oregon. But there would be no parting either.

What did he really want?

· · ·

Your daughter is very lovely, Señor Hildalgo," Porfiro observed. "She will make a very good marriage, no?"

"That is not what you are here to talk about. Are you prepared to follow Señora and Señor Farrell when they leave?"

"Si. By morning I will have my men just beyond the walls of the courtyard."

"Not too close. We don't want them to know you're behind them. I think it will be much easier to let them lead you to the mine."

"You are sure about the gold and the jewel? People have searched for the Lost Spanish Treasure for hundreds of years without finding it."

"I'm sure that both the gold and the ruby are at least two hundred years old. The setting for the jewel is Spanish, and the design is Old World. Yes. I believe we have found it."

Señor Hildalgo leaned back in his desk chair and gave a deep, satisfied sigh. He had considered sending for Porfiro a long time before. Already a wealthy man, he had visions of building an empire here where the territory of New Mexico and old Mexico joined. Soon more Americans would come, and if he owned the land, he would be as well-to-do as the father of the man his daughter would marry. He cut a sharp eye toward the Mexican bandit.

"You know, of course," the banker said, "if you get any idea of taking this all yourself, you'll lose all claim to your family's land."

"Si. I understand. We will split the treasure. You will buy all the land and I will return a portion of my treasure to you for the land that once belonged to my family."

"Fine. We are agreed."

There was a moment of silence before the two men returned to the courtyard.

On the couch Lawrence Small kept very still. He

didn't think that Tucker and Raven had any idea that the banker was about to try to cheat them. Of the three, Lawrence much preferred taking his chances on the big American and his wife to Señor Hildalgo. But what to do?

The newspaperman lay there contemplating the situation until he decided that he had to warn them. Perhaps if they appreciated his actions, they'd take him along. That was exactly what he wanted. To go on a treasure hunt himself.

He could see the story now, splashed across the New York City streets. Son of wealthy publisher finds long-lost Spanish treasure.

Once he was certain that his host had left the room, Lawrence stole quietly into the hall and up the stairs. Outside the Farrells' room, he knocked. Lightly at first, then more firmly.

"Mr. Farrell, open the door. It's very important that I speak with you."

Nothing.

He moved to the next door and tried the knob. The door opened easily to reveal an empty room, maid's quarters, he'd guess. Slipping inside, Lawrence closed the door behind him. Odd, the door between the rooms was locked. Next he tried the balcony, stepping out into the shadows. He moved silently down to the Farrells' room. That door opened easily.

Empty.

There were no sleeping forms in the beds, no portmanteaus or cases. No clothing left behind.

They were gone.

For a moment Lawrence was puzzled. Then he understood. It had been an elaborate hoax. Tucker Farrell had obviously drugged him with the wine to prevent his interference. Señor Hildalgo and a Mexican called Porfiro were planning to follow them the next day when they'd announced they were going to look at land. Obviously the Farrells had drummed up the injured ankle and the early retirement so that they could leave during the fiesta.

"Rats!"

Lawrence considered his situation. Maybe if he hurried, he could still catch up with the pair, warn them, and ask them to take him along.

But first he made up the bed to look as if someone were sleeping there. With a little finagling, he discovered the door to the balcony could be latched from the inside, then closed, leaving the room locked.

He'd found out before they came that they'd left their supplies at the livery stable. It made sense that they would reclaim them. Now all he had to do follow them, rent a horse, and find someone who could tell him which way they'd gone.

Borrowing a buggy wasn't theft, if he let the horse go at the edge of the small town. Lawrence watched the horse return the same way he'd come, then walked the rest of the way to the livery stable.

"Hello?"

The stable was dark. Nobody answered.

"I said, hello inside. I need to rent a conveyance."

A curse followed, then a thump, and the door opened. "Who be you?"

"I'm Lawrence Small. I'm a newspaperman and I'd like some information."

The door slammed. "Come back when I'm open."

"No, please, I'm willing to pay. I need a mount."

"Only got one sorry horse. He's an ornery old cuss, belonged to a priest till he had to sell him to pay for food for his flock of sinners."

Half an hour later, Lawrence was riding a bony horse and heading out of town, in the same direction he'd been told that an American and his lady friend had gone earlier.

It had cost Lawrence a large portion of his funds, but he was certain that the proprietor of the stable wouldn't tell anyone else what he'd learned.

Now if he could just get the horse to cooperate.

Suddenly the stubborn animal began a determined trot off the main trail in another direction.

Lawrence yelled and pulled on the reins. But the horse kept going, and Lawrence, holding on for dear life, went along.

So much for fame and fortune. He'd been tricked. He would be lucky to save his life.

As the trail narrowed and began to climb toward the mountains, Yank began to fight Tucker's control. The night, already cloudy, darkened even more. Black racing clouds fled across the sky in pursuit of the moon, shrouding it momentarily, then releasing it as a moaning wind hurled itself down the canyon.

In the face of danger, Tucker urged Yank forward. They needed to make as much progress as possible before they were missed. Even then, those in pursuit would know the direction they'd taken and be on their trail. He wished he had a better idea of where the treasure was, if there was a treasure. He wished there were another way other than returning to Luce's cabin.

Tucker had only the markings he'd transferred to the tin plate and Raven's mother's carrying bag—that and Luce's cryptic message, "Follow the water."

He wished Raven would talk to him.

But she was totally uncommunicative, almost as if she'd turned her back on him. Yank slung his head. Tucker swore. He'd hoped to find a place where they could leave the trail and find another way into the hills. But in the dark, that was a foolish wish. In the end he kept moving up in the same direction he'd traveled that first night. As they climbed higher the trail narrowed, the cliffs became steeper, and the moon disappeared over the summit of the sacred mountains, throwing the trail into complete darkness.

Suddenly Yank came to a determined stop. Tucker couldn't force him to go any farther. "What in the west side of hell is wrong with you, horse?"

"This is the spot where we go down," Raven said.

Of course. Tucker was so tired that he hadn't realized how far they'd come. Yes, they did need to go down, but he couldn't force himself to urge the horse forward.

It was Onawa who started the descent. Yank whipped his tail and followed. Finally they reached the bottom and stopped to allow the horses to drink from the Rio Grande.

Tucker felt a curious sense of déjà vu. He'd done this before. The last time, they'd found Luce beneath the ledge, hidden in the rocks. Tonight the ghosts of both Luce and the murdered Mexicans seemed to dance down the canyon. Tucker shivered and studied the cliffs. He didn't think that Swift Hand's or Porfiro's men were watching, but something, or someone, was.

"I don't think we'd better risk climbing up the other side in the darkness," he said.

Raven waited.

"We'll take cover for the rest of the night in the place where we found Luce."

As if she understood, Onawa moved down the canyon.

"I think," Tucker went on, "we have a good enough start that we can take a brief rest. Then if we leave at first light we can get back to the cabin before anybody learns we are missing."

"All right." Raven slid from her horse and hobbled her nearby. She then moved toward a patch of grass downriver and, with a knife she'd taken from her pack, cut huge hunks of the tender vegetation to feed the horses.

In the meantime Tucker removed their bedrolls and unfolded them side by side beneath the overhang. He filled his canteen, noting that Raven hadn't opened hers at all. By the time Raven returned, he'd made a cold camp and was waiting for her to bed down.

She didn't argue with his arrangements, rather it was as if she no longer cared. Moments later she was covered with her blanket and her breathing signaled that she'd already fallen into a light sleep.

Tucker felt a great disappointment. He didn't know what he'd expected, certainly not a request for a good night kiss as she'd made before. Not a gesture of remorse for her drawing away. Not the passionate woman he'd rejected back in her room. But he'd hoped for some sign that she remembered and that she, too, felt regret.

There was none.

For a long time, Tucker sat in the darkness, his head resting on his saddle, his hand on the holster beside him. Then, finally, as faint streaks of light swirled the sky, he slept.

Beyond his reach Raven lay, restless in that last sleep which brings the phantoms, the unknown messengers of the dark. She felt her body itching as if she'd stepped in a bed of fire ants. But it was more than that. There was an urgency, almost a fear. She had to hurry.

There was someplace she had to go, and she was being held back. There was no one there, but she couldn't move. Struggle as she might, she could not rise from her bed. Beyond the faint haze of darkness she could see them, the phantoms, writhing, beckoning.

"Please," she whispered urgently, under her breath. "Let me go. I must go."

Yes, you must go. But not alone. You must complete the

ritual. Follow the stream to the top. Together you will find the cave in the mountain. Heed my words and look for the sign. Beware the bronze dagger.

Raven came suddenly awake. She'd hoped for a reassuring dream, for another meeting between the raven and the cougar, for a message that told her where to go. But this suggestion of a cave was not reassuring. There were phantom figures beyond her hiding place. They weren't Mexican bandits and certainly not part of Swift Hand's band.

The figures in her dream had been bearded, their chests covered with gold and silver, their heads protected with odd helmets that caught the moonlight. She'd never seen people dressed like that. Were they gods?

Raven's heart was beating wildly. She sat up, afraid, alone.

Alone? She could see Tucker lying next to her, but she couldn't reach him. He was restless, moving about in his sleep. And then it came, suddenly and powerfully, the chanting, the low, distant drumbeats that announced a vision. But this time it was different.

Suddenly she could see through Tucker's eyes, feel the intensity of his thoughts and understand his fear.

He was not here. He was in a different place, a different time. There was a battle raging about him. Indians, crying, screaming in fear. Children afraid—alone. And there were soldiers, wearing blue uniforms, riding toward the camp. Pistols were drawn, rifles firing.

"No, stop," someone cried.

"We are only women and children," another called out.

"We have come here in peace," an old man pleaded.

But still the soldiers came, relentlessly, stabbing, shooting, mutilating. Like waves of locusts devouring everything in their wake, they came.

And people died.

Then she saw him, Tucker, bearing down on a child, sword drawn, eyes wide with horror. At the last moment, he picked up the little girl, and holding her beneath his arm, he rode away. And Raven became that child, felt her terror, felt her fear. Wildly Tucker urged the big black horse whose name she now knew to be Yank through the camp, across the shallow river, and into the hills beyond.

She could feel the big man's heart beating, his fear, the saliva dried in his mouth and how he could barely swallow. Finally, when they were far away from the battle, he let the child down, looking at her with great sad eyes.

"I can no longer do this," he said. "I renounce all of this and the life I have lived. From now on, I travel alone."

The little girl looked up at the golden man who had saved her. Wise beyond her years, she knew that he was as empty as she.

"You must not go back to the camp now, little one. Wait here. Someone will find you." And he rode away, leaving the child behind.

The little girl looked around, then started back the way they'd come. Raven, now flying above and watching her, whispered, "No, don't go."

But she went, putting one foot before the other until she was so tired that she could barely walk. Finally she topped the rise and looked down at the scene before her. The tepees had been burned. The smoke was thick, but she could see the bodies strewn across the camp like thistle blown by the wind. There was a smell of blood and fire, but there was no sound, only a great silence.

The little girl looked at the devastation and began to cry.

Overhead, Raven flew low across the site of the massacre, searching for one to care for the child. Then she heard a single shot. As she dipped her wings and reversed her course, she saw the child fall, mortally wounded. The soldier would never know that his heroism had all been for nothing. Twice she flew over the camp, then soared across the horizon until she saw him, the fleeing man on the black horse. She accompanied him as he rode for most of the day, then stopped by a stream and bathed the splatters of blood from his body. He made a fire and burned the blue uniform. When the last coal had died away, he put on civilian clothes, mounted his horse once more and started south.

From above the site, high on a ledge, a mountain lion leapt down and started toward the rider. Now all four, the cougar, the raven, and the dreamers, were one.

Tucker jerked and opened his eyes, finding the dark-eyed woman watching him. The eyes in his dream, the symbol of the future, the spirit child of his vision. She'd come to him again in the flesh.

Raven.

14

"Tell me what happened."

"It was only a dream," he answered, still caught up in the horror.

"I know. I shared the dream with you."

"I don't understand. How can that be?"

"I cannot say. Perhaps the spirits willed it, Tucker."

"Then you know what I did?"

"I know you were one of the soldiers and you rode away from the battle."

The confusion almost overwhelmed him. "Yes. I couldn't do it."

"Couldn't do what?"

He used every mental control he possessed to force himself to examine logically what he'd just experienced and answer her. "Kill people. First I was a Confederate soldier, too young to know what would happen in war. I did what I was ordered to do. Toward the end, wounded and sick of killing, I couldn't find the glory anymore. I went home and found out that the war had cost me my land and everyone I cared about. I just turned my sights to the west and kept riding. It didn't matter much what I did. Ended up in Colorado."

"What were you going to do out here?"

"I didn't know. Being a soldier was all I'd ever done, except live on a plantation where my father made all the decisions."

"What happened to your father?"

"He was killed in the first year of the war, before I even joined up with my fellow rebels."

"But you became a soldier again out here."

"Yes, I crossed paths with Colonel John Chivington. He was organizing the Third Colorado Cavalry, a new regiment of volunteers who'd been ordered to purge the savage Indians."

"And you joined."

"That was my last mistake. I had some crazy idea that if the West were rid of the savages, others like me could come here and start over. I needed to believe in a new future. I didn't know it meant getting drunk and killing innocent women and children."

Raven nodded, a sad expression on her face. "You weren't the only good man caught up in the persecution of Indians. Many of the soldiers had to get drunk to do it, even the bloodthirsty ones."

"No amount of whiskey could make me slaughter innocent people—or worse."

"Chivington," Raven said. "The Sand Creek Massacre. They attacked Black Kettle and his Cheyenne who'd made camp on the creek. You were there."

"I was there."

"But you didn't kill. I saw you. You saved a child, a child that could have been me."

Then, finally, he understood. She really had been there. Through his dream she'd seen what had happened. She knew the truth.

And she hadn't turned away.

Raven took his hand, not censuring him, but simply sharing the pain of his memory.

Tucker sat up, careful not to move his arm, but forcing himself leave to the dream behind. He let out a deep sigh. He was so tired. When he dreamed about the past, it seemed to suck the very life out of him, leaving him drained of emotion.

Yet this time was different. Raven's touch was a kind of balm, an anchor. Finally he acknowledged the connection between them. Not sensual this time, but spiritual and just as powerful. Everything about her touched him in some way. And every day brought a different woman to his side. The determined warrior at first had turned into the mystical spirit woman who changed into a passionate creature discovering how to be a woman. Now came the compassionate healer who made him bare his soul.

Tucker relaxed. It had been a long time since he'd been sure he had a soul. Because of Raven, it had sprung to life again. He didn't know what he thought about that. Life was easier when he could just drift without thought or responsibility. But was that really living?

Raven could feel Tucker's tension fall away. She was aware, even if he wasn't, of the importance of this moment. He had accepted that the spirits could influence their lives, and he was sharing himself with her, willingly, knowing that it was not a past he could be proud of. This understanding signified nothing in the larger picture. It didn't mean that they would find the treasure. But it was important to her as a woman, just the same.

"Don't you see, Tucker? All the bad things that happened are in the past. We can't change that. But we have an opportunity to change the future. We will find the treasure, buy land, and look toward a better life."

He gave a dry laugh. "I've heard that before. Every

commander since Moses has believed that he had some kind of divine guidance. I always thought it was a lie, Raven, that the only thing a man can know and control is what's inside himself. I'm what I am. You're what you are. The best we can hope is that I don't ruin you. Now, let's get moving."

As they mounted their horses, Raven felt a great sorrow in her heart for this man who'd lost his belief in the future. For a moment he'd shared his pain, and she'd learned that he was more of a crusader than he knew. Somewhere deep inside of Tucker Farrell was that promise of tomorrow that he'd spurned. He just needed help in finding it. She smiled at the thought of helping Tucker, convinced that, even more than before, their futures seemed entwined.

By the time the sun hit the floor of the canyon, they were almost back to Luce's cabin. The trip was easier this time, for they'd made it before.

As they rode, Tucker's spirits began to rise. He'd worry about the spirit world later. For now, he would concentrate on seeking the treasure, though he had no grand illusions that they would find it. And even if they did, they would never be able to get it out and take it back to Colorado. To succeed, they would have to face bandits and Indians, not to mention others who would hear about the discovery.

No, the treasure hunt would be a grand adventure, but the chances of his being able to buy land in Oregon after this was over were about as good as his chances of marrying Raven and making her the mother of his children.

Marrying Raven? Where had that come from? The only time in his life that Tucker had entertained the idea of marriage was when he was eighteen years old and going off to war. Having Lucinda pledge her undying love and promise to wait for him was part of the grand spirit of patriotism that swept the South. It had been an illusion. Learning that she'd already taken up with someone else when he returned hadn't even disturbed him.

She'd been part of a dream that had died, and he hadn't allowed himself to dream again. He'd deliberately closed off all thoughts of marriage, a family, the good things that might have been. Every day had been a new day, a new start. That was the way he had wanted it.

Until now.

Until Raven had invaded his dreams and his life. Now he had difficulty telling what was real and what was part of the spirit world she carried around with her. And, in spite of his skepticism, he kept running head-on into some kind of magic that deepened the connection between them.

He couldn't believe that he'd shared what had happened at Sand Creek, but he had. And she hadn't been horrified to learn that he was one of the soldiers who'd attacked the Indians who'd wanted only peace.

He felt dirty and ashamed about that part of his past. Now Raven made him feel strong and proud. Seeing himself through her eyes was hard to believe.

For the last five days, they'd ridden over half these mountains, being chased and being captured. Now they'd come full circle, back to where they'd started, as if they couldn't escape their destiny.

When they reached Luce's cabin, Tucker slid off Yank and removed his saddle and bridle. "We'll rest the horses and eat. I want to retrace our steps and see if we're being followed." He led the big black horse into the makeshift corral. He turned back to Raven, catching her just as she slid from Onawa.

"Careful, that ankle isn't back to full strength yet. We're going to need all our parts working to get through this."

"It's much better." Raven caught Tucker's shoulders and held him for a moment. "Tucker, will you do something for me?"

"Sure, what?"

"Until we find the treasure, can we get past whatever there is between us and just be friends, really friends? I've never been around a man alone, other than my father and my grandfather, and I'm not sure what I'm supposed to feel. And, like you, I fear this emotion could interfere with what we have to do. But for now, we must make a truce between us."

"A truce? Sure, and you and I will ride through the streets of Washington City leading a parade when we're done here. Maybe I'll even run for political office. A deserter and a do-gooding Indian, won't we be a pair?"

"I think we would make a grand pair," Raven whispered and watched him head up the trail on foot. "I think we were meant to be. Some things even Grandfather did not prepare me for, but I will learn."

Raven was very confused. Sometimes Tucker seemed to be deliberately cruel. She wished she knew more about being a woman. At the same time, a wave of guilt swept over her that she was even thinking about herself when she should be focusing all her attention on her mission.

"Oh, Grandfather, why couldn't you have come with me? I'm so uncertain."

You were chosen, Raven. The future is in your hands. Do not despair. The spirits will lead you in the way you are to go.

She'd heard that from her mother's people for most of her life, and she'd accepted it. Surely the Great Spirit hadn't intended the Arapaho people to be eliminated from the face of the earth. But that was what was happening. Their lands had been taken. The buffalo were being severely depleted, and now their own tribal numbers had dwindled to a pitiful few. How was she to change all this?

With a heavy heart, she turned toward the cabin, where she found a bucket to haul water for the horses. Then she brushed them down for the night. After unpacking their bedrolls, she built a fire to prepare a meal, and set a pot of water to boil for coffee. She cut chunks of salt pork and fried it in a skillet over the fire. Next she mixed up flour and grease and salt to make biscuits. Tomorrow she'd search for greens and perhaps a few spring berries, but tonight they'd fill their stomachs with pork and bread.

When the food was done, she walked out into the tiny clearing where she could see the late afternoon sun vault over the mountain peaks toward the west, above the pool where they'd bathed. There it was again, that peculiar formation in the peaks beyond the cabin. There was a slash of light, then a space of darkness, then light again, as if someone had painted vertical streaks of sun across a dark canvas.

The long hours of sunlight had warmed the granite and sandstone rocks. Now, as the sun slid behind them, the cool late afternoon air moved in. Raven couldn't be still. There was too much quiet. Even the birds had hushed. She started up the trail in the direction that Tucker had gone. Being alone had never seemed lonely before—before Tucker. Now she hastened her step, anxious to find the big tawny man. She needed to see his eyes, even though she knew they'd likely frost over when he saw her.

More and more often in the last few days, he'd let down his guard and she'd been able to see how he felt by watching his eyes. Tense, sometimes stern, but at other moments he'd unknowingly let a bit of yearning seep into his expression, and once he'd even laughed. Those changes in his eyes had been the measure of the growth of their relationship and what she missed most when he was gone.

She wondered what he thought about her. She wondered about her own sudden reversals of mood. From being the woman driven by her purpose, she'd changed into a woman driven by her newly emerging needs. Change was frightening, but it seemed almost stronger than she was.

Tucker didn't want a truce. He hadn't agreed to her suggestion that they be just friends. So, where did that leave her?

They were like a young mare and a stallion meeting for the first time, curious yet wary. Drawn to each other, yet not ready to trust their instincts. She sensed that they were behaving like the youths they'd never been.

Several hours had passed and she was growing more and more concerned. There'd been too much time to think about what happened. Suppose they'd been followed? Suppose this time it was Tucker who'd been captured? She'd started this journey alone, without fear. But now everything had changed.

Where was he? She didn't want to consider what would happen if he never returned. They were too much a part of each other's purpose to lose the other's strength.

Then she heard a whistle. As the sound grew closer she stopped and waited. Then she saw him, moving toward her, a smile across his mouth broadening when he caught sight of her.

"Tucker." She rushed into his arms as naturally as if he'd asked her to come to him. "Did you see anything?"

"Not a thing. Nobody."

The moment Tucker's strong arms closed about her, Raven knew that was what she'd been waiting for all day.

She realized that they hadn't yet defined their relationship. She was probably taking a foolish chance, but she couldn't turn away. She needed to be reassured, not about being followed, but about being cared for. For so long she'd been strong for the Grandfather, for their people, for her own sisters who never understood that beneath all her stoic calm was a restless insecurity. This time Raven Alexander very much needed someone to be strong for her.

Now she had somebody to share her uncertainties with, someone who made her feel protected. And she let go the last of her reservations and leaned against him openly, with no pretense of having too much wine, or too much fear.

"Did something happen while I was gone?" he asked.

She answered him honestly. "I missed you."

He swallowed hard, obviously at a loss for words. "You look very beautiful in the afternoon light. I didn't expect such a welcome."

She didn't answer. Instead she leaned against him, the warmth of his body bringing heat to the coolness of hers. They felt so good together.

"Nothing happened?" His voice was tight with emotion.

"Nothing happened," she echoed. Except something inside her had changed. He'd been gone and she'd been afraid. Now he was back and everything felt secure again. "Are you hungry?"

"Hungry? God, yes, I'm hungry. My stomach and my backbone are having a duel."

"Then let's eat." She slid her arm around his waist and adapted her steps to his as they walked back to the cabin.

The sun dropped lower in the sky until it fell beyond the ridge and a soft gray bank of shadows swooped across the narrow valley where the cabin was. Tiny night birds darted across the sky in search of insects, and in the distance they heard the mournful sound of a coyote.

"Something smells good." Tucker was reluctant to speak for fear that he'd break the peaceful mood they shared.

"Salt pork and biscuits," she said, "and coffee."

"No juice of the red berry?"

"No juice of the red berry." She smiled. "I'm saving that for a special occasion."

"What, to celebrate finding the treasure?"

Tucker's words were meant to be a continuation of the jubilant spirit of the evening. Instead they seemed to have the opposite effect. Raven tensed for a moment, then made an obvious attempt to throw off whatever bothered her.

"When we find the treasure, we'll invoke the spirits to join in the celebration," she said. "And you know what happens when a bunch of celebrating spirits get stirred up."

"No, what happens?"

"You never believed in fairies?" Raven asked as she started laying out the food.

"No. There was an old slave on the plantation who cast spells for the others, but so far as I knew, the only thing that happened was that she got fat from taking part of their food allotment and they went hungry."

"Well, my father was Irish and he believed in the Little People, leprechauns. He thought they were caretakers to the Irish. And my mother's people believe that every part of nature has a spiritual guide to oversee our lives. What do you believe?"

Tucker tried to answer Raven very carefully and with as much honesty as he could. "Raven, until I met you, I believed only in what I could see and touch and feel. Now I don't know. I wouldn't be surprised to find a mermaid in Luce's pool. But I'm still having trouble thinking that there are spirits who control our lives."

"Control isn't the right word." She tore the bread into pieces and laid it on the tin plates Tucker had bought back in San Felipe. "It's more that they know what will happen and they give us their wisdom, if we ask."

"Do you think they'd tell us where the treasure is if we ask?"

Raven poured the coffee and sat down. "I think they already have, Tucker. After we eat, maybe we can examine the carrying bag and the pan with the markings. The answer is there, if we can find it."

"And if we can't?"

Raven broke open her bread and slapped the salt pork inside. "Then we will have failed."

"Would that be the end of everything?"

She thought for a long minute. "I don't know. If we fail, it will be because we lost our sense of purpose."

"Did it ever occur to you that we could fail because we aren't supposed to succeed?"

Raven nodded. "Yes, but I don't believe that. We've come too far. The treasure is close by, I sense it, and we'll find it if we open our minds and our hearts."

Tucker ate the food and thought about what she'd said. If he opened his heart any further, it would shatter into a thousand pieces and he'd lose it entirely. His heart already knew how he felt about Raven. It was his mind that he was having trouble convincing.

After they finished the meal, Raven brought her mother's carrying bag with the symbols painted on it, and Tucker got the tin pan he'd marked with holes that traced the design on Luce's head.

On closer examination Tucker could see that the pinpricks of light on the pan matched the half triangles on the carrying bag. "These have to be mountain peaks,"

Tucker said. "But what about these odd lines between? They aren't parallel, so they aren't trails."

"They're wavy, almost like rainbows, or waves," Raven observed.

"That's it," Tucker exclaimed. "They're waves. Water."

The sun had set and they were examining the drawings by the light of the fire. When Tucker held the tin pan in front of the fire, the design shone like stars leading ancient travelers.

" 'Follow the water,' Luce said," Raven commented.

Tucker studied the design. "We thought that was only to find his burial place."

Raven nodded. "But the burial site was important for more than that. As keeper of the treasure, Luce had to be placed in the proper spot at the base of the sacred mountain."

"You can see the wavy lines above the cabin, and this circle here must be the pool."

"I think you're right. And if we travel in that direction, we'll be walking toward the odd formation of peaks I saw."

"But what about the butterfly? It doesn't seem to fit with the rest."

"I don't know. Maybe it was just part of my mother's totem. Each person has their own symbols, and they are private," Raven said.

Tucker folded the bag and put it inside the saddle-bags along with the tin plate. "Tomorrow we'll go back to Luce's grave and we'll start from there. We'll follow the water."

"Speaking of water," Raven said, "we have some dishes to wash before we go to bed. Will you go to the pool with me?"

"Will the spirits get me if I don't?" he asked with an easy laugh and began to gather their plates.

Raven picked up the skillet and the coffeepot. "Maybe not, but you'll be in trouble with me if you don't. And believe me, Mr. Farrell, that's a lot worse."

"Ah, Mrs. Farrell. We've only been married a few days and you're already turning into a shrew. What am I going to do with you?"

"I think you're just going to have to seal my lips, husband."

She stopped and turned toward him, her lips slightly parted, her warm breath lightly feathering his chin.

"I knew that I chose a smart woman." Then he kissed her.

15

Tucker's kiss was so light, she could barely feel his lips. With both hands full, neither Raven nor Tucker could touch the other, but Raven could feel her body reach out to him. Her fierce response staggered her. Excitement bubbled up her veins, sharpening her senses and making her pulse race.

Then, almost before it had begun, the kiss ended and they stood looking at each other like two young fools, grinning, balancing on the narrow edge of longing. Raven thought about her fears for their relationship, for the continuation of their mission, and knew that what they felt when they touched was too powerful to put aside. Whatever happened now, the mission and her feelings were all part of the same.

"Well, Mrs. Farrell, your lips are better than the sweetest red berries."

"And your kiss is more potent than Señor Hildalgo's wine."

"And if we don't get to that pool, we're going to scorch the food left in these dishes," Tucker said and swung around to find the path upward.

He didn't whistle this time, but Raven didn't need to hear his pleasure to know it was there. His quick steps spoke louder than words, as did the rapidity with which the dishes were scoured and laid on the rocky ledge to dry.

"Now, about that waking dream from our last visit to the pool and that one when we danced beneath the trellis at the fiesta," Tucker said wickedly. "Do you suppose we could doze off again?"

There was no rock between them this time, no chanting or distant drums. The only sound in Raven's mind was the pounding of her heart.

"Do you think the spirits are watching?" Tucker asked in a tight low voice.

"Of course."

"Do you think they mind that I kissed you?"

She grinned. "You've kissed me before. Were there rock slides?"

"No"

"Lightning strikes?"

"No."

"Hordes of locusts or birds attacking?"

"No."

"Then I think they were very pleased."

"Then I believe I'll do it again."

The stars twinkled. The stream plunged down from the hole in the rocks overhead and fell into the pool. A soft night breeze wrapped around them as Tucker kissed her.

The mountain seemed to sigh, and showed its approval in every physical way that nature could have designed. Silver moonlight drenched the rocks, casting a shimmering dreamlike quality to the night. The melody of the water filled the night around them like a hundred hearts beating in unison. And somewhere in the distance,

Tucker heard a kind of murmur, like a chorus whispering some repetitive musical cord.

The sound reached within him and loosened the last of his defenses, turning his insides into melted honey that licked his skin with heat and made every nuance of the night intensify.

Raven's lips were soft and warm; her body pressed against him, setting off a shivery motion. Beneath her buckskin he could feel her breasts tighten and harden. Her body was alive with response, her breathing fast and light.

"You take my breath away," he whispered.

"And you charge through all my restraints as if I had none, as if this were meant to be." Closing her eyes, she let her body experience the feel of him against her, strong and hard, vibrating with energy.

A dam of emotion broke inside her, allowing all her held-back fears and desires to run free. She felt flooded with fire, and suddenly her dress was gone and he was running his rough hands over her bare body. She let out a deep, long moan in her throat.

There was a sense of panic and overwhelming awe, and for a moment, she pulled back. But Tucker wouldn't let her retreat, not this time. He moved his lips down her face and to the hollow at the base of her neck, his fingers plying her breast and her bottom as if she were clay being molded into a sculpture and he were the artist creating the masterpiece.

She was gasping now for breath, tearing at his shirt, seeking the touch of his bare skin beneath her palms. Hot, then cold, she moaned helplessly. Her fingertips searched his chest, moving downward to his belt.

Then the belt was gone, along with his boots and his trousers. Softly Tucker whispered her name, making the word sound reverent, pure, his fingers plowing through the heavy mass of her hair, separating it, combing it across her shoulders and down her back. He brought a handful of it to his lips, brushing it across his chest and nipples.

His mouth devoured hers while her hands, wild now in their own exploration, ran rampant over his body. She could feel his heart beating, feel his breath hot upon her hair, feel his erection throbbing against her.

Then he lifted her and carried her to a mossy area beside the water. Whispering her name over and over, he laid her down and came down beside her.

"You're so sweet and wild," he said. "I feel the print of your lips across my body as if I've been branded in fire."

"You have, my golden mountain lion. I've put my mark on you for all time."

"Now it's my turn to brand you." His kisses continued to rain across her with sweet potency. The trail of fire swirled along the cords of her neck, across her breasts, and down her stomach to her navel and below, where the vortex of sensation was sending swirls of heat spiraling outward.

"Oh, Tucker," she cried out, "it aches. Why does it ache so much?"

"It's a need as old as time," he whispered. "Let yourself give in to it, let it wash over you."

"But I'll explode."

"That's the wonder of it, sweetheart. When it's right, in spite of all life's trouble and pain, we get rewarded with something that nobody and nothing can take from us."

Then he was over her, the hair on his chest brushing her breasts with fire, his heavy arousal throbbing against her thigh, his leg thrown across her.

In the moonlight, she could see his eyes, shimmering like smooth stones beneath crystal-clear water. Her hands were tugging at him, feeling the sinewy muscle in his arms and back, drawing him closer. Like a sleek statue, he rose above her, waiting for some kind of distant signal, holding himself back until she was about to die of want.

She moaned helplessly, whispering his name, asking, pleading, needing. Her voice caught in her throat, held by such tightness that she felt as if she would die.

"Raven, my sweet, you've never been with a man before."

"No."

"The first time, there is pain."

"Pain always leads the way to joy, else how do we know the pleasure?"

And then he was poised between her legs, probing, stroking until, just at the moment she was ready to scream, he plunged inside her, bringing a strangled cry of shock. Pain quickly turned into pleasure and she met him thrust for thrust. Savagely they moved together, his hands clasping her shoulders, her nails raking his back. Consumed by fire that raged higher and higher, she buried her face into his shoulder, crying out in pure animal ecstasy.

As in the waking dreams, she could feel Tucker. She was in his skin, feeling his need for her.

I'm being burned alive by this woman.

Raven delighted in being able to experience not only Tucker's need but his thoughts. *She's tearing me to pieces, then bringing me back together again. Christ, don't let me hurt her. Don't let it stop.*

It was back, the connection between them, the knowledge that came from some mystical world beyond. Raven lost all sense of self, of separation. She opened her mouth to scream, but it was Tucker's voice that split the night air with an unworldly howl. Then, just as she feared death and the transformation into the spirit world, it happened, the explosion she'd feared, sweeping them through a tide of fire that erupted in starbursts of heat. Together, breathlessly, uncontrollably, they were swept along until, at last, they lay spent, he in silence and she crying from the power of their journey.

"I'm sorry, Raven." Tucker planted little kisses across her face, still not understanding what he'd experienced, but afraid of the intensity. "I couldn't control myself. I've hurt you badly."

"No," she gasped, "it was wonderful—so very wonderful. Thank you, Tucker. Together, we were one being." Her body trembled with the last wave of fiery sensation.

She was lying in his arms, separated, yet still locked to him spiritually, reluctant to let go of a moment that could never come again.

"What in hell happened, Raven?"

"We became one. Does it not always happen that way?"

"Never. Never has that happened to me before." Tucker was having trouble dealing with what they'd shared. It was too powerful, too all-consuming. He was discovering that making love to her hadn't satisfied his longing. He wanted her now as much as he had the first time he'd kissed her.

More.

But the ground was cool and the mist from the waterfall fell across their body like silver fog. Raven began to shiver.

"We'd better get back to the cabin before you catch a chill," he said, coming to his feet.

She rose behind him, walking to stand beside the pool. At that moment a shard of moonlight hit the the bottom of the pool and reflected its beacon upward.

"Oh, look, Tucker."

He followed the beam and saw the light being threaded through a sliver of rock high on the mountain. Like an arrow it seemed to point to a spot near the summit. Then, as if a curtain fell, the light was cut off and the night went dark.

"A sign," Raven whispered. "A sign directing us where to go. It's the same spot as before."

"You think that has something to do with the treasure?"

"Do you have a better explanation?"

"No," Tucker said, rattled by more than just the signal. Everything that had happened was almost mystical in its power.

Everything except the beautiful woman standing nude in the moonlight, the woman with whom he'd joined in a celebration of desire.

To his surprise she slipped into the pool, splashing herself with the icy water. Then, rising like a sea siren, she climbed out, picked up her dress, and walked back toward the cabin, all shyness and restraint gone.

Quickly Tucker gathered his clothing and followed her, stunned by her beauty, by the honesty of her response, by the openness of her actions.

Once inside the cabin, she quickly built up the fire, warmed her body, then slipped into the blankets and held out her arms.

"Hold me, Tucker. I would keep the magic with us until tomorrow."

He fell down beside her. "You sound sad."

"I am. This night can never come again, and I will always hold it close."

He pulled her into his embrace. "Don't say that, my love."

"Would that I were your love." She closed her eyes.

But for Tucker sleep did not come. He lay reliving the night, trying to understand what had happened, trying to fashion a plan for the rest of their journey. In the end all he could do was hold Raven.

"Would that I were," she'd said. He'd heard her as clearly as if she'd spoken aloud. Yet she had never opened her mouth. He had to be so caught up in the magic that he was imagining something that could never be. Still, if what they'd shared wasn't love, then it was as close to it as he'd ever come.

Love. The very thought scared him to death. To love meant he had something to lose.

And Tucker Farrell always lost.

Porfiro checked his men as they mounted up.

"Make sure you have everything you need," he advised. "We won't return until we find them."

"But what about the Indians?" Juan asked.

"We'll take care of them as well. We are *bandoleros*. A puny band of ragged Indians won't stop us."

Porfiro's eyes swept the city plaza. San Felipe was his town. The banker's daughter would soon be his ticket to a complete hold on the area. She thought she would marry the son of a wealthy landowner. She was wrong. Porfiro would be her husband when he had the treasure.

Gomez Hildalgo believed he was being smart, keeping the secret of the gold and the ruby jewel from the town, but Porfiro had his way of learning. Long before the banker had told him, Porfiro had known. Nothing went on in San Felipe without his knowledge, including the escape of the Indian woman and her man.

He should have known when it happened. He would have had it not been for the engagement party. Losing the woman he wanted to another man had interfered with his attention for a time. But no more. Soon the wealth of the Spanish treasure would belong to him. He would take a wife and assure the importance of his station in the town.

He was a Romero, and the Romeros were descended from the Spanish who had come here generations ago.

Now Porfiro was ready to go after the woman and Señor Farrell. They'd lead him to the old miner who'd share the location of the treasure with him. For too many years Porfiro had waited. After all, it was his Spanish ancestors who'd originally acquired the treasure, acquired and lost it. Now power and success were at hand. Soon the Romeros would be respected again.

"Are we ready, Juan?"

"Si, Porfiro. Where do we go?"

"We go into the mountains, by the river, where we rode when the Indians attacked. We will follow the woman who hears the voice from the past."

"And what will we do when we find her?" Juan asked with a wicked grin.

"We'll find out what we want to know. Then we'll kill her."

Hot coffee, fried pork, and the leftover biscuits from the night before made their breakfast, and while Raven was packing up, Tucker checked the back trail.

An hour after dawn, they were moving up the mountain toward the spot where the beam of light had pointed. But distance was an illusion and by noon they were little closer than when they'd started.

"Don't you think we ought to stay close to the water?" Tucker asked.

"I don't know," Raven admitted. "The beam seemed to be a sign, but I'll admit that I'm as confused about that as I am about—"

"Me?" Tucker finished for her.

"No, I mean it suddenly seems so awkward." From the time she'd opened her eyes and found herself alone in the bedroll, she'd felt strangely uncertain. Making love in the moonlight had seemed so natural, but the harsh reality of morning cast everything in an uncomfortable light. They were no longer what they had been, but neither knew yet what they were.

Her shiver had nothing to do with the chill in the air. She felt Tucker's wariness and it made her nervous.

The rugged side of the mountain was steep and magnificent. Loose boulders dotted its stony surface amidst openings that might be caves or mines. Behind them, Raven could see the light reflecting off the broken mirror in the pool. For a distance she could see the stream as it threaded its way down the cliff.

But above the pool, the point where the water burst from the rock, there was no sign of the creek. Where did it go?

"Let's study our maps," Tucker suggested, sliding from his saddle.

Raven pulled the carrying bag from her saddlebags while Tucker removed the tin pan from his. Shading his eyes from the glare, he studied the markings.

Raven leaned against him, holding the bag up to compare it with the pan. "Do you see anything you can identify?"

"Nothing except the stream, or perhaps it's the pool. Do you see, right here, the wavy lines?"

She leaned closer, bringing herself into contact with his body. She could see the lines and what might have been a mark indicating a narrow valley. "That could be Luce's valley and cabin," she observed.

Tucker's concentration was immediately broken when he felt her press against him. "Yeah," he muttered. "But the only other thing we can be sure of is that we have to climb the mountain. And I can't see any way to do that just yet."

"Neither can I," she agreed, "but the spirits will guide us, never fear."

But he did fear. The only spirit guiding him was the spirit of the flesh. And now that he'd tasted the forbidden fruit, all he could think about was Raven's body, Raven beneath him, Raven's heat.

For the first few days, Raven had been a mystery, a challenge that came to him. She was alone, on an impossible mission with insurmountable odds. Somehow she'd gotten to him, made him feel responsible for her safety.

Almost overnight that protective need had changed to pure temptation. He wanted her and that want had grown with every hour, cresting to hot desire in that moment by the pool when they'd experienced what she called a waking dream. He'd been hopelessly drawn into her mystical world. Even as he'd tried to hold back, he'd been pulled in.

What did it all mean? Had Raven created some mystical spell from which he could not escape? Tucker felt as if he'd lost control, and he'd sworn never to let that happen again.

Then came last night and he knew he was lost.

"Let's move on," he said roughly.

Raven put her hand on his arm. "I thought we were going to be friends."

"Friends and lovers don't necessarily go together." Tucker climbed back into the saddle.

"Why not?" she said, following his motions.

"You can talk to friends. Friends explain and ask before they steal a man's soul."

She felt her heart lurch. She wanted to talk to Tucker. She wanted to hear the sound of his voice. It made her feel breathless inside. But she'd been so caught up in the magic they'd made that she hadn't realized how upsetting it was for him. "And lovers?" she asked.

"Lovers, you make love to."

The breathless feeling tightened, cutting off her air supply to her lungs. "Tucker, I am your friend, but I can no more explain what we felt than you can. I don't want to take anything you don't wish to give."

"It seems to be out of both our hands."

"I'm sorry you're confused. But I'm also your lover now and I'm not sorry about that. I'm yours to make love to whenever you wish. Do you wish to love me now?" She started to dismount.

"No! I mean, hell yes! I want to make love to you now and tomorrow and next year, and if your spirits don't take you away, I will. But now is not the time. I need to think about all this, to keep my wits about me. Half the people in New Mexico could be behind us. We don't have time for that—now."

"Whatever you say, Tucker."

By noon they were moving through an area so barren that Tucker doubted any man had been there before. There was no trail, no path, only rough, rock-strewn terrain that fought them every step of the way. And they seemed no nearer to the place where the light had pointed than when they'd begun.

Tucker pulled off his hat and mopped his face with his bandanna. A little farther and they'd reach the top of another ridge. What lay beyond was probably more of the same. At the rate they were moving, it would take them days to reach the peak they were heading for in the distance.

"I'd like to keep going," he said. "The area is so rough I'd hate to get trapped in a place like this with nowhere to make camp. Do you feel up to it?"

"I'll make it, Tucker. You lead the way."

She was doing it again. Putting him in charge, placing her faith in him. And he was accepting that faith, binding

himself even tighter to her with the foolish idea of finding
a treasure that had been hidden for two hundred years.

"Damn!"

Yank tossed his head, showing his complete agreement. Behind them Onawa neighed softly, quieting the
big black horse, who found his footing and moved off.

"She's got you just as hog-tied as I am," Tucker observed to his horse. "Never thought I'd see that time for
either one of us."

About midafternoon they finally crested the ridge,
and Tucker was dumbfounded by what lay before him. A
long, narrow valley hid an oval bowl-shaped jungle of ver-
dant meadows. Down the middle ran the elusive stream,
twinkling and bubbling through green grass. Hundreds of
yellow-and-black wildflowers dotted the landscape.

"What is it?" Raven came to a stop beside him. "Oh,
it's beautiful. But how, how could this be?"

"You're the one who speaks with Mother Earth; you'd
be more likely to get an answer from her than from me,"
Tucker said. "But I suspect that there are hundreds of
places like this tucked into these mountains."

"Look at the flowers, they're everywhere. On the
grass, in the trees. Their petals are caught by the wind like
leaves in the fall."

"Well, let's go down. We need to fill our canteens,
and this looks like a good place to camp for the night."
Tucker urged Yank down the ravine, between two massive
fir trees, toward the bottom of the valley.

As they grew closer they discovered that what they'd
thought were festooning wildflowers were instead gold-
and-black butterflies that swarmed up in a great flaming
eruption of color.

"Oh, Tucker. Butterflies."

Soon the huge brilliant wings were everywhere, on

their arms, on the horses' backs and heads. Like the petals of a million flowers being dropped by the gods, the graceful butterflies' sun-shot wings skimmed and dipped in the air.

Tucker felt as if he'd stepped into a fairy tale. This was some kind of wonderland, all green and lush and filled with magic. The last vestige of doubt vanished from Tucker's mind. Raven and her spirit world were truly magical. If he hadn't believed it before, he believed it now.

Raven climbed down from Onawa and stood still. Soon she was covered with the giant butterflies. They alit in her hair, on her face as if to kiss her cheeks; they decorated her buckskin dress.

Then, as if responding to a silent signal, they took flight, soaring across the sky in a wave, moving to the north like a golden blizzard. Clouds of the lacy creatures joined the flock and began to leave the valley.

"Oh," Raven cried out, "did we frighten them? Did our intrusion make them leave this beautiful place?"

Tucker watched their tremulous legions dip and sway across the sky, all moving in tandem toward the horizon. "No, I don't think so. See, some are staying behind. I believe it was just their time to go."

"I'm so glad they stayed long enough for us to see them." Raven turned around and around in the middle of a lush, flower-crested field. "I think we must have stumbled into Papa's fairyland. If we listen, we'll hear the Little People."

"Or maybe it was magic of another kind," Tucker said as he dismounted and came to stand beside her.

"Magic?"

"Remember the butterfly on your mother's carrying bag?"

Raven caught her breath. "Yes. It was gold and black, like the ones here. What does it mean?"

"I never thought I'd say such a thing, Spirit Woman, but maybe these butterflies are a sign that we're on the right track."

"Oh, Tucker, I was so afraid before, but now I understand that I was wrong. We do belong here. This is where we were being led all along. The spirits brought us here."

And there, surrounded by stately fir trees, sparkling water, meadows of wildflowers, and butterflies, Tucker kissed Raven as naturally and beautifully as the surroundings that created the moment.

Freed, the horses drank from the stream, then grazed nearby. Caught up in the magic, Tucker drew Raven down to the meadow and loved her. This time there were no chanting voices, no drumbeats, no waking dreams. This time they were just a man and a woman belonging to each other.

"I'm definitely beginning to believe in your spirit world, Mrs. Farrell," he whispered.

"I certainly hope so, Mr. Farrell. I wouldn't want to be traveling with an unfeeling man." Raven smiled, remembering their lovemaking by the pool. She could never accuse Tucker Farrell of being an unfeeling man. She just wondered if he understood how much she knew.

"Would that I were your love." Tucker repeated the words she'd whispered from her heart.

He knew.

It was late afternoon when the remaining butterflies came to rest in the trees and the flowers closed their petals to the encroaching darkness. Overhead the light of the moon crept over the trees in the east as the remaining rays of the sun leapt behind the next ridge.

"We'd better make camp," Tucker said.

"Why? I like it right where we are."

"The ridges will protect us from the wind, but it will still grow cool before morning." He came to his knees.

"Then you'll just have to warm me again."

"Not unless we get some food into this body. It needs fuel to perform, and we used it up hours ago."

"In that case, you make a fire and I'll cook. I'm afraid you'll have to eat bacon and bread again."

"I've had less."

Once Tucker had the fire going, he looked across the valley. "I think I'll ride back up to the ridge to check behind us."

Raven refused to believe that anyone might be following them. Everything was too beautiful, too perfect. As Tucker built the fire, she stirred up flour for bread and cut chunks of salt pork to be fried. Tomorrow she'd catch some fish, maybe find some wild onions and watercress.

After all, she mused, Tucker Farrell was a big man. He needed a lot of fuel. At least, if she had her way, he was going to.

But it wasn't the Indians or the Mexicans who intruded. It was nearing sunup when a mounted burro came charging down the ridge. Tucker sprang to his feet and pulled on his trousers. Raven quickly slid her dress over her shoulders.

As the burro came closer and saw Yank and Onawa, it broke into squeals of delight and rushed into the clearing.

"Tucker, it's Jonah the burro. What are you doing here?"

"I'm sorry," a familiar voice answered. "I didn't know he'd raise the dead with his caterwauling."

Tucker recognized the rider and swore. "A better question, Mr. Small, would be how'd you find us?"

The newspaper reporter's long skinny legs curved around Jonah's middle like a vise, holding on for dear life. "Be still, you old fool!" he called out, pulling on Jonah's reins, bringing the burro to a sudden stop. The jolt dislodged Small and freed Jonah to join the two horses. "I didn't find you, this burro did."

"And why'd you come after us? You could have been lost in these mountains and never heard from again."

Still sprawled on the ground, the odd-looking young man answered, "I came to warn you. You've been betrayed."

Tucker held out his hand to help the newspaperman stand. "By whom?"

"By Señor Hildalgo. He knows you're looking for treasure and he wants it."

"He and half the population of New Mexico know about the treasure. It's no secret," Raven said crossly. "What do *you* want?"

Mr. Small hesitated. "I want—I thought that you ought to know that a Mexican named Porfiro is looking for you. He's going to wait until you find the treasure and then take it from you."

"We're aware of that," Tucker said.

"But do you know he's working for Hidalgo?"

The confirmation of his suspicion came as no surprise to Tucker. Except he would have guessed the partnership included the bridegroom's father as well.

"I still don't understand," Raven said. "How'd you find Jonah?"

"I bought a scrawny horse from the livery stable. The animal had once belonged to a priest. When we started out of San Felipe, he took off across the mountain and ended up at the village where he'd once lived. A man named Benito took me to the priest."

"Benito." Tucker nodded at Raven. "And how did that get you here?"

"The friar accepted my donation to the church. When he learned of my mission, he suggested that I take this contrary animal. He insisted that if anybody could find you, Jonah would. I just let him go. Seems the priest was right. Have you found the treasure yet?"

Tucker was unable to conceal his dismay. "No. I don't suppose it may have occurred to you that you could be leading Porfiro straight to us."

"His men were still at the fiesta. I don't think they were to start out until morning. They planned to wait outside the walls and follow you. I left long before they did."

"And just what made you decide to warn us?" Tucker growled.

"It was stick with the banker or the two of you. You held more appeal. You don't have to share the treasure with me, Mrs. Farrell. I just want to come along. And I bought a gun, to help you defend yourself against the bandits. See?"

In a scabbard attached to Jonah's saddle was a rifle, new and shiny and almost as long as Jonah was tall.

"Oh, Mr. Small, you took such a risk. If you don't want the treasure, what could you possibly expect to gain?"

"This could be the story of a lifetime. If not, I still want to share the adventure. I have to do this. From the moment I stepped on that stage heading west, I knew that something was pulling me. Now I know what. Haven't you ever wanted something so bad that you'd do anything to make it happen?"

"Yes, I suppose I have," Raven answered softly.

"You're wearing an Indian garment, aren't you, Mrs. Farrell?" Mr. Small asked.

"I am part Arapaho," she replied.

"The dress you wore when you left the stagecoach." He nodded his head happily.

"Yes. Make yourself at home, Mr. Small. I was just about to make breakfast."

Food, she thought, fuel for the body. Though she was chagrined to think, at a time like this, that Mr. Small's presence might mean that Tucker wouldn't require so much fuel for the body.

For the first time in her life, beneath her breath, Raven Alexander let out an Irishman's oath.

16

"Sikya volimu
Hamisi manatu
Talasi yammu
Pitzazgwa timakiang
Tuve-nanguyimani."

After supper Raven stood by the creek singing softly as the last rays of sunlight disappeared.

Tucker came to stand beside her. "What does your song mean?"

"It's about butterflies. A Hopi Indian guest sang it once at our green corn festival."

"Sing it in English."

"I'm not sure I can. Sometimes the translation loses meaning, but I'll try.

'Yellow butterflies,
fly over the blossoming virgin corn,
with pollen-painted faces
chase one another in brilliant throngs.
Bring new life.'"

"The melody of the song sounded very sad, but the words are of hope," Tucker observed.

"Yes, remember I told you that pain precedes joy."

Tucker remembered and his gut tightened at the thought of what had precipitated her words. Across the campfire, Lawrence Small wrote in a notebook. Though he'd cajoled Raven all during supper she'd refused to disclose any information about the treasure they were seeking. Her only comment was that it was lost and she and Tucker were searching for it.

"It could be just a beautiful legend," she'd explained. "Nobody knows that the treasure even exists. You could be risking your life for nothing, Mr. Small."

"Please, Mrs. Farrell," he'd said, "call me Larry. No, make that Lawrence. I left little Larry back in New York with my family."

"Maybe," Tucker had suggested kindly, "that's where you ought to be, also. The West is a tough place for a tenderfoot."

"I really don't want to intrude," the long-legged man said, "but this is very important to me—even if—even if I die in the process."

He hadn't elaborated further. Now Tucker wanted to know more about Lawrence's motives.

"What are we going to do about Small, Raven?"

"I don't know. What do you think? Can he be trusted?"

"It isn't a matter so much of trust as of practicality. He's trouble. We'll have to look after him when we ought to be watching out for ourselves."

"Perhaps," Raven replied. "But there is more to the man than even he believes. He was right about our being pursued. And he is supposed to be here, I'm certain of that."

"Then I'm going to have to get some better answers

than we've heard so far." Tucker returned to the campfire, Raven's hand in his. "Why would you risk your life to come after us, Mr. Small?"

Eagerly the newspaperman closed his notebook, wrapped it in a protective oilcloth cover, and looked up. "It isn't the treasure that matters, it's that I helped find it."

"What will you do when we find the treasure?"

"I'll write the story. Lawrence Small will write a story for all the world to read. I know you don't understand, but that's what's important."

"Why is that so important, Mr. Small—Lawrence?"

He frowned and stared at the fire for a moment. "You may not understand, but I'll try to explain. My father and brothers publish one of the largest newspapers in New York City. They're very good at what they do. I'm not."

Tucker sat on a log he'd drawn to the fire and drew Raven down beside him.

"Why?" Tucker asked. "Why aren't you good at it?"

"I don't know. As a boy I was the kind who tripped over his shoelaces, who turned over the inkwell, who spilled the milk. I'm more like my mother. My brothers— they were exactly right to be newspapermen. They looked the part. They were composed and they fit in anywhere, with men or women, exactly like my father. I'll never fit into his world until I do something special."

"I should think that with proper training, you could learn to write good stories, Lawrence," Raven said. "Perhaps you need to practice writing little stories first. If what you have to say is interesting enough, people will take notice."

He gave a bitter laugh. "I wish that were true, but it isn't."

"Lawrence," Raven insisted, "look at me. I'm a mixed breed. My sisters and my father were white. But my mother was half Indian. I never fit in their world. I had to find my own. So will you."

"Ah, forget about Lawrence. Not even my mother calls me that. I'm just Larry. That's all I'll ever be. And it isn't just writing stories. It's writing stories that people want to read. The only things they'd let me write were advertisements and notices. I figured that if I came out here and wrote about outlaws and gunfighters, I'd prove to everyone that I'm a real newspaperman. That probably sounds silly to you, Mr. Farrell. You're the same kind of man my brothers are."

"No," Raven said softly, "that isn't silly. Everybody wants to be respected. Please, come with us. Whatever we find, you'll share. But promise me you'll wait until we tell you that the story can be told."

Tucker couldn't believe Raven's words. "You're going to let a newspaperman tell the world about the treasure?"

"Once we find the treasure, there will be no keeping it secret anyway. We have to sell it to buy the land. If we allow Lawrence to release the news, he'll do it properly and perhaps we can keep the location secret."

What she said made some kind of sense, Tucker decided. "And you'll agree to that, Lawrence?"

"Certainly, Mr. Farrell. Whatever you say."

"I say you're a lucky man, meeting Raven. We both are."

"Lucky? I like that," Lawrence said. "What would you think about calling me that? Lucky Small. No, not Small. If I'm going to change it, let's go all the way. What about Smith. Lucky Smith, that's a Western name, isn't it?"

"Lucky Smith it is," Tucker agreed. "And we can use another gun. Three people are better than two. All right, it's a deal. But you have to keep up. We don't wait and we don't take the easy way."

"By the way, Lucky," Raven added, "there's something else you should know. We don't know where the treasure is."

"If we never find it, I hope you won't be disappointed, partner," Tucker said.

"Not unless you're disappointed by my confession," Lucky said. "You'll have to show me how to fire the rifle. I've never used one in my life."

Tucker bit back a groan. "Didn't your father believe in teaching you to defend yourself?"

"Yes, but my mother didn't like firearms. The only thing I'm good at is fencing, and I don't think the bad guys out here know a foil from a fencepost."

It was hard sleeping next to Raven and not holding her in his arms. In fact, it was damned impossible. Once he knew that Lucky was sleeping soundly, Tucker rose and led Raven away from the campfire to the meadow where they'd seen the butterflies that afternoon.

"What are you doing, Tucker?"

He drew her down to the grassy carpet and lay over her, his elbows supporting his weight. "I'm just going to kiss you good night. You may welcome Lucky into our camp, but I don't."

"I don't think you have anything to be concerned about. He's a very sound sleeper."

Tucker toyed with a strand of hair that had escaped her braid. What was he doing? A grown man, sneaking a woman off into the night.

"How do you know that?" His voice was more ruthless than he'd intended. She'd turned to face him, her hands sliding up his back, digging into the fabric of his denim shirt while she was adjusting her body beneath him.

"Because," she said breathlessly, "while you were bedding down the horses, he made a big point of telling me."

"And I don't suppose you intended to share that with me?"

"Of course I did. You never gave me a chance."

And then he was kissing her, his tongue seeking the sweetness of her mouth. He rolled away from her for a moment and lifted her dress high enough to reach her bare breasts. For several moments he traced the shape of her body as if he'd never touched it before.

Then his shirt was unbuttoned and their bodies were touching, bare skin against bare skin, heat against heat.

"Raven, this is unbelievable. It's crazy," he murmured. "You shouldn't let me do this. I shouldn't be touching you."

"Why?"

"Because you're meant for more than this, more than just being Tucker Farrell's—"

"Woman? Why?"

"But what about your people, the treasure, your destiny?"

For tonight she was beyond caring about anything but this time, this moment. "Tucker, shut up!" When she touched the bulge in his trousers, he sucked in a breath and followed orders.

He never wanted to stop. He didn't even try. The only treasure he wanted was the one he held in his arms.

"Why didn't you tell me what Lucky said about being a deep sleeper?" Tucker asked later.

"I waited to see what you would do."

"I might have waited too. But I was too eager to touch you again, more eager than you," he said, knowing he shouldn't have let himself love her again.

"Are you sure?"

She turned toward him, throwing her leg over his muscular thighs, pulling herself half on top of him. She was sure he'd been mistaken about who was the most eager. Then her exploring hand found the part of him that was standing ready to disagree.

But disagreeing wasn't nearly so much fun as agreeing. She slid over him, taking him inside her body. Gasping from the sheer pleasure of the act, she held back the truth. She was just as eager, but she'd save that bit of information until a time when she wasn't learning about fire and eruptions.

Later, as they watched the stars twinkling overhead, Raven let out a deep sigh of pleasure. "Is it always like this, Tucker?"

"I hope so," he said softly. "And I hope we spend a very long time proving it."

"So do I." She laid her head on his shoulder and closed her eyes in sleep.

Finally, just before the dawn broke, Tucker pulled a sleepy Raven into his arms and carried her back to camp. He didn't have to hear the exaggerated snoring to know that Lucky had heard their return.

This time he lay down on the blanket and pulled it over them, continuing to hold Raven in his arms.

She was his and he was staking his claim. Nobody would know yet, except Lucky. But Tucker knew and that was enough.

The next morning they started up the valley, following the stream and focusing on the peak where they'd seen the curious slants of light. A band of butterflies danced across the sunshine, as if they were as curious about the travelers as the riders were about them.

"My goodness," Lucky observed, "there are a lot of those big beauties, aren't there?"

Raven held out her hand, upon which one very large golden pair of wings settled down. "Tucker says that this valley is probably where they spend their winters. We saw a great many of them flying north yesterday."

"Too bad I didn't bring my paints. It would make quite a picture, all this color."

Raven rotated her hand and the butterfly flew away. "You paint, Lucky?"

He blushed. "I used to. But the only artwork that a newspaper uses is pen-and-ink drawings, and I'm not very good at that. I just try to catch the feel of a thing. The exact mechanics don't always signify."

"Beauty of the spirit is always harder to express than fact," Raven agreed. "Just look at this place, hidden here for centuries. There is something powerful in knowing that you feel what you see. One day you'll understand what I'm saying."

"In the meantime," Lucky observed philosophically, "the butterflies are our symbols of purity of purpose. I believe they mean that nature approves of what we're doing."

Raven watched him bouncing about on the burro's back and wondered at that idea. For now she had to agree.

It quickly became obvious that Lucky's attempts at riding Jonah were pitiful. Allowing him to walk and pull the animal slowed the two horses down and made the burro frantic. Tucker was convinced that having the newspaperman along would be a hindrance, but he hadn't thought about this kind of problem.

"The only way this is going to work," Tucker finally said, "is for you to ride with me on Yank and let Lucky ride Onawa. Will she allow that?" he asked Raven.

Raven sat quietly for a moment, then nodded. "She will."

Tucker turned to Lucky. "Can you ride a horse?"

"Of course. I had two years of riding lessons. Though I haven't done a great deal of it. Usually I take a buggy."

"It doesn't matter," Raven said comfortingly. "Onawa will take care of you."

Jonah, happy to be rider-free, darted happily between the two horses and danced alongside.

Raven wasn't certain that her best interests were served by planting her body against Tucker's, but once the changes were made, the journey moved faster. She liked being in Tucker's arms, but it was disturbing all the same.

Her body's memories were vivid and she longed for the intimacy of the night before. Not once in her past could she recall hearing anyone describe the feelings between a man and a woman the way she felt about Tucker. Because she had grown up without a mother, these relationships were shrouded in mystery for her.

Of course, there'd been the coming-of-age celebrations in the Indian village, when the young Indian maids and boys danced together, choosing their partners amidst giggles and secret meetings. But even then she'd remained aloof.

Until now.

Happily she leaned back against Tucker and glanced up at him. "Do you think we'll find it today?" she asked.

For a moment Tucker was completely nonplussed. "Find it?"

"The treasure. Isn't that what we're doing?"

Tucker was no longer certain what they were doing. He was awash in sensations that he'd managed to ignore successfully for most of the last twelve years: desire, emotion, a state of constant arousal that no amount of making love seemed to dissipate.

"What makes you think the treasure is here?" Lucky asked.

"We—we don't know. But there were several signs that made us think that the location is up there."

Tucker indicated the mountains beyond the upper bowl edge of the valley.

" 'Up there' covers a lot of territory," Lucky observed. "Can't you be a bit more specific?"

"Not yet," Raven answered, wishing they could. "When we get there, we'll know. Until then we'll just enjoy the ride."

"I don't understand why this place is so green," Lucky said. "It can't be just the stream, for there are streams throughout these mountains and they aren't like this."

"He's right, Tucker. What kind of trees are these?"

"They're pines and fir. They've just been sheltered by the ridges around the valley and protected from the winds so they're full and straight and green."

"Back in New York, I did some research about the pollination of plants, for a story," Lucky offered. "They didn't publish it, but I'm wondering if the butterflies might not have a hand in helping all this grow. And the birds. I've noticed that there are a lot of them."

Tucker agreed. "The birds bring in the seed, fertilize them, and the butterflies pollinate the flowers. Without predators or the elements to interfere, the valley just keeps on replenishing itself."

"Fairyland," Lucky commented. "I'd like to describe it, but I could never do it justice."

Raven nodded. "Perhaps the mountains not only protect its secrecy, but keep it safe from the elements. The outside world can't destroy it if they don't know it's here."

At noon they stopped to rest the horses and allow them to graze and drink from the stream.

"I think I'll wander off down the stream a ways," Lucky said. "I believe I saw some ripe berries back there. You all just go on and do—whatever."

Raven felt her face flush.

"Do whatever?" Tucker grinned. "Do you get the feeling that our friend is trying to play Cupid?"

"I think so."

"Then perhaps we shouldn't disappoint him." Tucker pulled Raven into his arms and kissed her deeply. Finally he leaned back and gazed at Raven's face. Her eyes were glazed with passion.

"I think you'd better stop looking at me like that, Mrs. Farrell."

"Why?"

"Because you're a walking invitation to make love, and we can't keep doing that."

Raven moistened her lips and was rewarded by a second kiss. "I don't see anything wrong with kissing, Tucker."

"But desire takes too much of a man's attention. It isn't that I don't want you. God knows that's all I can think about, and that's the problem."

"Lucky seems to understand. He won't interrupt us."

"It isn't Lucky that worries me." Tucker thrust Raven from him. "When all my being is focused on you, Raven, I don't know what else is happening. Both the bandits and the Indians could be trailing us and I wouldn't know it."

"The spirits would warn us," she argued, not at all certain that her argument was valid.

"I don't know about that. We have a responsibility here too. Don't you remember your dream? The raven was caught in the rocks and the cougar had to rescue it. Think about it. Suppose something happens to the raven in the valley? I'm supposed to help you, that's why I was sent here. Remember?"

Reluctantly Raven had to admit Tucker was right. "Yes, you were sent to guide me to Luce, and you did."

"Then Luce charged me with burying him and finding the treasure."

"And we're doing that," Raven said.

"Yes, but there is more. I never believed in anything spiritual before I met you, but I've been thinking about little else since. Don't you see, all your dreams have been about a cougar, about your animal self, the raven. Your thoughts and dreams have become a reality."

"This is true. But why does that bother you?"

"I'm thinking about my dreams, too, about dreams of birds, of children, of war. There is much that I don't understand, and I don't like not knowing. I think we should turn our attention to our quest. We have to get that behind us before we can trust any of this."

At that point a large black bird flew over, breaking the peaceful silence with his raucous cry. It disturbed the horses and Jonah, who brayed in a shrill, complaining tone.

"You see," Tucker said in a tight voice, "even I can understand a rebuke. We've been warned."

A shiver ran down Raven's spine. Maybe Tucker was right. She was in danger of allowing her own needs to overshadow her mission.

A clearing of the throat announced Lucky's return. "Hello in the camp. Look, berries, red berries. I don't know what they are, but they're sweet and they really taste good."

"Red berries?" Tucker smiled at Raven conspiratorially.

"See," she whispered. "The signs are good. The heavens are watching over us, and the earth gives us pleasure." She took a handful of the berries and popped half into her mouth and handed Tucker the rest. "Trust the spirits, Tucker."

"What the hell?" he said. "Ever heard of a real honest-to-God feel-good tonic, Lucky?" he asked grimly.

"Not one that worked."

"Well, don't give up yet. It might happen someday."

But Tucker wasn't nearly as confident. The mood had been shattered. Realistically and spiritually, Tucker had lost control. He felt as if his essence were turning into liquid and being absorbed by the very ground they were standing on.

The thought was almost too real.

17

In the north, Swift Hand fasted for two days. He smoked the pipe of knowledge and opened his mind to a message from the spirits.

None came.

Angrily he finally ordered his braves to mount up. They'd return to the sacred mountains, to the cabin where their mission had begun. They'd follow the path of the spirit woman. He'd put his fear of the sacred mountains behind him. This time he would not fail. He knew that he was the rightful leader of the Arapaho and he would prove it.

After a day's ride from Luce's cabin, Porfiro reached Father Francis's village. He tortured the priest until Benito finally confessed that the treasure hunters were riding toward the peak of the sacred mountains in the west.

The next morning, leaving the priest badly beaten but still alive, they took Benito captive, forcing him to accompany him to show them the way.

After the second day of searching without finding

Raven, Porfiro was losing his temper. Benito, fearing for his life, finally told the Mexican about the secret valley.

"Señor, I can take you to the valley, but beyond that I cannot go. It is said that the valley is haunted by the Ancient Ones."

"You will take us there. And if I do not find the woman, you will die by my hands."

The valley was deceptively long. From the southern end, great storm clouds, heavy with rain, turned their third day of travel dark. The three travelers were protected from the winds in the low area where they rode, but as the black handfuls of clouds hurled themselves across the sky, Tucker worried. Still in the lowest part of the valley, he was concerned about shelter. In camping by the stream, they'd moved far from the ridges where they might find caves to protect themselves from the rain.

"We need to ride faster," he said, feeling an impending sense of disaster. "I don't like the looks of that sky. We're too exposed here."

"A little rain never hurt anybody."

Tucker dug his heels into Yank's side. "I'm afraid what we're in for isn't a little rain." He knew he was being cross, but he couldn't seem to recapture the carefree spirit they'd enjoyed on seeing the beauty of the hidden oasis.

The end of the valley was still far away when the first drops hit, big, cold drops that easily penetrated their clothing. Then the wind came, dipping over the ridge and slapping them from the side like a sharp hand.

"Whoa!" Lucky called out. "This is looking bad."

Onawa now matched Yank stride for stride, bouncing the poorly prepared Lucky about like the butterflies caught in the fury of the gale. Jonah squealed in protest as he scurried to keep up.

"Looks like the burro has the right name," Raven shouted in Tucker's ear.

"I think your spirits may be just a bit angry," Tucker yelled as he bent forward, wrapping both his arms around Raven. "The bird tried to warn us. Now we're about to get swallowed by Jonah's whale."

They were being drenched now as the storm broke over them in a fury. Thunder rolled. Lightning scissored the sky. Frantically now the horses plunged through the darkness, moving toward the safety of the mountains as if their lives depended on it.

And the rain continued to fall in torrents. For what seemed like hours, they rode, slipping, sliding, and being boxed about by the wind. Now, over the sound of the rain came a roar, distant at first, then stronger.

"What's that noise?" Lucky shouted out.

"I don't know." Tucker lifted his head to judge the distance to the bottom of the mountain. Not too far now. If they could keep the horses from stepping into a hole in their mad rush, they just might make it, but poor Jonah was falling behind.

Then, in a flash of lightning, Tucker identified the sound. Water. The stream was being fed from every crevice plunging down the mountains through the rimrocks, and the water was filling the valley like a bowl. They were about to be drowned by an angry flood.

"Hurry! We have to get up the ridge."

Straining with every ounce of their energy, the two horses plunged toward the rocks, found the first footholds, and started to climb. The three riders made it, but they couldn't see Jonah. As soon as they reached the rocks, Tucker slid to the ground, tugging Raven after him. He couldn't let her die, he wouldn't.

"We can climb better on foot," he said. "You too,

Lucky. Let the horses go. They'll find their own way."
Taking Raven's hand, he started up.

The rain pelted their faces, turning the rocks into
slick obstacles and the spaces between into mud-
entrenched rivulets. The storm rolled and the elements
fought overhead. Tucker gave silent thanks that he
couldn't see where they'd climbed. The trek had been
steep and they were high up the side of the valley.

Just as Tucker despaired of surviving, Raven pulled
on his arm.

"This way." She shouted. "A cave."

Tucker didn't ask how she knew, he simply followed
her, reaching back to make certain that Lucky was still
there.

Moments later they were inside the dark hole in the
earth. They were wet and cold, just like the first time
they'd met. Except this time there were three of them,
and the water below them was rising. Miserably they hud-
dled in the cave, protected from the elements by the
mountain.

Then, just as quickly as it had begun, the storm abated
and the sun shown out in giddy brilliance on the water-
soaked valley below. Like a million tears, the droplets spar-
kled in the sunlight. And even as they watched, the water
began to recede.

"There must be a huge cavern beneath the mountains
to take the water away that quick," Raven observed. "I've
never seen anything like it."

Lucky, still clutching his oilcloth-covered notebooks,
stood at the door to the cave, his eyes opened wide in
awe. "The valley is like a big round bucket with a hole in
it."

Tucker held tight to the edge of the cave and felt his
traitorous knees weaken at the height they'd achieved in

the rain. "So much for the valley being protected from the elements," he said.

"But it doesn't seem to be harmed, and the water brings new life as well. But what about the—" Raven's voice turned sorrowful, "the butterflies, the ones left behind. They couldn't possibly have survived all that."

But even as Raven spoke she saw splashes of yellow and black spring to life above the rain-washed meadows. Across the entire valley, there were hundreds of dots of color. And something more. "Look," Raven cried in delight, "a rainbow."

For Tucker it was too much to take in. Near death, then a rainbow. The three muddy treasure hunters stood in the mouth of the cave taking in the beauty of the scene before them.

Then Lucky frowned. "Where's Jonah?"

"The last I saw of him," Tucker answered, "was when we started up the ridge. He fell behind and the water began to rise. I don't know."

"What about Yank and Onawa?" Raven asked.

"They're somewhere above us," Tucker said with more confidence than he felt. "Let's see what we can do about moving up."

But the way was treacherous, and it was almost more than Tucker could do to force himself to climb. Only by planting his eyes firmly on what lay ahead could he reach back to make certain that Raven stayed alongside. Even Lucky commented that they'd picked the steepest part of the ridge to climb.

Finally, hot and sweaty, they reached the mesa at the top where Yank and Onawa waited beneath the last stand of fir trees extending beyond the greenery of the valley below. But there was no Jonah.

Reluctantly Lucky mounted Onawa as Tucker and a silent Raven rode Yank across the gray ribbon that snaked its way around the mountain and down the slight incline beyond. Once they got past that, they'd be on their way to the jagged rock that Raven was convinced was their destination. They moved slowly now, as if they didn't want to leave the valley.

"I suppose he could swim," Lucky speculated.

"Jonah? With a name like that, I'm certain of it," Raven answered. "He'll probably show up before we camp for the night."

But he didn't and it was obvious that Lucky's appetite was affected by the burro's absence, for he ate sparingly. Finally he stood.

"I think I'll walk back down the trail and see if I can find the rascal. He has my bedroll and food. Would you mind? I'll catch up with you tomorrow. Jonah will know where you are."

Before Tucker and Raven could answer, Lucky was moving off at a rapid clip.

"I'm surprised," Tucker said. "The man isn't used to physical exercise, and he's been in the saddle for two days."

"He has a good heart and he's worried about the burro. I'm worried about him too."

Tucker poured coffee into the pot and breathed in the smell of the strong liquid brewing over the fire. "I'd be a lot more worried about Lucky than Jonah. That burro can take care of himself."

But the burro's disappearance put a pall over the night, and even with Lucky gone, Tucker made no move to be close to Raven. Instead he unfurled their bedrolls apart but close to the fire to dry out the lingering dampness.

He'd have to think about providing food for Raven. They would soon use up the salt pork and flour they'd brought, and so far Tucker hadn't foraged for food in the most lush marketplace they'd encountered. He didn't want to give voice to his reasons. Finding game meant using his pistol, and he couldn't bring himself to disturb the silence with gunfire.

Gunfire carried, and if they were being followed, he'd be pinpointing their location.

Nightfall came and Lucky didn't return.

There was little sleep for either Raven or Tucker that night. Raven slipped inside her blanket, disappointed, but understanding of Tucker's reasons for keeping his distance. Already she was missing the feel of his big, strong body. How would she get along without him now that she'd learned how he made her feel? Waiting in the darkness, she hoped he'd change his mind and reach out for her. But for the first time, he didn't welcome her. There was no heart-stopping kiss. She missed being in his arms and she couldn't forget about the long-legged newspaperman who had been reborn as Lucky Smith. The darkness lay heavy on her heart.

"I hope he is lucky," she whispered. "Please, Mother Earth, look after the man. He only wants to write about your goodness. And look after Tucker, because I care for him."

Swift Hand crested the ridge overlooking the valley before sunset. He looked at the lush green growth in awe. There would be animal life in such a place, food and water. He thanked Mother Earth for her bounty and started toward the floor of the valley. The storm had washed away any trace of Raven, but she was nearby; he could feel her strong presence.

• • •

It was nearly dark when Porfiro and his men viewed the astounding sight of butterflies roosting for the night against the purple hues of the setting sun. He was stunned by the valley, but even more delighted by the possibility of catching up to Señora Farrell and her *americano*.

He was not a superstitious man, but what if Benito were right about this place? With the darkness the valley grew eerily quiet, except for the sound of the night birds. After what had happened back in the village with the birds, it was always better to be safe. They'd make camp at the top and begin their search again in full light.

Quickly he gave the orders. His men tied up Benito and began setting up a fireless camp. Sullenly they ate cold tortillas, cheered only by the wine they'd slipped away from the fiesta. Porfiro chose a dry spot beneath a large tree, wrapped himself in blankets, and went to sleep dreaming of gold and jewels.

Farther down the valley, Swift Hand looked up at the Mexicans and made a gesture of loathing. He was not the only one after the spirit woman. He'd learned enough Spanish to understand the leader's orders. They meant to take the treasure and harm Raven and her man. Swift Hand had no love for the woman who'd usurped his place in the tribe, but she was one of his own, and a good leader looked after all his people.

The fat little man hadn't even set a guard for his own camp. Swift Hand gave a signal to his braves and settled down to wait. At full dark they would water and hobble the horses at the stream below. They were outnumbered. They'd have to take advantage of the Mexicans' being full of wine.

And his men would be quick and silent.

•   •   •

Near the top of the peak, Raven lay in her own bedroll, missing the warmth of being in Tucker's arms. He was only inches away. She should have felt safe, but she was uneasy. She attributed her restlessness to her unfulfilled mission and the ease with which she allowed her feelings for Tucker to interfere.

"What's wrong?" Tucker asked quietly.

"Nothing."

"I don't believe that. You're the calmest person I know and now you can't be still."

She was lying with her head on her arm, looking at the mountain peaks before them. "I guess it's because Lucky and Jonah are missing and I still don't know where the treasure is. I thought we'd have a sign by now. The map shows the valley, the stream, and the peaks, but there are so many. Even my mother's carrying bag doesn't speak to me."

"I know. After we saw the markings on the stones where we buried Luce, I thought we might find them again. But if they were ever there, they're either gone now or we've missed them."

The sun had already passed behind the valley summit and the watery light of the moon had not yet lit the peaks. Already the stars were beginning to blink in the sky. As Raven studied the shadowy ridges she began to feel a shiver creep up her spine.

"Tucker, get that tin pan."

"You want to look at the map in the dark."

"It isn't that dark, and for what I want to see, I won't need light."

Tucker rose and fumbled through the saddlebags, handing the tin pan to Raven as he reclaimed his spot beneath the blanket.

Raven held the plate out in front of her, lifting it

over her head so that she was looking at it against the sky.

"Look, Tucker, these markings we've been studying match up with the stars above the ridges. The spots on Luce's scalp weren't peaks, they were stars!" She kept moving the pan around, changing her position as she looked through it.

"So, what does that tell us? There is no X where the treasure is buried. And besides, the earth turns and the stars move."

"No, we're in the right place. Just look here at these two holes close together. You can see the light of the setting sun through both of them. The others to the left are faint."

"So the stars aren't out yet. The sky is too light."

Raven was getting excited. "No, that isn't it. Flying Cloud told me that Luce would guide me to a place where the light of the moon meets the light of the sun. The two holes on the right have sunlight and the first and second holes on the left have moonlight. Now, the second hole is growing lighter. The light of the moon has caught the light of the sun. It's there, Tucker. There, where they meet. That's where the treasure is hidden."

"And where is that, Raven? I don't have a marker to draw a line downward from that spot, and it's too dark to identify the place."

"But it won't be in the morning. All we have to do is lie right here, where I'm lying now, and hold the plate up to the sky. At the point between the two circles is where we'll find the treasure."

"Sure. Nothing to it."

"We won't know exactly, but as long as we head for the area, we'll find it."

"Let me look," Tucker said, taking the plate. "I can't see a thing. It's all moonlight now."

"And your position is wrong. It has to be seen from where I am. The rimrocks catch the light and throw it back. Oh, Tucker, I'm certain of it. When the light of the moon touches the light of the sun. Tomorrow we'll reach the place. Somehow we'll get a sign."

Tucker dropped back on the ground, uncertain of his feelings. They'd come so far. Raven was convinced that the treasure was really up there in the rocks, waiting for them to find it.

Then what would happen? The thought that their mission was over brought cold chills to his heart. Until now Raven had been caught up in the heat of the chase and her awakening as a woman. Once it was all over, would there be room left in her life for him?

She folded her arms across her chest, holding the tin plate close to her heart, and gave a big sigh of satisfaction. "Oh, Tucker. We're going to do it, find the treasure and buy the land. The Arapaho won't have to go to the reservation, and the spirit of my grandfather will be at peace."

A tight "Yes" was all he could manage. He wanted to throw the pan away, forget about the treasure and—

What?

Raven hadn't been the only one indulging herself in the euphoria of the search. He'd been just as bad. Loving her at night and spending the days searching for a dream come true. The two of them against the elements and their enemies. With their passion to bind them.

Even Lucky hadn't changed anything. For a time, he'd been welcomed into their little fantasy. Where was the man? Tucker had wanted to go back and search for him, but Raven had said no. He was all right. He'd find them sooner or later. And Tucker was forced to bow to her wisdom.

But now all that was about to come to an end. And

Tucker Farrell, cowboy and drifter, would become a drifter again. Except before, what he did and where he did it was unimportant. This time he felt empty. Empty and full of longing. Without a purpose, he hadn't cared what happened.

The cold hard truth was—now he cared.

Lucky, still searching for Jonah, slipped and sloshed across the meadow. It was very late when he finally faced the fact that he was lost.

He had to rest. The lower valley was too wet to bed down in. He headed for a section of rock that shone white in the moonlight. Nearby was an elevated stand of trees. With any luck he could find a spot there where the water had receded. By fashioning some kind of bed made of boughs, maybe he'd get some sleep, then retrace his steps in the morning.

But the white rocks weren't just rocks; the color came from a coating of slippery mud. His first attempt to cross over sent him rolling down the gooey substance, covering him head to toe with a shimmering coating of white. He even had mud in his eyelashes.

"Ah, heck!" He'd done it again, fallen on his face. Now what would Raven and Tucker think? He'd better wash the mud away before it hardened.

He trudged back toward the stream. Exhausted almost to the point of dropping where he stood, Lucky stopped worrying about being careful and, pushing his way through a stand of brush, came out on a huge rock overlooking the creek.

At that moment the moon, just about to drop behind the trees, slanted a sharp light across the valley. A gust of wind swept down from the north, its sound becoming a low moan in the silence as if the valley were speaking.

"Mother of God!" he exclaimed, his voice echoing eerily across the valley.

Lucky was stunned when five shadowy figures sprang to their feet and drew their rifles. They were Indians, not Mexicans, watering their horses and caught completely unaware.

Then the Indian leader saw Lucky and fell to his knees. The braves were pointing up at him and backing away in terror. He looked down at himself and understood. When the moonlight struck the mud, it picked up traces of silver and made his body look as if it were sprinkled with stardust.

"The keeper of the sacred mountains," Swift Hand called out. "The Ancient One."

Lucky didn't know what the Indian meant, but it was clear that he thought Lucky was some kind of god or spirit.

Why not make them really believe it? He started to moan, softly at first, then louder. He waved his arms and stomped his feet.

"Aio ooo ohhhh. Um bah. Um bah. Aio ooo ohhhh."

As Lucky lapsed into a mock Indian chant, the Indians cried out in terror.

Across the valley, Porfiro, already awakened by the unidentified curse, heard the war chant, then the screams. "Indians." He swore. He and his men were too close to the treasure to turn back. But they weren't the only ones following the spirit woman.

"Spirits," Benito contradicted. "These are sacred mountains. You are being warned away."

Porfiro considered his situation. He didn't believe for one minute that what he'd heard was ghosts. There were Indians in the valley. Obviously they were unaware of his presence or they would have attacked the camp. He didn't know what they were doing, but so long as the noise continued, they were safe.

"Take cover," he ordered.

The frightened bandits, half asleep, searched for rocks and bushes to hide behind.

Porfiro didn't know how long it was until morning, but he feared that the Indians were holding some kind of battle ceremony, perhaps a war dance. Having already met a band of renegades who'd killed too many of his followers, he didn't want to take any chances. Still, his own men were about to bolt.

"Don't soil your trousers. The savages don't attack at night," he said in a low voice.

"No," Benito chided, "but the spirits do."

Porfiro swallowed his uncertainty. "Be silent, old man!"

Before Benito could argue, they heard the frantic sound of ponies galloping away in a mad withdrawal. The sound of their hoofbeats receded as they headed into the cover of the trees and up the valley, cresting the ridge beyond.

"What was that all about?" the bandit called Juan asked warily.

"Indians," Porfiro answered. "Spirits don't ride horses."

"No, I mean before. What made that unholy sound I heard?"

"I told you," Benito said softly, "it was the keeper of the sacred mountains. Those who come to this place unwanted, die."

"Gag him before I decide to kill him," Porfiro ordered.

Once Juan had complied, they settled in to wait for morning.

By the time the sunlight slid across the valley, Porfiro knew that the bandits were bordering on giving up the treasure hunt. He couldn't deny that he, too, felt something spooky, as if they were being watched. But by whom? The Indians were gone. Raven and the *americano* were no threat against such great odds.

And he refused to believe in any spirit keeper.

"Mount up, men. Let's find that treasure. Just think of all the señoritas and wine we can buy. We will be rich!"

Sluggishly they complied. For most of the day, they fanned across the valley, until they found Raven and Tucker's campsite on the mesa. By that time it was nearly dark, and Porfiro decided they were close enough to pull up. If they were going to allow the spirit woman to lead them to the treasure, they did not want to interfere with her search.

They made a cold camp and, fearing the return of the keeper of the sacred mountains, each man slept with his rifle loaded and laid across his chest.

Tucker was growing more and more uneasy. Raven slept quietly beside him. Lucky was still gone. Yank and Onawa moved about restlessly. Tucker's eyes felt as if they were filled with river sand when he finally closed them. The moon was high in the sky. When the dream started, he wasn't sure for a moment whether it was real or whether he was asleep.

They were in a cave, a dark cave with walls and a ceiling like those of a room. The walls were all gray and damp, except for the wall directly ahead. It was lighter in color and smooth. They couldn't go forward and they couldn't return. Raven leaned against the wall, crying. He started toward her when the earth began to move and the floor of the cave cracked open, swallowing her up in the fissure that formed.

Crawling to the side, Tucker peered down. He could see her at the bottom of the crack in the earth. She was standing in an odd yellow light, surrounded by brightness.

"Tucker, we've found it!" she cried out. "I told you we would. A mountain of gold and jewels! Come down and get yours!"

"Raven, come up!" he called out. "It isn't safe. You could be crushed."

"No, we've found the treasure. Tucker, you have to help me."

But he couldn't. His knees buckled and his lungs collapsed. He couldn't draw air into them and he was frozen where he lay.

Then the earth began to tremble again. Raven would be trapped down there with her treasure. She'd found what she was seeking, but he was about to lose her and there was nothing he could do.

Panting and terrified, Tucker awoke and sat straight up. It was morning. Raven was holding the plate in front of her, then moving it away and studying the ridges before them.

"I think I've spotted it," she said. "Look there, where the light-colored peak joins the jagged edge of the black rock. Do you see it, in the middle, about halfway up?"

"I see it."

"Let's move out quickly." She began to scatter the fire.

"No, stop." He grabbed her arm. "I've changed my mind. You aren't going up there."

She turned toward him, her face filled with surprise. "What do you mean? Of course I am. If you wish to remain behind, I'll understand."

"You think I'm afraid?"

"I wouldn't hold you responsible if you changed your mind, Tucker. You've already done more than I had any right to expect."

"You don't understand." His voice was so low that she could barely understand the words. "You'll be hurt."

"Tucker, I've already been hurt. I've been captured by Swift Hand and I've survived a flood."

"But this is different. You're going to fall and I—I can't—"

She put her hands on his muscular arms and searched his face. "What's wrong, Tucker?"

"I had a dream. I saw the treasure and I saw—"

"You saw me get hurt?"

"No, not really. I just saw you fall and then I woke up."

"Thank you," she whispered, and leaned up to kiss him. "I know you care for me, but I have to go on, with or without you."

Tucker was defeated. He couldn't stop her. He couldn't let her go on alone. The forces of nature had set things into motion, and nothing could stop them.

"Then we must eat," he said, building up the fire. "We don't know how far we have to go or what will happen."

Reluctantly Raven prepared the last of their salt pork and made a skilletful of bread. They drank their coffee and ate quickly. Then Raven, regal and stoic, was ready to go. Tucker, reluctant and silent, accompanied her.

By midmorning they'd reached what appeared to be a dozen dead ends, only to find at the last minute a space where the rocks seemed to open up and they were finally able to get through. They were halfway to the rocks that Raven had marked. At noon they rested the horses, ate the last chunks of the bread, and washed them down with water from the stream that ran along beside their path. At sunset they'd reached a flat area at the base of the rocks she'd kept in her sight for the entire day.

Tucker figured they were within an hour's climb of their destination. Lacy patches of clouds floated low, swirling around them and moving down the valley behind. An eerie sense of forboding settled in with the fog. Even the birds had hushed. Tucker had spent the last two hours searching the rocks overhead and the slope behind.

He couldn't explain the feeling he had. But if the area weren't so barren, he would swear that they were being watched. The dream, he decided. It had spooked him and he couldn't get rid of the image of Raven at the bottom of that crack in the earth.

"We'll camp here for the night and wait for good light before we go higher," he finally said.

"But we're so close," Raven argued.

"And in our haste we could make a mistake. We haven't come this far to do something foolish."

She could tell by his tone of voice that arguing would be useless, so she agreed. "We have nothing left but coffee."

"I'll see if I can find a rabbit before dark." He checked his pistol and started across the side of the ridge, moving quietly but steadily. It was almost dark when he spotted the deep pool that bowed out from the stream. Two shadows flitted about the water.

Fish would be just as good as a rabbit, and they didn't require him to fire his pistol. He didn't want to call attention to their location. Besides, he hadn't seen anything moving until now. He studied the pool. If he dislodged the rocks at the lower edge of the enclosure, the water would drain out. If he did it just right, he'd capture at least one of the fish.

He was lucky. The downward pull of the water kept the fish from moving back toward the stream, and by placing the rocks he moved at the upper edge of the pool, he kept most of the stream water from refilling the hollowed-out space. In less than ten minutes, he had two big trout, dressed and strung on a limb for carrying. Supper without firing a shot.

That was important. He knew in his bones that they were being followed by something or someone. He wished he knew whether it was the bandits or the Indians.

While Tucker was gone, Raven explored the area. The ridges were made of red boulders rolled downward from the red-and-tan limestone cliffs. Layers of clay seemed to hold the rocks together. Nestled among them were little pockets of greasewood and prickly pear, a cactus that promised retribution if they made the wrong move.

Tucker had been wise to bring them to a stop. Falling was probably the least of the potential dangers ahead. The silence was broken by a swarm of Mexican swallows swooping toward one of the cliffs protected from the sun by another ridge. The birds had built mud nests on the face of the rock, and she could see little heads poking through holes in the center of the cones. When the birds flew near, she could hear the tiny fledglings screeching to be fed.

As she headed back to camp, Raven was pleasantly surprised to come upon a patch of glistening green-leafed plants. With the wandlike blades thrusting out in all directions and a single stem in the center holding up clusters of white blossoms, she recognized the plants as sotol. With a knife she dug the dirt away from the bulb from which the roots dug down into a rare patch of rich earth. She chopped away the leaves, revealing a pineapple-shaped cone, which she buried in the coals of the fire. It would make a good meal if Tucker did not find meat.

When he returned with fish, she set a spit to cook them over the open fire. Later they split open the sotol bulb, peeling away the scorched and blackened exterior to get at the layers of fruit circling the core like that of an onion. Blowing on their fingers, they ate the particles of hot, sweet-tasting food.

"It isn't something I'd go out of my way to get," Tucker admitted, "but it's filling."

That, the fish, and the coffee satisfied their hunger, leaving enough for tomorrow. After eating, they laid out their blankets, determined to get a good night's sleep in order to get an early start.

In spite of her growing excitement, Raven willed herself to concentrate on her goal. Tonight she refused to have any fears or worries. She refused to think about Tucker or tomorrow.

Success meant buying the land for her people. Success meant Tucker could have his ranch in Oregon. Failure meant that the Arapaho would have to go to the reservation and Tucker would have no reason to go far away.

Success meant losing Tucker. Failure gave her a chance to keep him.

Success could bring great happiness—and great pain.

Tucker slept fitfully. Even when Raven moved over to his blanket, slid her thigh across his, and snuggled close, she felt no reassuring warmth as she had in nights past. But finally she slept.

At some point Tucker came suddenly awake. He couldn't hear anything, but he knew that Raven was in his arms.

Where she belonged.

Still, he couldn't rest easy. Were Swift Hand and his braves still looking for Raven? Where were Porfiro and his men? Where were Lucky and Jonah? Tucker made up his mind that if the newspaperman didn't turn up by morning, they'd go back and look for him.

Where would they be tomorrow night?

The tone of their journey had changed the moment

Raven discovered the secret of the map. And tomorrow, if his dream became reality, their journey would end.

Tucker felt a great pain tear at his heart. Moisture gathered in his eyes. In the distance he heard the lonely sound of a mountain lion, voicing his feelings for all those listening to know.

Tucker understood the big cat's pain.

18

It was just after dawn the next morning when a wet but reasonably clean Lucky heard Jonah's weak squeal of outrage.

The feisty little animal was knee-deep in the wet sand left by the flood. Lucky's first attempt at rescue resulted in his losing one shoe and almost getting stuck himself.

Remembering the hours of reading he'd done in his father's library, he recalled his fascination with quicksand. This mess wasn't that kind of mire, exactly, but it was the same principle. What he needed was something he could hook into Jonah's saddle so that he could pull the burro out of the labyrinth.

There seemed to be nothing at hand.

Finally he tried laying fronds of brush across the sand. They floated. From broken leaves, he went to tree limbs. While not floating exactly, they managed to remain on the surface. Jonah seemed to understand that Lucky was trying to help him and, for the first time in their acquaintance, waited uncomplaining.

By laying the limbs in a grid pattern, Lucky was able to lie flat across his creation and inch himself forward until he could reach the beast. After an initial flurry that threatened to pull Lucky into the mush, he managed to tug Jonah across the end of one of the branches. When he didn't sink, the quick-thinking burro allowed himself to be pulled by Lucky, who backed away from the trouble.

Finally back on firm ground, Jonah paused long enough for Lucky to grab bread and cheese from the pack before he took off up the valley toward the place where he'd been swept away. Lucky, wearing only one shoe, was forced to travel more slowly.

As if he knew what he was doing, the burro stopped to graze, allowing Lucky to catch up. Nightfall brought them to a flat ridge at the base of the peaks where he discovered Raven and Tucker's camp. From its location he guessed it was from the night he went back for Jonah. Lucky decided to make camp there. Walking in the daylight was bad enough. The dark would only bring him a broken leg. At least, with Jonah's return, he had his bedroll and supplies. After writing up his extraordinary adventure in his notebook, Lucky bedded down for the night.

It was the next morning when he heard the ponies approaching. Quickly Lucky came to his feet and searched for Jonah, who was nowhere to be seen.

Lucky started up the slope, then, realizing not only that he'd be seen, but that he'd leave a trail, he backed down the way he'd started until he reached a stand of fir trees. Tree climbing was another activity he'd never learned, but when in danger of being caught, he found it was easier than he'd expected.

Perched near the trunk of the tree on a limb with heavy foliage, he watched in the olive gray of the dawn as four bandits passed beneath his hiding place.

Porfiro, in the lead, rode slowly, studying the ground. Suddenly there was a call from someone riding closer to the stream. The four riders turned under the tree and rode out of sight.

All Lucky understood from their conversation was the word "Raven." Porfiro's men had found something that drew their attention. Obviously the bandits had found Raven and Tucker's trail.

At that moment he caught sight of Jonah, just barely visible, halfway up the ridge. He seemed to be moving in a circular direction, and as Lucky watched, the burro disappeared from sight.

Taking a deep breath, Lucky slid back down the tree and took off, following the tree line as far as it went, then crouching behind the rocks until he found a narrow path.

Lucky took a quick look back and saw the Spanish ponies about two hundred yards across and halfway down the ridge. The bandits had dismounted and were studying the ground.

Lucky didn't know what had held up their ascent, but he said a small prayer that he was ahead of them. He'd reached a point where he could zigzag back and forth behind the rocks and not be seen. Beneath his feet, in the soft mud, he could clearly see Jonah's hoofprints.

For better than an hour, he climbed before coming to an open place with little shelter. He could be seen by the Mexicans below. Did he dare risk exposing himself?

Did he dare not?

If they attacked him, he'd just fling his arms about and yell like a madman. It had worked for the Indians. If the picture of a man going crazy in the wilderness didn't scare them to death, at least it would warn Raven and Tucker—if they were still alive—if they were anywhere around.

He took a deep breath and slipped the last few feet and climbed into the open space, pausing for a moment as he listened for a sign of recognition.

None came.

But he did find Jonah, waiting behind an outcropping of rocks.

"All right, Jonah, let's find our friends."

As if on command, the scrawny beast took off an at angle away from the Mexicans and headed up.

Lucky almost made it to the rocks.

Almost, but not quite.

A shout from below said that he'd been seen.

"Did you hear something?" Raven asked, inclining her head to listen.

"Just falling rocks and the wind," Tucker answered, wiping the perspiration from his face with his bandanna. "Are you sure this is where we ought to be? It seems too easy."

After the flat section below, the travel up had followed a wandering trail, steep but reasonably open. Tucker attributed its smoothness to the mountain goats that occupied the area.

"If the treasure is concealed in a mountain, it has to be a place where the treasure could be carried," she said.

"Who had it, and who carried it?"

"Flying Cloud said that his people took it from the conquerors who stole their land. That's all I know."

"Well, I'm beginning to think that the whole bunch of them dreamed this up during a peyote party."

As she turned to answer he saw it, on a rock just over her head. A crude red drawing of what appeared to be a sun being blown off course by wavy lines. "Look, Spirit Woman. You were right."

She turned back toward the side of the mountain. It was there, the symbol on her mother's carrying bag. Worn by the elements, chiseled into the uneven pattern of the rock, but still there.

For a long second, she just looked, her knees wobbling, her breath caught in her throat. "You were right, Grandfather. You were right."

As she stood an even greater weakness swept over her. The familiar sound of drums and chanting began. Then came a thrumming in the earth beneath her feet. She could feel them, the clip of hoofbeats, the movement of animals up the same trail they'd just covered. The air grew thick. Sunlight faded to a blur of hazy movement. And suddenly she was there beside the burros, watching them as they moved into the mountain, one by one, each burdened down with the spoils of the armor-clad thieves who had stolen the treasure from the Indians in the South and West. After raping the area of treasure, they were moving it to the ships along the Gulf of Mexico, taking what they'd stolen back to Spain.

"No," she whispered, "it isn't yours."

"Raven? What's wrong?" Tucker asked. But she didn't answer.

Then, as if she were alone, she began to move through the rocks, leaving the present behind. Tucker let go of Yank's reins and followed. Sliding through crevices and into space that wasn't there one moment and seemed to open up before her the next, she moved.

Driven. Drawn. Finally she reached a low, narrow opening that looked as if an animal had scratched it out. As if she suddenly remembered Tucker's presence, she stopped and turned back to him.

"We need torches."

"How? What?"

"Use my petticoat. Tie it on a limb. Dip it in the jar of bear grease in the saddlebags and bring it here. And get the shovel," she instructed. Then, inclining her head, she listened. "Someone comes. We must hurry."

Tucker didn't question how or what she'd seen. Too many times she'd been right in this crazy adventure. If she said someone was coming, someone was coming. He hurried back to the horses, removed the saddlebags, and searched for the necessary objects, wasting precious minutes before he found a limb.

At the last second, he swatted Onawa and Yank on the rear, sending them up the trail around the mountain peak. Whoever was coming behind them should follow the horses, leaving him and Raven behind.

Quickly he returned to the spot where Raven waited.

"We have to crawl through this hole," she said. "Can you do it?"

He looked at the hole and down at himself. "I'll make it."

"Good. I'll go first. You light the torch and hand it to me."

"I'll go first."

"No, Tucker. It must be me."

He wanted to argue, but something about the set of her shoulders told him that would be futile. He nodded.

She dropped to her knees and started through the opening. There was little clearance for her. Tucker wondered how he was going to follow. He wasn't sure he could even force himself to try. Then she disappeared into the mountain and he knew he had to do it.

He lit the torch and handed it through the hole, then pushed his head inside. His shoulders touched the sides. He couldn't even lift his head to look. A moment of panic swept over him. He was about to get stuck, and both he and Raven would be trapped forever in a tomb of treasure.

Then, as he inched forward, the sides of the rock became slick, as if they were greased. After what seemed like an eternity, the darkness began to grow light, and suddenly he was through the hole into a chamber. Raven was holding the torch high, lighting the small, cool, empty cavern with a vaulted ceiling.

"Look, Tucker. What do you make of this?"

She was standing before the far wall, moving the torch up and down.

Tucker joined her, studying the smooth light-colored surface. "It looks like some kind of clay wall. But it's almost too smooth."

"That's what I thought. Somebody built it here."

Tucker ran his hand over the surface. "But how? And why?"

"There are pockets of mud throughout these mountains. The swallows build their nests in them. Someone probably brought the mud in here to build this wall. The treasure is behind here. I know it."

Tucker put his head against the wall and tapped. He moved down a few feet and tapped again. "I believe it's hollow behind, at least for a section in the middle."

Raven lifted the torch and stood back. "Use the shovel. Break into it."

"Are you sure that's a good idea? Remember Luce's warning."

" 'Beware the bronze dagger.' " Raven looked around again. "I don't see any sign of a bronze dagger, do you?"

"No, but suppose it isn't what we think it is. It could be some kind of trap."

Raven leaned against the wall and closed her eyes. "I don't think it means us harm. We're supposed to do this, Tucker. I feel it."

"Maybe we shouldn't be in a big hurry. Let me look around some more."

"No! We don't have much time. Give me the shovel. I'll use it."

"No you won't, Raven. If you insist, I'll do it."

Using the shovel like a pick, he broke through the thin layer of mud with little effort.

"I feel like one of those swallows, pecking a hole for a nest," he mumbled as he reached into the space behind. The mud was dry and easy to crumble under the pressure of his strength. Their torch was beginning to die as he widened the hole. Soon he had a hole large enough to poke his head through.

"We'll take a quick look, then we'll have to go back and get more light."

"Let me see," Raven said.

He stepped back and let her go. It was her quest, her treasure. It was only fitting that she have the first look at whatever was beyond.

"Tucker, there is a very large statue standing in the entrance. I believe he's made of bronze. Maybe that's what the warning is about. He seems to be guarding the treasure."

The shadow man he'd seen in the vision at Luce's pool. It was real. "We have to have more light."

"I can get to the outside and back quicker." Raven turned toward the entrance. "Wait for me."

"The saddlebags are hidden outside the hole," Tucker said. "I sent the horses up the mountain so that if someone is behind us, they'll follow them."

"What if it's Lucky?" she asked.

"He'll probably fall in the hole and find us by accident."

"Wait here," Raven ordered and disappeared outside.

"I wouldn't dream of leaving." Tucker gave a snappy salute. As soon as she was out of sight, he began to dig in earnest. If there was danger from the statue, he wanted to find it before she returned. Widening the opening, he exposed two huge feet, laced in sandals. Two massive legs were attached to a short skirt. Above the torso were two hands folded across the warrior's chest.

No, he decided as he broke through the upper section of the hole, not folded, they were holding some kind of crossbow, set with a dagger, ready to be fired.

A dagger.

The bronze dagger.

There was a creak and Tucker dropped down instinctively. He didn't know what he was facing, but he wasn't taking any changes on having that thing topple over on him.

At that second the torch burned out, leaving the cave pitch-black.

Tucker closed his eyes for a long moment. Logically he knew where he was. Raven would return with another torch and they'd be fine.

If she returned.

If she could fashion another torch.

He might have remained calm, except for the sudden rush of movement somewhere overhead. Rocks fell. There was a large creak and the statue seemed to groan. Something, or someone, was up there.

He had to protect Raven.

Tucker opened his eyes.

An unexpected faint glow of light inside the hole he'd just made kept the cave from being totally black.

He heard the sound of Raven's return behind him. She handed him another torch.

"There's light inside." She hurried to the opening and wiggled through.

"Wait, Raven. We don't know—"

"Tucker," she said in a voice filled with awe. "We've found it. It's really here, the lost treasure of the Arapaho people. Can you get through?"

Throwing caution to the winds, Tucker quickly widened the opening and pushed through, sliding around the bronze body into a cave washed with a stream of light from overhead. Sitting in the midst of gold and jewels was Raven. She'd dropped the unlit torch and was holding a golden cord laced with rubies in one hand and an elaborate Spanish comb of gold and jewels in the other.

For a moment Tucker was so stunned by the opulence of the treasure that he couldn't speak. The baskets that had once held the bounty had partially disintegrated over time, allowing coins and nuggets to spill across the floor. There were jeweled crosses, bowls, statues, and swords, all glowing in the dim light.

"Where'd the beacon of light come from?" he asked.

"Look up."

Overhead he saw a fissure in the roof of the cavern, through which the sunlight slanted. A man couldn't get through the crack, and unless he were on top of the spot and looked through at exactly the right time of day, the cavern would never been seen.

Tucker couldn't refrain from touching the jewels. For just a moment, he was giddy with a feeling of euphoria. He'd never truly believed that the treasure existed. And even if he had believed in it, he would never have expected to find it.

There were gold pieces, pearls and rubies as big as robin eggs. One huge ruby was attached to the point of a crown, with other jewels forming an elaborate design along its crest.

Raven took the crown and plopped it on Tucker's head. Lifting an emerald-encrusted sword, she tapped each shoulder, then his forehead. "Tucker Farrell, I proclaim you king of the sacred mountain."

"And I declare you to be my queen." He planted the prongs of the Spanish comb in the weave of her braid.

Around her neck he draped ropes of pearls, and on her slender wrists, he threaded bands of golden bracelets.

"I didn't believe you, Raven," he said. "I'm sorry."

"You didn't have to," she answered. "I knew we would find it."

"And did your visions tell you how we're going to get all this back to civilization?" he asked curiously, only now beginning to realize how remarkable their find truly was.

"We aren't. One of the first things an Arapaho learns is that the earth provides. We take what we need, but we do not take more."

Her reply was as beautiful as her bejeweled body. Tucker knew as they looked at each other that it wasn't just the treasure that was remarkable, it was the woman and what they'd been through together.

He'd feel humble in her presence if they'd never found the treasure. Then it suddenly hit him; the search was over. Their time together was about to end.

He felt a pain squeeze him, twisting his insides until he thought he would die of it.

"No," he whispered. "I don't want this."

"I don't understand," Raven said. "This is what we set out to find. Why don't you want it now?"

"Because—" *Because I'll lose you*, he thought, realizing that what he felt for Raven was more than just physical, more than admiration, more than need. He'd turned his back on possessions, on any kind of future. He'd lost everything he once loved and he'd worked hard at not filling those dark places in his life. Now his tightly protected life had been ripped open.

Raven had slid inside and wrapped herself around his heart. It hadn't just been about protecting her; he'd been healing the pain of the past and now he had nothing to hold on to. The hate was gone, replaced with responsibility and desire. The past was dead and the future was laid out.

A ranch in Oregon. A new life.

Alone.

No, that wasn't what he wanted. He wanted Raven— forever.

"I don't want the treasure," he said, "because we'll never get out of the valley with it."

Her eyes widened, dark and wet. "We must, Tucker."

"No. This time the voice inside of me is saying 'Go.' This is too big a risk, Raven. Always before I—"

Always before, he'd gone, left before he was confronted with taking a chance. That's what he'd done since the war. That's what he was urging Raven to do, take the safe way. Give up without trying.

Why hadn't he realized it before? If he left before he had to take a chance on happiness, he would avoid the hurt that he might feel instead.

But we have to feel the pain, else how will we appreciate the joy? That's what Raven had said when he'd made love to her. She understood that all along, and she was willing to take the risk. Still, this was her life he was talking about, not his. And he didn't want her to take the risk.

"Let's get out of here. We don't need this, Raven. I'll find a place for us. I'll take care of you. I—"

She reached out and took his hand. "I know that you want to spare me pain. Thank you for that, Tucker, but I have to see this through. What I might want is unimportant. This is my destiny. Whatever happens was meant to be."

He was going to lose her. The very thing he'd tried to avoid was going to happen. "What about us?"

"If we are to be together, we will be. If not, we will survive."

"Raven, I don't want any spiritual answers. I'm just a

man and you're a very special woman. All this has been some kind of dream, from the moment we ended up on that ledge together. I guess what I'm asking is for us to wake up and be ordinary people."

"It's not a dream, Tucker. Look around you, it's real. We're real and there is nothing ordinary about either of us."

Nothing about what was happening seemed real except the cold spot in his heart. Not even the tremor he felt beneath his boots. Not even the creaking that had begun in the walls of the mountain.

"I think your sacred mountain is angry, Raven. I thought I heard something earlier, now I'm sure of it."

"What?"

"There was someone overhead. Loose rock must have fallen through the crack and set off tremors inside the cave."

"An animal, a mountain goat." She looked up at the crevice, hoping it was an animal and not their pursuers.

"Hello, down there," a low whispery voice called out as a shadow fell across the opening. "Mrs. Farrell?"

"Lucky? Is that you?"

"Yes. How'd you get down there?"

"There's a small tunnel in the mountain. I'll come and get you." Raven started back toward the statue.

"No, don't do that. Porfiro and his men are headed toward us. I just climbed up here to hide. You stay put and I'll try to lead them away."

"No, Lucky. You don't know the mountain. You'll get hurt."

"Don't try to stop me, Mrs. Farrell. This is the most exciting thing I've ever done."

There was another tremble, another crackling noise as the mountain seemed to shudder. Next came a noticeable ripple in the rocky floor on which they stood.

"Raven, I think we'd better get out of this cave."

Raven was torn between her concern for Tucker and Lucky and fulfilling her mission. Surely Mother Earth wouldn't let them find the treasure, then keep them from using it to save her people.

"You must leave, Tucker. Removing the treasure was never your responsibility. I don't want you to be hurt."

"Sure, I'll just step outside and tell Porfiro that the mountain is unhappy with his presence. He'll have to go."

Tucker was making a joke, but she was only too aware that Porfiro's men were behind them and the tremors were getting worse. Overhead, particles of earth sifted down. Beneath their feet, cracks were beginning to etch across the floor.

"I can't leave, Tucker. I can't come so far and fail. It wasn't meant to be like this."

"You can't know what the spirits planned," Tucker argued, studying the interior more carefully. If the bandits were behind them, they might have to find another way out. The cavern was large, but there seemed to be no tunnels leading away. Only the rift in the ceiling.

"Remember my dream, Raven. I think it was a vision. You're going to fall. Please, let's take our chances with Porfiro and get out of here, now!"

And then they heard it, a shout in the small cave behind them. It echoed across the cavern, bouncing off the walls.

"Porfiro!" Raven said, defeat written across her face. "He's found us. All was for naught."

"Not so, Spirit Woman," Tucker said. "There's one thing that we know that Porfiro doesn't."

"What?"

"To beware the bronze dagger."

19

Raven looked at Tucker with fear in her heart. She'd brought him to this place and now he was going to die. All her life she'd been convinced that she was destined to do something remarkable. Flying Cloud had never told her what the future held for her, only that she'd been chosen by the spirits, that someday she'd understand why.

But she hadn't known that it would mean such sacrifice. Losing Tucker would take a piece of her heart, but she would survive if the spirits ordained. Being responsible for his death was different. How could she sacrifice someone she cared about?

Yet she had.

And now she was going to lose the man she loved.

Love.

When had that happened? Gradually, without her even realizing it, he'd made a place for himself in her life. Announcing that he'd stay around to protect her, that they'd see the treasure hunt through to the end, taking care of her.

She'd watched her sisters fall in love, each in a different way. But she'd never thought about what it meant. To love a man was to give him every part of yourself.

Raven Alexander could never do that, for she had a higher calling, a goal she was putting in jeopardy. The spirits were angry with her. She was being punished.

Now her throat tightened and her heart thumped wildly. She wanted to put her arms around Tucker, hold him, tell him how sorry she was that she'd brought him here. If he died, a part of her that she was only just now discovering would die with him.

She wanted to tell him she loved him, but she couldn't. The feelings were too new.

And she'd never know his heart, never know if what he felt for her was anything other than a responsibility and a physical attraction.

The earth rumbled, its growl intensifying. Overhead, Lucky said that Porfiro had set a guard, then disappeared into the mountain with his men. Lucky couldn't move without either falling or being discovered. Then there was a scuffling noise in the outer chamber.

"Look, amigo," a voice called out, "there is another passageway beyond."

Raven backed away from the statue. But there was nowhere to run. Belatedly she wished they'd followed Tucker's suggestion that they leave the cave and the treasure behind. But she'd been so consumed by their discovery that she hadn't thought she might endanger Tucker or that they might die.

"Look, there is a pale light through the hole in the wall," one of the bandits yelled.

The constant shifting of the earth beneath them rattled the bars of gold, clanking them together. The sound signaled to the intruders that there was something more than light through the hole.

Any minute now the bandits would be inside, and Raven's quest would be over. They'd come so far.

There was a loud crash and a wrench of the rock overhead. Mother Earth closed the two sides of the ceiling together, shutting out the light from above.

From outside came curses and heavy thuds as the men were flung about in the darkness.

"Porfiro, I cannot see. What shall we do?"

"We strike a match."

There was a scratching sound, then a feeble light flickered for a minute and died.

"It is no use, Porfiro, the match it's not big enough. I think we need to go back."

"Juan, I will not lose the treasure before I've found it. What we need is a torch. Crawl through the hole and fashion one, quickly."

Another tremble of the earth set off dust and debris that fell in chunks from the ceiling.

"Raven." Tucker started toward her.

At that moment the ground shifted violently. A portion of the overhead rock gave way, dropping a startled Lucky into the midst of the treasure with a thud.

As the dust settled, Tucker and Raven made their way to Lucky's side.

"Are you hurt?" Raven asked, trying to maintain her balance with the very earth heaving beneath their feet.

"No, I don't think so. But—oh my, look at all this!" Lucky gathered handfuls of the jewels, letting them trail through his fingers. "You found the treasure!"

"We found the treasure," Raven said.

Sunlight slanted down through a newly formed large hole in the ceiling, catching the jewels and reflecting the light across the granite walls. The shaking walls caused the patterns to flicker, casting a ghostly illusion around the cave.

"We found it, Lucky," Raven said. "But the bandits have found us. And now you're in danger."

Scuffling and more curses filtered through the opening.

"Light the torch," Porfiro directed. "And you, you take it inside."

Raven watched as an arm extended into the cave. An arm, followed by a familiar body.

"Benito!"

"Señora, is it you? And you, Señor Farrell."

Quickly Luce's cousin stepped farther inside the cave, glanced around at the treasure, and let out a strangled cry of amazement.

From outside, the bandit called, "You there, Benito. What do you see?"

The bronze statue swayed ominously. Tucker slid his arm around Raven, and the three treasure hunters and Benito backed away from the warrior. As they watched, the false wall began to disintegrate, thundering to the floor, exposing the full height and majesty of the giant bronze figure.

"Forgive me, Mother Earth, for offending you," Raven whispered.

Speechless, Porfiro and his men stared up at the ancient warrior.

The earth continued to tremble, setting off a maelstrom of dust. Another section of the ceiling fell, grazing the bronze idol's back, bouncing off a protrusion at its waist, dislodging a piece of the ancient metal.

With that action the arms of the statue creaked and began to move.

In horror they watched as the dagger shot across the space and speared Porfiro in the chest, pinning him to the wall above the opening. For the others, awe turned to

shock, then to fear. They shoved their leader aside and
scurried back through the hole and out of the mountain.

The statue teetered precariously until it toppled forward, carrying earth and rock with it. When the dust settled, they could see that the exit was totally blocked.

"Christ, we're trapped in here," Tucker said.

"The top," Raven suggested, "let's try to climb up
there."

They started toward the rock pile that had formed
beneath the opening above. But like a bucking bronco,
the earth beneath their feet continued to heave, making
it impossible to find a footing.

One screaming jolt split the earth between Tucker
and Raven, and before he could pull her back, she and
most of the treasure slid down a crevice.

A clod of earth grazed her arm, leaving a red welt.
Her eyes and nose filled with grit, but she came to a sudden stop. She and part of the treasure were trapped halfway down the rift.

"Raven, are you hurt?"

"I'm all right, Tucker. It's just a bit narrow down here.
What about you?"

Tucker glanced at Lucky and a wide-eyed Benito.
"We're fine." Cautiously he crept to the edge and looked
down. "It's just like in my dream. I saw this happening."

Lucky moved to the edge beside Tucker. "How are
we going to get her out?"

Frantically Tucker looked around. There was no rope,
nothing that could be used as a ladder. Even looking down
at the jagged rocks between Raven and the top turned
Tucker's stomach to a quivering mass of jelly. How could
he get down there?

"Hang on, Raven, I'm coming to get you."

To the sounds of Benito's frantic prayers, Tucker slid

over the edge and began to work his way down, every step a potential disaster as the earth continued to shake.

"I'm right behind you." Lucky blocked Tucker's light as he started to climb over the side above.

"No, stay there. I might need you and Benito to help me."

The rocks dripped with moisture, making it difficult to hold on. Every step set off small tremors, and the way grew narrower.

"I'm sorry, Tucker," Raven said. "If I'd known what I was getting you into, I'd never have offered you a stake in the treasure. I'm responsible for you being in danger."

"I didn't have to come with you. It was my choice."

She shifted slightly and heard the sound of coins falling even deeper into the earth. "I think there's another cave below where we are, Tucker. There's an opening. I can hear the coins falling through."

"Don't move," he instructed as a rock tore from the earth and fell away beneath his feet. "Look out, Raven."

Lucky was leaning dangerously over the edge. "What do you think is happening, Tucker?"

"Earthquake. I've heard about them, but I've never been in one like this. Usually they come and are gone in minutes."

"It's the Ancient Ones. We're going to die," Benito said.

Tucker reached the ledge where Raven and a large amount of the treasure had landed.

"Do you have some kind of attraction to ledges?" Tucker asked.

"I seem to, don't I?"

"We've got to find a better place to meet," he said, covering his fear with teasing as he pulled her into his arms.

"Yes." She snuggled against him. "You're much too big for ledges. Why'd you do it, Tucker?"

"Do what?"

"Climb down here. How will we get back?"

"You two okay?" Lucky called from above.

Another tremor threw Tucker and Raven against the side wall, dislodging a bar of silver and more coins, which slid from the ledge and fell in silence. Then he heard a splash below.

"Water," he said. "I think I heard water down there."

"The valley drain. Maybe that's how the flood water got out of the valley."

Tucker didn't want to think about where the water went, or what would happen to them if they fell farther. Climbing down was one thing, but getting a grip on the wet, moving rocks was going to be almost impossible.

But they couldn't stay here. If the rumblings got any worse, they needed to be as far away from this place as possible. He didn't look forward to being sealed up inside a mountain with the treasure.

"We've got to climb back up, Raven. This whole area is unstable. We don't have much time."

"But the way out is blocked by the statue and the collapse of the wall."

"There's still a crack in the top. If we can work our way up, we have a chance. Let me get you started."

Raven looked up and then back at Tucker. He was right, they were in danger of being crushed or sealed up inside the mountain. She reached for a handhold, feeling Tucker lift her to the first ridge in the surface of the wall.

With Tucker behind her, pushing and encouraging her, they clawed their way up. They were almost there when the tremors intensified. With falling rocks hitting their faces, Tucker and Raven held on, pressing themselves against the damp wall of rock.

But this time the shaking didn't subside. It grew.

The fissure widened. More of the treasure slid into the abyss below. And then the entire wall they were clinging to fell, carrying them, Lucky, Benito, and the treasure straight down into the icy water below.

For a moment Raven was stunned. Then she struggled to raise her head above the rapidly moving water. Where was Tucker?

"It's an underground river," he yelled, close by. "Hold on, I'll get to you."

In the darkness he could only hope that Lucky and Benito had survived the fall. Then he heard a roaring sound as something hit the top of the cavern, something bearing down on them. The branches of a tree touched his arm.

"Grab the tree," he yelled. "We'll float down the river."

Lucky's voice came from Tucker's other side. "What if there's no way out?"

"This mountain is going to collapse. We'll have to take a chance." Tucker reached out in Raven's direction. "Raven!"

"I'm here," she answered. "I've got it."

"I too!" Benito's strangled voice came from behind.

Tucker worked his way back through the limbs until he could feel Raven. He hauled her against him, securing her with one arm and holding the thrashing tree with the other.

The shock of the cold water turned Raven to ice. She felt Tucker's hand lifting her up on the tree trunk as he pulled himself up beside her. The tree was bucking and whirling through a darkness so terrifying that she accepted their imminent death.

Mother Earth was displeased. They were being thrust

from her like bad children. They were going to die before she ever told Tucker that she loved him.

Then, in the vortex of whirling motion, everything went still. It was as if a cocoon of silence encased her, and she heard it, the sound of drums, then chanting voices, low at first, then louder. There were fires, along a ledge where warriors danced. She could see their ceremonies, the ancient drawings on the cavern walls. At the end of the tunnel, the water tore through the mountain and plunged into the rocks below.

"Tucker, there's a waterfall ahead. We have to get to the riverbank or we'll be swept over the edge."

The tree was still swirling, bouncing from one wall to the other side, but Tucker could see a definite glow of light from the outside ahead.

At that moment there was a great rumble. The river heaved up, pushing the walls outward, then receded, leaving a strip of earth alongside the water.

"Quick! Everybody let go and jump for the side." As the tree curved toward the bank, first Benito, then Lucky took a flying leap and landed in the soft sand edging the wall. The tree wasn't going to turn its trunk to the side. They'd have to let go and swim.

Raven looked up at Tucker, stricken by what he was asking. She'd never learned to swim, only the current had kept her afloat in the beginning. And she'd never seen water like the angry current they were caught up in.

"Don't be afraid, Raven," Tucker said. "Trust me, I'll catch you."

He let go of the tree, and without a thought, she followed, her head going under, her shoulder scraping a rock as she was flung about the roiling water.

This time she was too cold to kick or keep her head above the water. As she was going under for the second time, she felt Tucker's hand on hers, holding on, pulling her slowly toward him. Finally, giving out a groan of exhaustion, he pulled himself onto the bank, drawing her alongside Benito and Lucky.

The tree was swept toward the tunnel of light and upended, disappearing from sight.

Crashing rock and the groans of the mountain forced Tucker to his feet. "Come on, we've got to get out of here, fast."

Moments later they were fighting their way along the wall toward the light. At the opening they stepped out onto the highest ledge Tucker had yet encountered. The river plunged over the ledge onto the rocks far below. Beside the ledge, rocks and mud were being gouged from the earth and began sliding down the mountain. They'd be thrown from their perch if they stayed. But they might be crushed by boulders if they left.

Then, in the valley below, Raven saw them, Yank, Onawa, and Jonah. They were dancing about nervously, uncertain whether to flee or stay.

"Look, Tucker, the horses!"

"They don't look too happy about the situation," Tucker observed, noting the movement beneath his feet. He knew the worst of the quake was still to come.

"They know something bad is happening," Raven said.

Tucker studied the trembling rocks. "Think you could convince Mother Earth to be still long enough for us to get down?"

As if on command, the ground grew still. The air, already hot and heavy, seemed to thicken as they tried to breathe.

"I'm thinking we'd better make tracks," Lucky said. "This may be the calm before the storm." He took off, slipping and sliding down the mountain beside the waterfall.

"Si, señor," Benito agreed, rushing down the mountain with a surer step than Lucky, who'd already lost his footing.

Raven hesitated only for a moment, then followed.

Tucker fell in behind. The treasure was lost. For whatever reason, the spirits didn't want them to carry the riches away from the sacred mountain. So long as they were alive, Tucker didn't care. He refused to lose Raven.

All he wanted was to get her to safety. A slower descent would have been safer, but the threat of having the entire mountain come down on top of them precluded that.

At one point the earth gave way beneath them and they slid the rest of the way to the bottom sitting down. Raven's buckskin dress would never be the same again.

"The horses," Tucker called out. "Let's get out of here."

Tucker mounted Yank, pulling Raven up behind. Lucky rode Onawa, leaving Jonah for Benito. But it was Benito and Jonah who led the way, fleeing the trembling rock now rolling down the mountain behind them. The water was forming a lake as it toppled trees to dig out a shell. Their escape was a ride from hell, but by giving the animals free rein, they were able to ride to safety.

The tremors stopped.

The earth stood still.

They were alive.

20

Lucky was the first to dismount. He slid to the ground and looked around. "It's stopped."

Raven, with her arms around Tucker's waist, was dazed. She finally stopped shaking, lifted her head, and glanced around. It was a miracle. They were in a familiar place, a place she'd never expected to see again.

"Luce's pool," Raven whispered, her voice filled with wonder. "We made it back."

Tucker let out a long breath.

After all the devastation they'd seen, she'd never expected to find anything still the same. But it was. The water still cut through the rock and fell in a musical stream into the pool below.

Jonah let out a squeal of delight and began to drink as though they hadn't almost drowned. Raven dropped her arms and slipped to the ground. Tucker followed.

She looked around at the place where she'd shared the first waking dream with Tucker. "I can't believe that we're still alive and back here. It seems so long ago." She made her way to the boulder she'd hidden behind while he shaved.

She sat down, leaning against the rock, grateful to feel the rough surface against her. Looking at Tucker, she felt the pain of reality begin to filter back. They were all the worse for wear now.

With a stubble of a beard, he was still a magnificent-looking man, proud and wild. His clothing was torn, as was Lucky's and Benito's.

They were alive.

But she'd failed.

As if she were a sleepwalker coming awake, she leaned her head back. Her eyes were open and filled with anguish. Tears rolled down her cheeks, but she made no attempt to wipe them away.

"We found the treasure," she said, "but we left it behind. My people will have to go to the reservation."

"Reservation?" Lucky questioned. "Is that what all this was about?"

"I was to find the treasure and use it to save the remaining Arapaho. I found it, but it's still inside the sacred mountain."

"Not all of it." Tucker came to stand beside her. "There's this. I don't know what kept it from being washed away, but it wasn't." He lifted the jeweled comb that still clung tenaciously to her braid. "And the golden chain."

The delicate, jewel-encrusted chain still hung around her waist, where she'd playfully hung it when they'd first entered the cavern.

"But that isn't enough," she said sorrowfully. "It's just a reminder of what is forever lost. Not only did we not bring it back, now it's at the bottom of a river in the middle of a mountain."

Tucker dropped to the ground beside her. "Maybe Mother Earth gave us only what she wanted us to have."

"I don't think the comb and the chain will buy land

for the Arapaho and a ranch for you in Oregon. I'm sorry, Tucker."

"You're wrong." Lucky made his way toward Raven. "In all the excitement, I forgot about all these. They happened to make their way into my pockets. I wanted to be able to prove that we found it," he said sheepishly.

He put his hands in his pockets and began removing loose jewels: rubies, diamonds, emeralds, and pearls. He dropped them into her lap. "You don't think I angered the mountain, do you?"

"I don't think so, Lucky. Without you the jewels would be lost. Thank you."

Benito, standing beside them wide-eyed, gathered a handful of the precious gems in his gnarled fingers. "This was what Luce did, stand guard over the treasure of the sacred mountain."

By the time Lucky finished emptying his trousers and his jacket, Raven's lap was filled with jewels. "Oh, and there's this." He reached inside his shirt for his notebook.

"Your notebook?" Raven asked, puzzled. "How did it survive the water?"

"It was wrapped in oilcloth. But it isn't the notebook. Look what's inside." He opened it to reveal a slender statue of a butterfly, carved from a sheet of solid gold, its wings encrusted with tiny slivers of black stones.

She began to smile. "My mother's butterfly."

"Raven's wings," Tucker said. "Lucky, it's worth a bloody king's ransom. How could you forget about it?"

"Didn't seem nearly as exciting as what was happening. Do you realize that we've had an adventure that most people only read about in fiction?"

"I guess we did," Tucker admitted, his eyes filled with the sight of Raven, her lap heaped with jewels, her eyes filled with tears.

Lucky beamed. "What I'm wondering, is how on earth did that enormous bronze statue get inside the mountain?"

"Luce always said there was a treasure," Benito said solemnly, "but we never believed him. He was told that the treasure belonged to the Spanish who sailed across the ocean. They came to Mexico, stole the ancient statue and the jewels from the people who lived there, and moved it north into the land where my people once rode. Then the intruders found gold and silver which they stole from the earth that belonged to the Ancient Ones."

"But how'd it get up here?" Tucker asked.

"The Spanish started to transport the gold and jewels back to the Gulf by burros."

"So they wouldn't have to sail around South America," Tucker said. "But your people might not have known that."

"No, my people, angry that their lands had been usurped, stole the treasures from the Spanish and hid it in the mountain. But that statue? I don't know."

Tucker picked up the butterfly and examined it. "So the Arapaho people were the holders of all this wealth, and yet they were starving."

"Money never meant anything to an Arapaho," Raven said. "It was the land that mattered. Besides, that was nearly two hundred years ago. Only Flying Cloud and Luce knew there was a treasure. But Flying Cloud didn't know what it was."

Lucky's eyes were wide. "Why not?"

Benito continued the story. "During the Spanish reign, half the Arapaho moved to the north. The others, my people, stayed behind. They began to marry into the Mexican families nearby. Only Luce knew the truth. He learned it from his father, who learned it from his."

"And," Raven went on, filling in the only part of the

story she knew, "it was tradition that a member of the tribe left in the south be charged with guarding the sacred mountain. Those in the north were to pass on the secret of the treasure to one member of each generation. Flying Cloud was the holder of the secret. Luce was the guardian of the mountain."

Lucky was scribbling madly in his notebook. "And now, Mrs. Farrell, you're both the guardian of the mountain and the holder of secret."

"No, not me. I've completed my mission. Benito must be the keeper of the mountain now. And Swift Hand will keep the knowledge alive. He knows where the valley is. He knows about the treasure. If the spirits want it found again, it will be Swift Hand who will be shown the way."

"But I thought that he was less than honorable," Lucky argued. He remembered the shock of the Indian when he'd appeared before him covered with white mud. "And he certainly isn't very brave."

"Swift Hand could have harmed us and he didn't. In my heart I know he was only doing what he thought was best for our people."

Tucker refrained from arguing with her. Whatever was left in the valley had been buried by nature's shovel. It would take Mother Earth to reveal its location. He didn't believe that Swift Hand would be chosen as the messenger, but he might well pass the secret to one who was. Tucker could say with certainty, if not full understanding, that the future was up to the spirits.

Tucker looked around. They'd done it. They'd found the treasure and survived an earthquake. The bandits had been defeated. Only Swift Hand was still out there, standing between Raven and the completion of her mission. Raven might think that the Indian had undergone a change, but Tucker wasn't at all certain. He wouldn't rest easy until they were back in Denver with the jewels.

The hot sun beat down on the rocks. A strange hush had settled over the pool, and the air grew heavy and oppressive.

"I think we'd better go, Raven," Tucker said. "I feel something wrong about this place now. We no longer belong here."

"Yes," she agreed. "The jewels must be packed so that they won't be seen."

"Jonah," Lucky said.

"No," Tucker corrected, "he will return to the village with Benito."

"No," Benito protested. "You will need the burro to carry the treasure. I will return to my village on foot. I must go. My wife will believe that I am dead."

Raven rose and, cradling the jewels in her dress, walked over to the old man. "You must have some of the jewels, Benito. Your people need so many things."

Benito fell to his knees, crossing himself in awe. "It is with deep humility I accept these jewels. I will give them to Father Francis, who will use them wisely. Now that the bandit leader is dead, his men will leave us alone."

"Look after the mountain, Benito," Raven said. "I don't think that even you could locate the treasure now, but we'll always know it is there."

"Si," Benito agreed. "And if the Ancient Ones mean for us to find it again, it will be so."

They watched as the old man stuffed the gems inside his shoulder pack. He solemnly shook hands with Tucker and Lucky, then bowed his head to Raven and left, walking slowly back the way they'd come.

They packed the jewels in Yank's saddlebags. And Onawa's held the butterfly. Eager to leave now, they chose the trail north, toward Albuquerque, leaving all that had happened behind.

Lucky climbed back on a calm and obedient Jonah, Raven on Onawa, and Tucker on Yank.

They camped by the river at nightfall, at the spot where they'd first discovered Luce. When a light rain started to fall, Raven walked down the canyon and removed her dress, allowing her body to be sluiced free of the evidence of their journey. Her dress was ruined, but with one of the nuggets, she could buy a new one for her trip back.

She wondered about the valley of the butterflies. Had the earthquake destroyed it? What about the treasure that hadn't fallen into the river? Was it waiting for another seeker?

Now, standing nude in the soft, warm rain, Raven felt life and hope return to her body. They hadn't needed all the treasure. What they'd found was more than enough. Their lives had been in danger, but Tucker had saved them.

Over and over, she'd put her life in his hands and he'd protected her. It came to her that love was trust, the giving and accepting of it. If she really loved Tucker, she'd ask him to stay with her.

But that would be selfish. And she'd spent her life being selfish, for Flying Cloud and the Arapaho. No, she'd let him go to Oregon and start his ranch. Even if her heart would break, there would still be enough money for her to return to her people in Colorado. She'd buy land enough for all. They would be free to live and die on their own land.

Lucky would write a story that the world would want to read, and his family would be forced to see him in a different light.

Everything was settled. Why then was she so despondent?

As the rain continued to fall she made her way toward

the cliff and sought the shelter of an overhang. As she sat she began to feel an odd prickling energy settle around her. There was an alien flutter of wings in the night air, and in the distance she heard the cry of a mountain lion.

Through the rain she could feel him, the essence of the man she'd called her mountain lion. There was a warmth in the coolness. It brushed against her at first, teasing, then more boldly painting her with heat.

Since the beginning she'd been able to reach out to Tucker, connect with him and share his thoughts. But this was different. This was a conscious effort to meld with him. Her need was deep and desperate, not to join with him so much as to become a part of him.

The energy around her became a delicious reminder of Tucker's kisses, an urging that grew as she sat in the darkness. In her mind she brought him into view, tall and beautiful, not in darkness but in the light. Tucker belonged in the sun just as she belonged in the darkness. He smelled male. He tasted male. Every nuance of his presence swept over her like hot fog.

He was leaving, soon. She understood that. This might be their last night together. Distance would weaken the connection, eventually killing it. Tonight might be all they'd have.

Tucker, my protector, my cougar, I love you.

Down the river Tucker felt a stab of need in his gut. He'd washed himself and stood out in the open, letting the salty moisture from his eyes be rinsed away with the rain. The adventure was ending. Tomorrow they'd reach Albuquerque, and once their jewels had been banked, Raven would go one direction and he'd go the other.

This was their last night together. Lucky was already sleeping. The horses were bedded down and Raven had left the camp.

She was taking his heart with her, and he didn't know

how to stop her from going. Even entertaining the idea of keeping her was selfish. Grand things were in store for Raven. She might not understand yet, but he did. Swift Hand might take over the tribe, but Raven was its heart, and without her they'd wither and die.

The pain in his gut intensified; his head throbbed. The backs of his knees tingled and his heart beat faster. Every part of him trembled as if he were standing at the edge of a cliff, staring down, knowing that at any minute he would fall.

And then he felt her, through the soft rain, through the night. Tentatively at first, then stronger, her spirit was reaching out to him. *I love you.* There was a curious uncertainty in her words, an asking that he couldn't comprehend.

Raven?

Tucker?

Down here.

She was down the canyon from the cliff on which he stood, asking.

What do you want from me, Raven?

Only you, Tucker. Only you.

Tucker started toward her, his steps slow but unfaltering. As he walked the thrumming in his head grew quiet; his knees were firm and his heart full. He knew even as he walked that he'd conquered mountains for this woman. She'd taken his pain and now his fear, replacing it with confidence, with need. He could want again. He did want.

He wanted Raven.

Their spirits melded first, creating a circle of warmth that transcended time and place. Along the walls of the canyon, the shadows of the Ancient Ones watched. Overhead and beneath, the spirit world joined to enclose them in a place of joy.

And then they were together in the flesh, touching, silk against sand, rough against soft, dream against reality. There was a song in the rhythms of their touch and their breathing, a chant that caught in the rain and intensified as it hit the textures of the valley. The murmur of the river, the high, sweet sound of the wind and the baritone of the rocks. All became the music of their love.

Tucker asked and Raven gave, riding the currents of their desire, caressing the sure softness of their acceptance. Turbulence followed gentleness, until the fever of their dance erupted into one final firestorm of love that exploded the cocoon and joined them with the elements. Nature accelerated their climax into an explosive tempest that melted every painful memory they'd ever kept. Then time stood still as the rain stopped and the moon moved out from behind a wall of gray.

"Oh, Tucker—" Raven said, her voice tight in her throat, "I don't understand how this happens to us, but I don't want it to be over."

For a long time, Tucker did not speak. Then, finally, he raised up on one elbow and looked into Raven's eyes. "This isn't over, Spirit Woman, and this isn't a dream. You've taught me something about myself."

"I have? What?"

"Everything I ever cared about was lost to me, so I quit caring. When I did that, I quit living. You came into my life with an impossible goal. Nothing stopped you and you reached that goal."

"Yes," she said softly, "I did. But I learned something from you as well."

His face was washed with surprise. "What could you possibly have learned from me?"

"That a person can't be single-purposed."

"Single-purposed? I don't understand."

"I never thought that I might have a life for myself.

I was so careful to close off anything that might interfere with my duty, I forgot that I'm a woman."

"So what did I do to change that?"

"You made me see that riches shared are twice as rewarding. Flying Cloud never told me to rely on anyone else to find the treasure. He said the spirits would send me help but the responsibility was mine alone."

"It was," Tucker agreed. "I'd have quit long ago—or at least *once* I would have. When I saw how strong and dauntless you were, I began to see that I'd given up on my life too easily. If I'd given up this time, I would have lost you."

She simply looked at him, not daring to ask what he meant. He might not have lost her, but he would leave and the end result would be the same.

"You made me believe in the impossible—a future."

"I didn't do that, Tucker. You've always had a future. You just had to work through the past to see it." She took a deep breath. "When will you leave?"

"Leave? Where would I go?" His surprise was too great. As she watched she could see a little quirk in the corner of his mouth.

"Oregon?"

"Now, why would I want to go to Oregon when the woman I love is going to be in Colorado?"

"The woman you love?"

"The woman I love. I can't imagine leaving you. Who will protect you? Besides, nobody else knows the secret of the red berries."

"You'd really come with me, knowing that the land I buy will be for my people?"

"The way I see it, there's going to be too much land for one man to ranch. I thought we might make a deal with Swift Hand and his men. They run the tribe and give us a hand on the ranch. In return, we can deal with the government on their behalf."

"You'd do that?"

"I'd do that," he said, "if the woman I love loved me too."

"Oh, Tucker, of course I love you. I love you so much I think I would die if you left me."

"There's something I have to clear up first, before we can find a preacher," Tucker said in a low voice.

"What?"

"When I rode away from Sand Creek, I never went back. I have to square myself with the army before I can help anybody. I don't know what they'll do to me, but I'd like to think that there is someone who would wait for me if I have to serve some time in jail."

"Someone will, your wife. Remember, Mr. Farrell. Father Francis is God's representative, and in his eyes we are already married. You have a wife who loves you spiritually, even if we aren't legally married under your law."

Tucker grinned. "A wife who loves me?"

"Of course, Tucker. I loved you before I even knew you. It just took me a while to know what that kind of love meant." She reached out and touched his face. "I'm not sure I understand it all yet. Do you suppose you could show me some more?"

"I wouldn't dare refuse a spirit woman," he said softly. "But I think it might take years to complete your education. What do you say?"

"I say I wouldn't have it any other way."

Epilogue

The following article appeared in the September 1, 1877 issue of the *New York Daily Journal:*

The *New York Daily Journal* announces the publication of the first book by new fiction writer Lucky Smith. Only after the book, already wildly received by the public, sold out for the second time was it revealed that the writer is a member of the famous Small family, publishers of this newspaper.

Mr. Smith, interviewed by his brothers, claimed that his material came from personal research. He went on to say, "Not many people have the good fortune to take part in a treasure hunt. Not many lost treasures are ever found. But there aren't many people like Raven and Tucker Farrell left in the world."

Lucky Smith's book is a fictionalized account of the search for ancient Spanish treasure by Raven Alexander Farrell, an Arapaho from Colorado, her husband, Tucker Farrell, and Swift Hand, the current leader of the Arapaho tribe.

The treasure hunters faced the greed of Mexican bandits and the forces of nature to find the Lost Spanish Treasure, only to lose the majority of it in an earthquake. At this time, the location of the treasure is unknown. The seekers managed to retain enough gold and jewels to secure the future of a small band of Indians who only wanted land that was rightfully theirs.

But according to Mr. Smith, his story isn't about the search for treasure. It's about two people who believed in the impossible and each other. This is a story of destiny, of commitment to the land, and of trust. This is the story of Raven and her cowboy, and the real treasure of love.

ABOUT THE AUTHOR

Bestselling and award-winning author, Sandra Chastain has written thirty-four novels since Bantam published her first romance in 1988. She lives with her husband just outside of Atlanta and considers herself blessed that her three daughters and grandchildren live nearby.

Sandra enjoys receiving letters from her fans. You can write to her at P.O. Box 67, Smyrna, GA 30081.

DON'T MISS THESE FABULOUS BANTAM WOMEN'S FICTION TITLES

On Sale in June

MISCHIEF

AMANDA QUICK, blockbuster author of ten consecutive *New York Times* bestsellers, dazzles with her newest hardcover. Only one man can help Imogen Waterstone foil a ruthless fortune hunter—and that's the intrepid explorer known as "Coldblooded Colchester."

____ 09355-X $22.95/$25.95 in Canada

RAVEN AND THE COWBOY

SANDRA CHASTAIN, praised by *Affaire de Coeur* as "sinfully funny and emotionally riveting," serves up another western delight when mismatched lovers Raven Alexander and Tucker Farrell embark on a perilous quest for treasure.

____ 56864-7 $5.99/$7.99 in Canada

THE MAGIC

A deposed heiress with the "Sight" enlists a returning Crusader's help on Beltane Eve to regain her lost kingdom, in this spellbinding tale from dazzling new talent JULIANA GARNETT.

____ 56862-0 $5.99/$7.99 in Canada

DON'T MISS THESE FABULOUS
BANTAM WOMEN'S FICTION TITLES

On Sale in July

From the electrifying talent of
SUSAN KRINARD
leader in fantasy romance

PRINCE OF SHADOWS

Beautiful, dedicated wolf researcher Alexandra Warrington agonizes over the plight of a gorgeous wolf she discovers in the wild . . . until it vanishes, leaving a darkly handsome stranger in its place.

_____ 56777-2 $5.99/$7.99 in Canada

WALKING RAIN

by the highly acclaimed SUSAN WADE

This impressive debut novel is the haunting, romantic, and richly atmospheric story of a woman on an isolated New Mexico ranch being stalked by unseen forces.

_____ 56865-5 $5.50/$6.99 in Canada